A DEVIL'S
JUDGEMENT

Have you read?

The Joslin de Lay Mysteries I:
Of Dooms and Death
The Joslin de Lay Mysteries II:
A Pact With Death
The Joslin de Lay Mysteries III:
Hell's Kitchen

Other Point Crime books by Dennis Hamley:

Deadly Music
Death Penalty
Dead Ringer

The JOSLIN de LAY MYSTERIES

A DEVIL'S JUDGEMENT

DENNIS HAMLEY

■SCHOLASTIC

Scholastic Children's Books,
Commonwealth House, 1–19 New Oxford Street,
London WC1A 1NU, UK
a division of Scholastic Ltd
London ~ New York ~ Toronto ~ Sydney ~ Auckland
Mexico City ~ New Delhi ~ Hong Kong

First published in the UK by Scholastic Ltd, 1999

Copyright © Dennis Hamley, 1999

ISBN 0 590 19769 X

Typeset by Falcon Oast Graphic Art
Printed by Cox and Wyman Ltd, Reading, Berks.

10 9 8 7 6 5 4 3 2 1

*The Joslin de Lay Mysteries
are written in memory of
Tony Gibbs (1938–1966)
of Falmouth, Jesus College, Cambridge
and Langwith College, York,
who loved the Middle Ages
and would have been one of the greatest of
scholars and writers about them.*

The scream pierced Margery's eardrums and its knife-sharp echo made her clap her hands over her ears. Where was it from? Half of her wanted to run away and hide. The other half wanted to find out.

It only took a moment for the brave half to win. She was wandering alone, away from the cottage in Greyfriars Street in Coventry where she lived with her mother and father, down Little Park Street towards the city wall, Little Park Gate and the open land beyond. She'd been on this earth for seven summers and winters and so she could wander alone if she wanted to.

There was the scream again. Oh, someone must be going through such pain. She had to find out where. She wanted to help.

She was at the end of Little Park Street. In front of her stood the Gate. The cry came again, nearer. Was it from the other side?

Again. Now her stomach turned cold. The cry came from down Dead Lane. AND NOBODY EVER WENT DOWN DEAD LANE, NEVER HAD, NEVER WOULD. Dead Lane was where all the dead souls of Coventry met before being taken off to Hell and everlasting torments. When the great plague came, years before she was born and half the people in Coventry had died, everybody in Dead Lane was carried off. Not one was spared. So nobody had lived there since. The old houses were just left to fall to bits and become one with dust and earth. The folk believed that it was from here that all the souls of Coventry claimed by the devil started their journey. Everybody shunned Dead Lane, both by day or by night. So she would as well.

But that terrible scream came from Dead Lane and she had to help.

She set out, turning left down this deathly quiet, ruined track with roofless houses, window spaces like empty eye-sockets and doorways like toothless mouths. No cry now, nor sign of what made it.

Then came an awful thought. Such a cry must be from a dead soul, a lost soul being hauled away to everlasting torture. Her father and the priest had told her that devils and fiends lurk behind every corner ready to snatch you away to fiery pits where you'll stay in torment until the last trumpet call to judgement. And especially in Dead Lane. Whoever made that scream must have been seized like that. A fiend was close by, lurking round the corner, FOR HER.

That was enough. She'd run away. But then she thought – wouldn't it be nice just to see a little devil all red and bristling, with stings on his thrashing tail, eyes glowing, teeth sharp like razors? That would be something to tell her friends. As long as no devil saw her.

She crept on, quietly so the devil wouldn't hear. The cry came again. Where was it from? Not in the lane itself. She looked up little alleys and entrances. She was almost at the end of Dead Lane. Just one little

2

entrance left, tucking right up to the city wall. Here was the crumbling wall of an old house. Was somebody trapped behind it where she couldn't see? She carefully looked round and behind the wall.

She caught her breath in horror. No, it wasn't just one little demon. IT WAS HELL ITSELF COME DOWN TO EARTH. What else could that gaping mouth be, those huge, sharp teeth, that red tunnel leading through it to who knew what terrifying depths?

It was getting dark. But she must find who had screamed – and perhaps catch just a glimpse of a fiend.

Oh, if this was the mouth of Hell, it was a terrible place. It glowed in a dim shifting red as the fires far below cast their light upwards to tell her what to expect if she did not keep the commandments and look after her soul. What were these things wedged between the great teeth? Legs? Arms? Heads? She dared go no nearer. She'd run home to tell her father that Hellmouth really was here in Coventry and she'd seen it.

And then Margery heard a sound which froze her blood. A low, retching moan started quietly, got louder. She had found who screamed.

"Help me!"

No, she couldn't run away. We had to help those who asked. Like the Good Samaritan. Margery turned back. "Where are you?" she whispered. All she could see were those dreadful teeth with heads and legs of dead people wedged between.

But were they dead? Something moved in the darkness, something close to – no, not close to but in between – those teeth. Though every nerve shrieked and muscle trembled, she came nearer.

And then she saw a sight she knew she would remember in her dreams for every night she had left on the earth. A man lay in front of her. Blood dribbled from his mouth. His fingers tried to grip the air. His legs and feet jerked feebly.

Margery looked closer. Though the red glow was dim she knew what she saw. The man was impaled on one of the teeth of the mouth of Hell. Its sharp, stained point pierced through his body and stuck out with fresh blood on it – as if the devils were too lazy to take him all the way down so had spiked him on the nearest handy object like an insect wriggling on the end of a thorn.

But Margery was brave. She made herself look.

"Help me. . ." said the dying man again.

"What can I do?" said Margery.

"Get word to my friends waiting in the *Tavern Where the Ways*. . ." His voice died. Margery bent low. "They mustn't . . . they mustn't. . ."

"Yes?" said Margery. "They mustn't what?"

"They mustn't come to Cov. . . There's a man with the head of a monster . . . he deals in death . . . they must keep away from. . ."

The man's voice ceased. His eyes were wide open and his mouth hung agape. Margery knew, though, that those eyes saw nothing and never another word would that mouth utter.

Now she was really frightened. She must run home, away from Hell, away from this Lane of the Dead. She must tell everyone what she had seen. But she had not taken three steps before a great darkness seemed to fall on her. Neither her father nor anybody else would know for a while yet about these terrible happenings round Hell-mouth.

Three whole weeks and a day before little Margery

had her adventure at the Hell-mouth in Coventry, Joslin left the comfortable town of Banbury, miles to the south on the road from Oxford. He reckoned that judging by the distance he'd covered since *The Merchant of Orwell* had landed him in Ipswich, he must be halfway to Wales. And about time. So far his journey had taken eight months. Three weeks getting well again after his trials in Oxford, then more time lost in Banbury – why, it was a week into May already. He would have to do better than this.

But the urge to sing where his songs were welcome and the coins flowed free was too great. Ten nights had passed in Banbury, singing in taverns and under Banbury Cross. Now his money bag was full with more in his panniers. In ten days his fame had spread. Folk came from cottages and fields and from lords' domains to hear him. Nobody seemed to worry that he was French. Perhaps news of the war never came this far. Or they forgave anything for a good song.

There would be no more stops except when he needed money. Bodies could be piled six deep around him and he wouldn't bother. He'd been too anxious to help and too likely to find trouble. Trouble – huge, awful trouble with a skull face and empty eye-sockets – had stalked him from the moment his father's servant had woken him in his chamber in the castle in Treauville. How many times since had he faced Death – his own and other people's? No more, he vowed. If Death approached on the road, he'd walk past on the other side.

"You be careful how you go, young Joslin," the landlord of the tavern at Banbury had said. "Envious eyes watched. I know these people. I wouldn't trust some of them with their own grandmothers."

"I'll be all right," Joslin anwered.

"Take my advice," said the landlord. "Keep your eyes open. To make for Wales, get off this road at the Fosse Way. Don't risk going in the Forest of Arden. If you keep up a good pace you'll find the Fosse Way by late afternoon. Turn right and follow the Fosse. The next turning takes you to Coventry."

Coventry. He remembered Matt on the road to Oxford. "Fine Corpus Christi Plays in Coventry." Matt thought Joslin ought to go and make a lot of money. But that was the trouble. It was a temptation, to stop there and sing with the actors in the plays on Corpus Christi Day. He'd seen plays like them in France and he loved them. The colour, the acting, the noise, the music, the excitement – as soon as Matt mentioned them he had decided he'd be in Coventry when Corpus Christi Day came.

But he daren't. It would waste time. This journey should only have taken a month. Anyway, Corpus Christi Day was in June. He'd be past the city by then.

"Don't carry straight on whatever you do," said the landlord. "You'll be heading into that Forest of Arden. It's a dark, twisting place with robbers behind every tree. You've done well for us here in Banbury. I shouldn't like to think of you coming to harm."

"I'll remember," promised Joslin.

"Don't ride alone," said the landlord.

"Who else is going to Wales?" Joslin replied.

"Nobody here, I fear. But there'll be a few going part of the way."

At that moment a huge man led a small, well-loaded horse out of the stables. "The very one," exclaimed the landlord.

"What do you want?" the man said.

6

"Nothing much, Gyb. Except to guide our young travelling minstrel here as far as Fenny Compton and keep him out of trouble on the way."

"It's not in Fenny that he'll find trouble. And I'm not going a single pace further, mind," replied the man.

"It's a start," said the landlord. "This is our Gyb. He's a journeyman mason He's used to tramping the roads for work and he can look after himself. I'd trust him with my life. He's on his way to a job in the manor at Fenny Compton. Aren't you, Gyb?"

"I could have told him all that myself," Gyb replied. "And we'll be on our way now, if you don't mind." He clicked his tongue and the little horse ambled out of the tavern yard. Joslin followed on Herry.

Over a mile had passed before Gyb spoke again. "Where are you bound for, then?"

"Wales," Joslin answered.

Gyb considered this. Then: "Rather you than me. You're from France, aren't you? I heard that in the tavern. Well, I travel, see, so I know things. There are some who'd like to see you on the gallows for an enemy." Joslin shuddered. He'd been there once already. But Gyb continued. "This lot round here, though, they go nowhere except over their little plots of land so they're ignorant. And you needn't fear me. Let the lords fight their wars among themselves."

"I'm still here," Joslin replied. "Besides, there's more blood in my veins than just French."

The vision of his father dying on the deck of *The Merchant of Orwell* sprang into his mind. "*You'll never know where your true loyalty lies. That is the curse your mother has bequeathed you.*"

You were wrong, Father, Joslin thought. *So far it's been a blessing.*

"I suppose you want to go back to France," said Gyb.

"Yes," said Joslin. "Yes, I do."

Gyb sniffed. "Rather you than me."

Silence again. Then: "I heard the landlord talking to you. He's right. You want to keep out of Arden Forest. If you don't. . ."

Joslin waited for, "I'd rather you than me." Instead, Gyb said, "If you end up in there, you'll never see Wales."

"Why not?" Joslin asked in a small voice.

"Oh, terrible things happen in it. Great ravenous wolves. Wild boars with tusks fit to run through two men together. Robber bands so clever they've tamed all the animals to their bidding. The robbers have the goods off the travellers' backs while the animals have the flesh off their bones. And if you don't meet them, there's Herne the Hunter charging through the forest on his ghostly hunt. One look at him is enough to kill you from fear. That's what happens in Arden."

Joslin said nothing. "Rather you than me," said Gyb.

"But I'm making for Coventry," said Joslin.

"You mind you get there," said Gyb.

They were the last words spoken. The few miles to Fenny Compton were covered. "Mustn't be late for Sir Piers Langley's bailiff," said Gyb. They were in a tiny village which Joslin saw would yield neither travelling companion nor food to buy.

"Well, I'll leave you, then," said Gyb. "And don't forget. Keep out of the forest. Keep the sun to your left. You'll reach the Fosse Way before you know it."

Then he was gone and Joslin travelled alone.

The further north he went, the more deserted and rough the road, the smaller the settlements, the thicker the woods on the low hills. Barns were ruined, cottages deserted, fields overgrown. The few serfs were sullen and half-starved. Twenty years before, the plague had ravaged the land hard and its marks were worse than anywhere he had seen in England. Herry ambled through this desolate landscape and Joslin sat thinking of all that had happened.

He had no idea how long they walked. Evening was here. He'd noticed no turning or crossroads. The road dropped into a valley where a smart, sizeable town lay. On a commanding hill, was a great castle, larger than Treauville or Stovenham. Castles meant trouble. People in them would not like him being French. Nobody had said anything about a castle in Coventry or a town before he reached the Fosse Way. Was this Coventry? He had no idea. So he found a tavern.

"What town is this?" he asked the alewife.

"Warwick," she replied.

"I've come from Banbury. Where's the Fosse Way?"

"I'm sorry, lad. You've passed it."

"I can't have." But he knew she was right. He had ridden in a dream and let Herry find the way for him.

Well, he wouldn't go back in the dark. He asked the alewife, "Can you let me have a bed tonight?"

"If your money's good," she answered.

He wasn't minded to sing. He hid his harp in a pannier. He'd better not let his French voice be heard here. Besides, he was very tired.

Anyway, there was a minstrel singing already.

A tall man with dark hair and a jowly, bristly face, square so it reminded Joslin of an axe-blade, was playing a wooden pipe. His large, long fingers danced up and down the holes and the shrill, high notes kept everyone quiet. This man had no harp. Besides the pipe, he played small drums and sang in a strong, gruff, yet tuneful voice. His songs had more rhythm than melody and Joslin could feel the listeners taken up in their insistent beat. This was a music as different from his own as it could be. At first he wanted to close his ears to the harsh sounds. But gradually the rhythms got inside his head, he listened fascinated, and thought: *I could learn from this man.*

For over an hour the minstrel sang. Then he looked at his audience almost threateningly. "I've done enough," he said. "You'll not make me play more."

There was a disappointed moan. He continued. "But remember the name until I pass here again. Crispin Thurn. If a snatch of melody comes to you, remember Crispin Thurn put it there. But I'm tired and thirsty and my tankard's empty. You'll have to wait for another time to hear my tale of Gamelyn."

There was an immediate shout: "Gamelyn. Give us

Gamelyn." Crispin Thurn put up a great ham-like hand palm outwards as if warding off wild animals. "Nobody makes me do anything," he roared. "I'll smash the head of the man who dares try."

They backed away. He grinned and large white teeth showed almost fiendishly. "Anyway, why should you want to know that story?" he said. "The things that happened to Gamelyn would enrage you so much you'd go straight out and burn every manor and hang every lord in Warwickshire. And we couldn't have that, now, could we?"

Joslin sat unseen at the back. *That was clever,* he thought. *Crispin Thurn will always be welcome here.* He watched the tall figure surrounded by locals and his tankard refilled time and time again. He wanted to tell him, "I'm a minstrel too." But he feared a contemptuous look and the answer, "You? Don't make me laugh."

Joslin's bed was in the straw over the stables. He had asked for this: since Herry was stolen in Abingdon he always stayed near his horse. For a long time he lay in prickly, sweet-smelling straw with Crispin Thurn's rhythms winding round his head. With it came a peculiar fancy, of Crispin and he singing together in a play in Coventry, with the townsfolk watching and cheering. But no, that would never be. By Corpus Christi Day he'd be miles to the west, perhaps in Wales itself. But there was a terrible barrier yet to be avoided. The Forest of Arden. The thought of it lay, harsh like Crispin's songs, and wouldn't go away.

He didn't know what time it was when he heard a noise outside. Why should one noise worry him? But this one was odd: it made his nerves tingle with the sense that something was wrong.

A horse clipped quietly across the yard. Whoever led it had wrapped cloth round its hooves. Joslin looked through a gap in the stable wall. Two men stood talking. Something about them suggested urgency and secrecy. One was very tall. At length he clapped the other man on the shoulder in a gesture of farewell. The other man turned and led his horse silently out. The tall man came back into the tavern.

Joslin was sure this man was Crispin Thurn.

But it was nothing to do with him. He lay down again and fell into a deep and dreamless sleep.

Next morning, he left early. The sky was overcast. A fine drizzle soaked his cloak slowly. Herry passed under the castle walls, which cast a pall, making the morning even darker.

If he saw a turning to the right he would take it. It might lead to Coventry as well as the Fosse Way would. The castle worried him. He feared that a soldier might spring from nowhere and shout, "We know you. I arrest you as a French spy." The castle was far behind before he breathed easily.

Was there a turning to the right? Perhaps he had taken it and was on the right road already. The cloud was so thick that no glimmer showed through. Settlements were sparse: cultivated strips few. Joslin felt uneasy. So often in England he had thought he was watched. Was that a movement behind a tree, a rustle in the grass, a snap of a branch too strong for bird or animal? He shook his head. He was on the road, free of murders, free of enemies. Why build up fear where none existed? But was he going the right way?

An hour later, he knew. In front of him was a mass of trees stretching far to either side and deep in front of him further than imagination could tell. He knew what he had done. Despite every warning he had received, he had blundered straight into the Forest of Arden.

Margery was hustled forward. A rough sack over her head stopped her seeing. Her feet scrambling on wood, then she was lifted up for a moment. She heard footsteps, then she was put down and pushed along again. Now there was stone under her sandals. She imagined the sharp claws of the demon's hand gripping her shoulder and the evil sting on the end of his tail.

Then she was thrown on the ground. The sack was pulled off. She blinked. How lovely to be free again. But what had they done to her? She was still blind. She couldn't see a thing. Did she dare speak to a demon? How should she talk to one anyway? "Why can't I see, Master Devil?" she asked faintly. But the demon didn't answer. She heard him shuffle away, she was sure she could hear that terrible tail bumping heavily along the ground.

So this was Hell? But she wasn't dead, even though a devil had taken her. She was all intact. But then, didn't we stay in our bodies even when we were dead, so we could rise again on the Day of Judgement?

Then she thought – if this is Hell, why is it so cold?

Suddenly there was sort of half-light above her. It was gone as soon as it came. Was a curtain pulled back and then closed? For an awful instant, SHE SAW THE DEVIL WHO BROUGHT HER HERE. AND HE WAS FEARSOME WITH HIS HUGE GOAT'S HEAD.

She shuddered. What would happen next?

She soon knew. The half-light came again. Now there were two devils, just like those in paintings on the walls of St Michael's Church. Her father had shown them to her, and also in the bright pictures in the book of psalms and prayers he possessed. Plenty of devils in that. These two were carrying something which she knew at once was going to spend all eternity in Hell because it was definitely dead.

She knew who. The man who died on the teeth of Hell-mouth.

What else could Joslin do? Go back to Warwick and find a road to Coventry? His heart sank. He'd lost so much time already, so why not just miss Coventry out? At least he'd lose the lure of Corpus Christi. Why not carry on westwards? Wales would be there just the same and perhaps he'd get there sooner. The forest couldn't be *that* big.

But it was. Soon it seemed as dark as night. Branches of ancient trees hooked down as if to pull him up, smother him and make him one with their gnarled trunks. Scurrying, creaking, splitting sounds were all round – unseen animals and trees living their strange lives. Sometimes he thought he heard wolves howling. Once he saw a huge boar. Deer moved between trees. He came face to face with a huge stag which lowered its antlers, then turned and crashed away from him. He half-feared the phantom shape of Herne the Hunter would follow. But his biggest fear was of stealthy human shapes, not phantoms but deadly and vicious. Herry was frightened. Joslin leant forward and whispered encouragingly in his ear. Before long even that wouldn't work, so he dismounted and led the horse forward.

What a great fool he'd been.

The half-hour he'd spent in the forest seemed a full day. He daren't look behind. If he kept going, perhaps they'd come out the other side in one piece.

Without warning, his hopes were shattered. He hardly heard the shout of "Now!" before he was hurled to the ground to lie winded. Something rough and evil-smelling was thrown over his face. Herry whinnied. Joslin lashed out with his feet. He groped desperately for his dagger. It felt as if an army had set on him. They kicked him in the stomach, cracked on the back of his neck with a staff. He tried to crawl away. There was a sudden, searing pain in his side. He tried to stand, staggered, swayed and, as warm blood coursed down his body, was beaten down again. He lay helpless, heart pounding in his ears, trying to stay conscious, waiting for a squalid death. But before blackness came, he heard curious things.

First, metal jangling. That must be his hard-earned money? Then a fight went on – thuds, grunts of pain, breathless swearing. Then running footsteps. The cloth was pulled off his head and, as mist filmed over his eyes, he stared at a face he knew.

"That's got rid of them," said his rescuer.

Joslin registered who it was before he slipped into dark unknowing. Crispin Thurn.

When Joslin came to he was lying on a heap of soft moss and leaves. Crispin was staunching blood from a wound which throbbed unmercifully. A short sword lay on the ground. Joslin tried to gasp his gratitude.

Crispin laughed, showing large, white teeth. "I knew you'd get into trouble," he said. "I watched you on the road, though I kept out of sight. You'd no idea where you were going. When you reached the forest, I thought I'd better catch up."

"So you followed me," said Joslin. "I knew it."

"Oh, no," Crispin replied. "It wasn't me you sensed. Not if you were frightened. You don't worry about friends following, even if you don't know they're friends yet. It's them after your blood that you worry about."

"What do you mean?" asked Joslin.

"I saw six creeping where you'd not see them. They knew you were a stranger. They thought that once you were in the forest, they'd do what they liked. They'd not touch me. I know how to keep out of sight."

"And you put all six to flight?"

"They were nothing. Puny cowards, that's what."

"Were they robber outlaws?" asked Joslin. To be set on by them and escape would be a proud boast.

"Like Robin Hood of Sherwood, do you mean?" said Crispin. "Once, perhaps. Not now. There are those lurking in the forest who don't worry where their livings come from. I'd not get rid of them so easily. Yet better men than them live under these trees."

Joslin had been so thankful to get out unharmed that he'd not thought to see what he had lost. He tried to raise himself up. Before he collapsed weakly back he saw Herry next to Crispin's own sturdy brown horse. The panniers and his clothes were scattered around and the harp lay up against a tree. Crispin picked it up and ran his fingers along the strings, making a sudden liquid chord. "When I saw this on your back, I knew I had to help you," he said. He gave it back.

17

Joslin remembered that metallic jangle. "Where's my money?"

"Sorry lad," said Crispin. "I couldn't stop them taking something. They shook it out, scooped it up and escaped before I could get at them. You'll not see it again, I fear."

"That was ten nights' work in Banbury," Joslin groaned.

"Don't worry," Crispin replied. "We'll be minstrels together."

"But I've got a long way to go," said Joslin.

"So have I. You won't be on your way for a while yet."

"I have to." Joslin tried to shout but his voice died inside his throat. "I'm bound for Wales."

"Go one more mile and you're dead with the effort," said Crispin. "You've a bad wound and harsh bruises. You need care."

Joslin lay back in despair.

"Don't worry," said Crispin. "I'm known here. I'll find you shelter, food and good people to see to you. When you're fit we'll journey together for some of the way. Together we'll make twice as much money as one."

"Where are you bound for?" Joslin asked.

"I thought I'd try my luck round the cities of the Marches where England meets Wales. Besides, I have business in those parts. Priests and bishops might not like my songs and lords certainly wouldn't. But one thing I know – the folk will."

Joslin remembered the night before. "You mean that song you wouldn't sing, because they'd burn every manor and hang every lord?"

"Aye, the tale of Gamelyn. It means a lot to me, that does. Maybe you'll hear it before our ways part. Where in Wales are you bound for?"

"I don't know." He remembered his father: "*The blessed Saint Ursu. . .*" – and Dafydd in the tavern in Henley on the way to Oxford: "*I fear you'll have a long search.*" "It could be anywhere. I'll just have to ask."

"Perhaps I could help."

Joslin told him about the elusive saint. Crispin thought, then said, "No. I can't say the name means anything. But then, I'm an Englishman so I wouldn't know." He caught at his horse's bridle. "Now then, Joslin, we must be on our way."

He lifted Joslin up as if he were a baby and helped him on to Herry's back. Then he sheathed his short sword, picked up the panniers and slung them over Herry's back as well. Finally, he took each horse by its bridle, one in each hand, and led them slowly away.

"As I remember, there's a woodman's cottage near here," he said. "I knew the people well once and they knew me. We trusted each other. They'll look after you better than their own brother."

Even though Crispin led the horses slowly, the bumping made Joslin's wounds hurt worse. He hardly knew when they stopped. But he heard words of greeting and knew that Crispin and another man carried him gently until he was under a roof and lying on a mattress which smelt fresh and felt soft, while warmth and wood smoke caressed him so he felt more like sleep than fainting.

"You're with Lew and Mab," said Crispin. "A wood-cutter and his wife. We know each other well. You're in the best hands."

Joslin dimly knew what came next. "See," Crispin said. "He's suffered a shrewd strike. A little deeper and he'd be dead. His bruises are bad. But he's strong: others might have been laid low by them."

19

"Don't worry, Crispin," said a woman's voice. "My broths are nourishing and my dressings will make his wound right. I'll feed him the herbs of the forest so he'll be strong again. Leave him with us."

Crispin bent over Joslin. "I'll go now," he said. "I'll look in from time to time to see how you are. I'll not journey further until you're well enough to go. I mean it when I say we'll travel together."

Joslin looked up at the square face like an axe-blade and saw the strength in it. "Where will you be meanwhile?" he asked.

"Ask me no questions," said Crispin.

There was one he must. "How long will I be here?"

"Two weeks. Three. Maybe more. You must be strong for the road. Though I don't doubt you will be with Mab to see to you."

Already Mab was feeding him with a hot broth with a curious savoury taste. He felt goodness flood through him and he drank the whole bowl like a baby. Then Mab said, "Let me look at that wound."

Joslin could stay conscious no longer. He heard Crispin say goodbye and the door close. But before he gave himself up to dreamless stupor he had one last thought. Three weeks here. In time to be in Coventry for Corpus Christi Day – but another delay in a journey which seemed to be taking half his life.

Deep in the forest, in a place which few knew, a frail man rested on a fur-lined bed under a deerskin blanket and a tent roof hidden by trees from prying eyes. He sat up as another man entered.

"He's here, in the forest," the arrival said. "The man who did you such wrong has come back. Say the word and I'll kill him for you."

"I know you would, Seth," said the frail man. *"But leave him. I want to be there when it happens and I want it to be in the place and at the time when it's fitting. You know when and where I mean."*

"You're right," said Seth. *"But it's hard to leave him unscathed."*

Now began a frustrating but comfortable time. Mab nursed him well: Lew left early each morning and came back at night after hard work. Joslin had the daily routine of dressing the wound, rest, rich broths, fresh bread and wild fruits from the forest. His wound healed and strength returned. After six days he was on his feet, weak but getting stronger. After ten days he went outside and saw to Herry. He knew his horse chafed for the open road as much as he did.

Every three days, Crispin came to see him. After twelve days, Joslin said, "I'm well enough now, Crispin. We can go now, surely."

"I'll say when, not you," Crispin answered.

After a fortnight, Joslin wanted to walk in the forest. All three, Lew, Mab and Crispin, were horrified. "You'll do no such thing," said Crispin. "Arden's no place for a stranger on his own."

"I need to stretch my legs," said Joslin.

"If he wants to he can come with me," said Lew.

So now Joslin went every day with Lew and the woodcutters. He noticed they were armed: longbows on their backs and quivers full of arrows at their sides. One always kept watch.

One day, Joslin knew why. The sharp axe blows at the base of an oak tree stopped and the woodcutters scattered as it began to topple. Suddenly an arrow embedded itself deep in the bark.

Lew cursed violently. "What do they want us for?" he muttered. "They know we have nothing."

The woodmen had disappeared. Lew pulled Joslin down behind a tree-trunk. His bow was at the ready. He let an arrow fly at a movement, just as a burst of arrows fell all round them. Other arrows from hidden woodmen returned the attackers' volley.

"These wretches never let us alone," said Lew.

"We're surrounded, Lew," a voice cried softly from somewhere a few paces to their right.

And then a curious thing happened. A tall, indistinct figure rose up from behind where the first volley of arrows had come. A voice called, "Back off. Leave them alone."

There was a tense silence except for the oak tree creaking as it teetered before its fall. Joslin thought he saw shapes stealing away into the forest. Then another shout: many men chanting together. It sounded like: "*Randall Stone shall come into his own.*"

Lew remained still for some minutes. Then he rose and one by one the other woodmen appeared as with a huge crash the oak fell and the forest was full of flying leaves, splintering wood and the shrieks of frightened creatures. The work of stripping the tree of its branches and sawing them into logs started. Lew looked at the trunk, saying, "I'm sorry to tell you this, Joslin, but a good ship lies somewhere in that oak fit to take yet more soldiers to France."

Joslin had a strange thought. The figure which called the attackers off was indistinct but the voice was familiar. It sounded like Crispin's. He said nothing to Lew. Next morning he was sure he was mistaken. Three days later, Lew asked if Joslin would like to swing an axe. At first, three puny efforts exhausted him, but soon he grew used to it. He would never strike like the rest but at least they didn't laugh.

All the time, good food, care and exercise were making strength course back, wounds heal and bruises disappear. Each night when supper was cleared away, prayers said and Lew and Mab were sitting either side of the fire, Joslin would sing and play and their rapt faces showed him they had heard nothing like it in their lives.

When he could sing no more, Joslin asked them about the forest and who it might have been who had attacked them. Were there really bands of outlaws like Robin Hood?

"There were. Not now," said Lew. "Now there's a rabble you should keep away from: renegade soldiers who know how to kill and don't care who they skewer for a couple of groats, peasants starving on their own land and turned to thieving and killing, men dispossessed and banished."

"Like Randall Stone," said Mab.

"Who's he?" asked Joslin. He remembered that chant.

"Let me tell you a story," said Lew. "Years ago, Randall Stone was the outlaw king. He was loved by the forest folk and the common people round about, but hated by the barons. But things change. Now, Randall Stone is the greatest scourge of all. The worst of thieves and killers. Mothers frighten their children with him when they're naughty. It's not 'the devil will come for you if you don't be good' round here. No, Randall Stone will come instead."

"Why?" said Joslin. "How can a man change like that?"

"Is it the same man? I doubt it. Randall Stone's

name lived on even after the forest rang with the news that he was dead. A new outlaw leader took on his name and carried on his work."

"Ah," said Mab. "It changed, when the invaders came."

"That's right, wife," said Lew. "Without any warning the forest was overrun with these people. Where had they come from? There are rumours, but no one knows because they won't say. We just try to keep out of their way. And they butchered the old outlaws until the last few survivors went into hiding. Then they had the gall to take on the name of Randall Stone and use it for their own villainy."

Joslin thought about this for a while. Then he asked, "And Crispin? How do you know Crispin?"

"We've known Crispin a long time," said Mab.

"But how?" Joslin persisted. "He's a minstrel. He's like me, on the road all the time, far away from here."

Lew and Mab looked at each other. Neither spoke. Had he overstepped some mark?

"We know him," Lew repeated after a full minute. "Ask us nothing else about Crispin."

They closed up, as if gates were slammed to in front of their faces. Joslin said no more. There was more to Crispin than he knew. Just as there was about the mysterious Randall Stone – if he existed at all.

"Another song?" he said and their faces opened into smiles again.

After three weeks, Joslin was strong again. As the first day of the fourth week dawned, Crispin came. "Are you ready, Joslin?" he called.

Joslin's farewell to Lew and Mab was heartfelt. "I wish I could pay you," he said.

But Lew raised a hand to forbid him. "No money," he said. "Your pleasure and Crispin's good opinion of us are reward enough."

Crispin was impatient to be off. Joslin wondered why. He must have been close by for three weeks, when he could have been on his way to the Welsh Marches. What had he been doing?

He put the panniers on Herry's back and then sprang up with them. He looked down to Lew and Mab standing there. "Goodbye," he said. "I'll never thank you enough. I'll never forget you."

"Perhaps, one day we'll meet again," said Lew.

Joslin turned to Crispin. "Where to?" he asked.

"Where the road takes us," Crispin replied. "Carry on the way we've come. We'll find the edge of the forest. Then we might make for Coventry. It could be well worth our while."

Well, why not? He did want to be at the plays and he needed money badly. Besides, what did a few days matter after all the months he had taken already?

Seth was back with the frail man. "He's on the move again," he said. "His name is different and he has a companion."

"He can call himself the Archangel Gabriel and walk with the Apostles, but I'll have his soul," said the frail man. "Watch him, Seth."

After three weeks spent in it, the Forest of Arden was to Joslin a friendlier place. Sunshine pierced the leaves and dappled the ground. Young deer peeped shyly through undergrowth. Red squirrels chattered. Woodpeckers drilled at tree-trunks and birds seemed to wake up and fill his ears with song.

"You don't want to believe half of what you hear about this place," said Crispin. "All right, there's danger like there is in every forest. But to one who knows it, the forest holds few terrors. Just worry when the barons go hunting here."

The road carried on ahead. Far from getting out of the forest, they seemed to drive further into it. They talked less and less. Even with Crispin there, Joslin longed for open skies and a clear way. As the day wore on, overhanging trees oppressed him again. The horses walked slower. It seemed as though the Forest of Arden covered the rest of the known world, with no human being except themselves in it.

Soon, Joslin lost track of time. Above, clouds gathered. The forest was gloomy again. Now and again, Joslin cast a look at his companion. Yes, he was a big man. His jaw jutted grimly from his square face, so that Joslin was again reminded of an axe-blade.

A strange suspicion crossed Joslin's mind. How accidental was his rescue from the robbers? There were so many questions he would like to ask. What about that strange encounter he'd seen in the tavern yard? Could the horseman have been a forest outlaw? What else could those half-hints and sudden silences from Lew and Mab mean? For now, though, Crispin had to be trusted. And why not? He'd saved his life, found him good shelter and help, never forgotten him. Yet there was a mystery about him and Joslin had learnt enough during his months in England never to trust mysteries.

They rode steadily for hours seeing nobody. Sometimes Joslin thought he saw shadows behind trees and wondered if they were watched. Late in the afternoon, Crispin pointed ahead. "Look there," he said. A lone figure was walking ahead along the road. "He must be very brave," Joslin replied.

"And lucky. Let's see why," said Crispin. He urged his horse on at a canter. Joslin made Herry follow.

The figure, turned, saw them and ran. But he was no match for the horses. From a hundred paces, Joslin saw there was something familiar about this figure. As they overtook, he saw what – a man wearing the minstrel's tunic, its yellow and red faded and dim. How strange. He'd hardly seen another a minstrel in England, yet now here were two almost together.

"Stop, friend. Don't fear us," Crispin called. "We're all in the same line of business."

The man stopped and turned. "What do you mean?" he asked suspiciously. Joslin knew voices like his after so long in London.

"We're all three minstrels, we're travelling to make money, so we should stick together and help each other, like any guildman would do."

The man pondered this. He was small and thin, with lank black hair. "Yes," he said at last. "You're right there. But how do I know you're minstrels? You en't wearing minstrels' tunics."

"There's only one way," Crispin replied and burst into "*Sumer-is-y-cumen-in*" in his deep bass voice. After a second's hesitation, Joslin joined in, a high descant in harmony which he improvised as he sang.

The new minstrel said delightedly, "You are, en't you!" He joined in, a tune in the middle which stayed true and bound up the other two into one. Then they changed tunes, so Crispin sang Joslin's as a bass, Joslin took the middle line and the new minstrel the melody. Then change again, and again, altering and varying out of pure joy in the music, as the horses walked on and their new friend trudged alongside.

They lost track of time until Crispin said, "That should warn every thief in Warwickshire." Then he added, "But what are we thinking about? Why should such a fine minstrel have to walk? Share my horse. He's strong enough to take us both."

"I'll take your bags," said Joslin.

With barely a break they carried on their way singing, changing songs, each saying, "Do you know this one?" and starting off, the others joining in if they did, making it up if they didn't. After nearly an hour, the new arrival stopped in mid-tune and said, "All right, I believe you're minstrels, but *who* are you?"

So Crispin told him about himself and Joslin followed. Then Crispin said, "What's your name?"

"Lambert, en't it," said the new minstrel. "I come

from Shoreditch, just outside the walls of London."

"I was in London," said Joslin.

Lambert eyed him critically. "Oh, yes? Not as long as me, though. Born there, wasn't I, and I had a good place singing in an alderman's household till he found he wasn't as rich as he thought he was. That was two years ago, and I've been on the road since. Not easy."

"It's not bad, either, if you know what you're doing," said Crispin.

"Were you kicked out by your master?" said Lambert.

Crispin ignored the question. "Where are you bound for?" he said.

"Meeting some people, aren't I," Lambert answered. Then his voice perked up, as if he'd thought of something. "Come to think of it, they'd like to meet you as well."

"Who are they?" asked Joslin.

Lambert put a finger to his lips. "Just wait," he said.

That stopped both singing and talk. The horses walked on over paths which never seemed to lighten. But, as the light dimmed, Crispin said, "We're nearly out. I smell open land."

They came to a clearing at a crossroads. In the middle was a low, ramshackle building made of wood except for a thatched roof. Over the entrance, a sign swung. THE TAVERN WHERE THE WAYS MEET.

"I know this place," said Crispin.

Joslin thought seeing a tavern at the end of a day's travelling should give him a welcoming glow. Instead, he shivered. He wanted to say, "Let's not stop here." But Lambert spoke first. "There's providence for you," he said. "They're here already."

In front of the tavern was a small two-wheeled cart.

Its shafts rested on the ground. A young man of about sixteen was pulling its load of bundles to the ground. A large man with long hair and tough, weather-beaten face stood impatiently at the tavern-yard gate. He was not helping. A young woman stood by him. "Hurry up, Sym," the man said. "You know Miles wants our tackle in before dark and the cart in the yard. Then we can run through the Adam and Eve play for the folk."

"I'm doing my best, Jankin," the boy muttered. When the bundles were on the ground, Jankin bent, picked three up at once and bore them off into the tavern. The boy lifted the shafts and trundled the cart into the yard. The woman took hold of a shaft. "I'll do it, Peg," said the boy.

When they had gone, the Tavern Where the Ways Meet stood like a bat's shadow in the deepening gloom. But Lambert chuckled and said, "You see? Fortune's always smiling. The very ones I've come to meet."

At the same moment as Sym and Jankin were unloading the cart, Margery was in a very cold Hell watching the devils bear their prize away to everlasting fires. But they would be a long time gone. The fires must be far away, because it was *so* cold here. She was surprised when they were back in a moment and speaking among themselves.

"Well, we know where the rest of his crew are," said one voice.

"So what do we do?" asked the other.

"Keep them away from here. The same way as we dealt with their friend. You know what these people possess which mustn't come here for Corpus Christi Day. Though the one we've sent where he belongs was the worst."

"But this girl's seen too much. She'll have to go the same way as the other."

"Don't worry. Let her go home. She'll say nothing."

Suddenly, in the darkness, Margery knew that a devil was very close AND TALKING TO HER.

"Go back to your good folk. Come with me."

The same rough sacking descended over her head. She was pushed back up a flight of stone steps and a slope made of wood. At last she felt fresh air. They took the cover off her head.

"Go home and be happy," said the voice. "Forget what you've seen. It was a dream. There are no devils in Coventry."

And then she was in the deepening dusk, the other side of the wall, running away from that hidden Hell-mouth as far as her legs would take her, down Dead Lane and into Little Park Street, with no idea of what the demon was talking about.

"Who are those people?" asked Crispin.

"Actors, en't they," Lambert replied. "Travellers like us. They travel all over. They've just journeyed from far away in Norfolk."

"How do you know them?" said Crispin.

"I met them in Cambridge. They were on their way from Norwich. It's hard being an actor. The money the folk pay gets shared out among six, not straight into one pocket, like it does for minstrels like us."

"So why go with them?" asked Joslin.

"I'm telling you," said Lambert. "They were doing their plays in an innyard and they asked me to sing. They liked what they heard. They said they were going to act in a castle, then go to Coventry to play on Corpus Christi Day. People come from miles around."

"You're right about that," said Crispin.

"There are always good pickings when the plays are on," Lambert continued. "The Aldermen might pay them so they wouldn't have to depend on how deep people's pockets are. Their leader had been there before. One of the actors would go on ahead to arrange things. The others would go to the Tavern Where the Ways Meet and wait there until he came with his news. If I joined them there, they said, I wouldn't lose out. Well, I said would. We'd all go the last few miles into Coventry together. Well, don't let's just stand here. Let's go in."

"I know this for a place where the welcome's not always what you hope for," he said Crispin.

"What do you mean?" asked Lambert.

"There's honest woodmen here who live by sweat and toil and there's rogues with knives hidden about them. And when you look at everyone gawping back at you, you won't know which is which."

"Have you been here before?" asked Lambert.

"I have," Crispin muttered. "Is it like it was?"

"Only one way to find out," said Lambert.

The Tavern Where the Ways Meet was a dark place inside, with walls of wood and low beams. Arnulf Long, the landlord, fitted it well. His hair was long, straggly and fringed round his eyes. His mouth was hard and his voice harsh. His eyes were not welcoming. One had a slight cast so he seemed to squint at them suspiciously. "I shall have to think about it," he answered when Lambert asked for beds for the night. "Months go by and no travellers come, so I make do with my regulars for a living. This inn may be at a crossroads, but it's not a main route where travellers follow like church processions. The robbers have seen to that. Nobody passes for months. Then you come in a rush and expect me to turn about just like that."

Crispin muttered to Joslin. "This isn't the landlord I know. Yet I've seen him before. Who could forget that squint?" Aloud, he said, "We'll sing for our suppers."

"Will you now?" The landlord showed no sign of recognizing Crispin. He waved his hand towards where the boy had dragged the loaded cart. "We're full of folk wanting to cheat free suppers out of us. Well, nobody cheats Arnulf Long. Five actors with their women and three minstrels is more than an archangel could bear."

"But they expect me," began Lambert.

"We'll see about that," replied Arnulf Long. "They were here first so they have first right."

He left. "He doesn't know you," said Joslin.

"Don't be so sure," Crispin replied.

Lambert was angry. "That landlord's only got to ask Miles," he muttered. "Miles will tell him I deserve as much as any of the actors."

"This Miles is not landlord here," said Crispin.

"Miles is the leader of the actors. His wife is Molly. There's Sym, the boy, and Jankin with his woman, Peg. You saw them out the front. There's Alban who Miles thinks is the best bar one, Hob who limps, and Bartholomew, who they sent on to Coventry and are here to meet. He's Miles's real favourite."

"Bartholomew? Who mentioned Bartholomew? Is he here yet?" The voice behind them was deep and rich. They turned and saw an imposing figure. He wore a once-red cloak, now faded and patched. Its shabbiness could not disguise the nobleness of the face, the hooked nose, firm chin and keen, steady blue eyes. His voice was deep and sonorous. Joslin imagined it filling market squares and castle halls. Next to him stood a motherly, comfortably-built woman with greying hair. Molly, Joslin supposed. Behind him were four men, including Sym and Jankin.

"About this rat-faced midget who's turned up. You know him, then?" said Arnulf.

Lambert bristled and nearly jumped on him. Crispin held him back. "Let it be," he whispered.

There was no hiding the pleasure of the four men and two women at seeing Lambert. "You're here," said Alban, tall, fresh-faced and no more than twenty.

"I knew you'd come," said Sym.

"I never thought you'd be daft enough to bother with us," said Jankin. His weather-beaten face looked at Lambert almost with pity.

"Then you were wrong," said Peg. "As always."

"I hope you never regret meeting up with us, Lambert," said Hob. His voice sounded too weak to be an actor's. "You wouldn't be the first who've joined us and soon wished they hadn't."

Miles had taken no notice of Arnulf's insult to Lambert. "So, lad, you're here," he said. "Well met."

Suddenly Lambert was so pleased that if he'd had a tail he would have wagged it. "Yes, I am, Master Miles. I'm right glad to see you all again. I've got two more minstrels with me. We can travel together."

Miles ignored that. "Landlord," he said to Arnulf. "We'll give the play of Adam and Eve tonight. We need to get it right if we're to take it to Coventry."

"Adam and Eve? Is that all?" said Arnulf. "My customers won't like that. What about a good laugh, and some barons and bishops falling flat on their faces?"

"I'm sorry. The only one who has skills to make people laugh isn't here. Even if he was, we wouldn't do what you want, we'd do our Day of Judgement play, ready for Corpus Christi. There are some laughs in that with Bartholomew at the mouth of Hell. If he comes back in time we'll think again."

"Not another one of you?" said Arnulf.

"Yes. Bartholomew. He's gone to Coventry to prepare the way for us and talk to the aldermen about the money they'll pay us for our Corpus Christi plays. We'll stay here until he joins us."

"When were you in Coventry?" asked Arnulf.

"Three, four years ago. Why?"

"Times change. Travelling actors aren't welcome."

"Why not?" Jankin demanded.

"You'll find out. I've had troupes of actors stay here on their way happy as young lambs and trudge back like old sheep bound for slaughter because the Guilds have said they don't want them any more."

Miles was crestfallen. "I might have known it," he said. "Do the folk want to act the Corpus Christi plays themselves? Are we up against the Guilds and their money?"

"So they tell me," Arnulf replied. "You can't blame them, can you?"

Miles looked weary. "Times are changing," he said. "It's the same in York, Chester, Wakefield, Lincoln, Norwich, who knows how many other towns? They all want to do it themselves and a right mess they'll make of it. There'll soon be no place for the likes of us travelling players. We'll scratch a living in taverns and little villages but the great times in cities on Corpus Christi Day will be barred to us."

"It's the way of the world," said Arnulf.

"Why should we put up with it?" said Miles. "We're good at what we do and no matter what Bartholomew tells us when he returns, we'll go to Coventry and they can turn us out if they dare. There's a great difference between people who know what they're doing and people who don't, and by God above we'll show them what that difference is."

"You'll have your work cut out," Arnulf grunted.

"We'll see," Miles answered.

ord must have spread through Arden to wood-men and foresters and outside to settlements on the edges that the players were here. As darkness came, people thronged into the tavern yard. A small, mousy-haired man appeared from the brewhouse at one side of the innyard and complained that he doubted whether he'd brewed enough beer.

"Water it down if you have to, Slad," said Arnulf.

Meanwhile, Miles, Molly, Jankin, Peg, Alban, Hob and Sym set up the play of Adam and Eve. They pulled the cart to one end of the yard as a makeshift stage and extended it either side by planking resting on barrels. They hung a once dark-blue curtain at the back painted with a silver moon, golden stars and a vast sun also in gold. On a dais above the curtain was a chair covered in gold cloth. Everyone would know that, though poor and makeshift, this was the Throne of God. A gold-painted ladder leant against the dais for God to climb to the throne with dignity. Flaring torches on the walls threw garish light on the stage.

The folk jostled for good views. Joslin felt the

excitement he knew as a boy when the actors came to the Count's castle at Treauville. For a moment, nothing happened. The stage stayed empty: the sun, moon and stars winked down from the curtain on to a bare world which, the folk knew well, God had not yet made.

Then a figure appeared. Lambert. He gave a roll on a small drum. Then he shouted: "Now see the play of Adam and Eve, how God made the world and Lucifer tempted Eve to the destruction of men, so God threw them out of Paradise."

There was quiet throughout the yard. From behind the curtain came a figure everybody knew. The quiet became an awed hush. The figure wore a white robe and its face was painted gold. Joslin knew that this was God. He came up to the throne and gravely sat. Though the voice was that of Miles, yet also it was God himself speaking. Everybody in the tavern yard knew this and felt it deep in their bones.

> "*I am the Lord enthroned.*
> *I am the first, I am the last.*
> *All things are made by my own will.*
> *What I decide, I will fulfil.*"

He made a wide gesture at the moon and stars on the curtain.

> "*Darkness I shall call the night.*"

Another grand gesture towards the sun.

> "*Day will come when it is light.*"

Now Miles spread his arms wide.

> *"These waters that are so widespread*
> *I bring together to a head.*
> *What I make dry, the Earth shall be.*
> *The waters I shall call the Sea.*
> *The sea will nourish the fish swimming,*
> *The earth will nourish the beasts creeping,*
> *Walking or flying on high.*
> *Now multiply on earth and be*
> *Safe in my blessing. Live happily*
> *For ever from this day."*

Miles rose from the throne and left. Joslin and everyone else knew that they had watched the world itself being created. They knew what would follow, but that did not stop an expectant intake of breath.

Miles had gone out on the right-hand side of the cart. From the left, round the other end of the curtain, came three more figures robed in white – Alban and Hob on each side, Jankin in the middle. Jankin wore a crown, once bright gold. Alban's voice filled the yard.

> *"Lord, you gave us everything.*
> *It was all made at your bidding."*

Then Hob spoke. His voice was thin and cracked.

> *"Why, you are so full of might*
> *That you made Lucifer so bright."*

Here, he indicated Jankin.

> *"We love you Lord, for bright are we,*
> *But none of us as bright as he."*

Now Jankin spoke.

> "*Indeed, we are his angels bright.*
> *But you must understand aright –*
> *The mastery belongs to me.*
> *From me alone comes this great light.*
> *Now, comrades, how would it seem if I*
> *Should sit on the throne of God most high?*
> *I am so strong in every limb –*
> *At least as strong and fair as him.*"

Hob answered.

> "*You seem so perfect to my sight*
> *I think you should sit there by right.*
> *For ever count me as your friend.*"

Alban threw his arms in the air, backed away in horror and cried:

> "*I fear you'll come to no good end.*
> *Approach that throne no Angel dare*
> *For fear of God who should sit there.*"

Hob answered, his voice dripping with contempt.

> "*Oh, no? It seems to my sharp wit*
> *By right as Lord should Lucifer sit.*"

Now Jankin's voice was harsh and triumphant as he asked Hob:

> "*My worthy comrade, think you so?*"
> "*Yes, and others do, I know,*" Hob answered.

Alban countered:

> "*Among that number, don't count us.*"

Jankin came to the front of the cart, raised his arms and shouted:

> "*Do you think for you I give a curse?*
> *Since I shine with such a blinding light,*
> *Just watch me as I take a flight.*"

He tensed himself like a hunting animal about to spring, then made a prodigious leap for the throne. He missed, sprawled on the floor, and somehow overbalanced out of sight behind the stage.

There was silence, then an unexpected snigger. "He thinks he's frightening us," said a voice. "If only he knew," said another. "Randall Stone would eat him alive," said a third, and everyone nearby laughed.

Hob followed Jankin. Everybody knew that they were Lucifer, now the Devil, and a fallen angel and they had gone down into Hell. Alban remained alone, then gravely left on the same side Miles had used.

Jankin and Hob reappeared. Their white robes were gone. They wore black rags and their faces were daubed with soot. Hob cried out:

> "*Lucifer, what made you fall?*
> *You were the fairest angel of all.*
> *We, once so mighty, strong and fair,*
> *Winging our way around the air.*
> *Now we are soiled with pitch and tar,*
> *Ugly, tattered, foul we are.*
> *Once we were rich, now we are poor*
> *And racked with pain for evermore.*"

Then Hob left, limping, crouching like the meanest beast. But Jankin as Lucifer stayed where he was, slowly stood up and stared at the empty stage. Lambert made a roll on the drum which echoed like tiny thunder. Miles entered again. He majestically climbed to his throne, and faced the audience. Once again, the deep voice rolled out.

> *"I shall make man in my likeness*
> *To rule the beasts, both great and less."*

He beckoned gracefully towards the side of the stage. Alban reappeared. But the soot had gone from his face and the rags from the rest of him. He wore only a brief loincloth. He crouched before Miles.

Miles placed his hands on Alban's head.

> *"Spirit of life in you I blow.*
> *Good things are all that you will know.*
> *Rise, Adam, and stand by me.*
> *All beasts in water and on land*
> *Shall eat gently from your hand.*
> *Their sovereign you shall be.*
> *I give you wit, I give you strength*
> *Over all you see, by breadth and length.*
> *But it's not good to live alone,*
> *To walk in Paradise on your own.*
> *So a rib from you I'll take,*
> *From your rib a maid I'll make –"*

Here Miles seemed to take a bloodstained rib bone from Alban's side. He threw it off the right-hand side of the stage. Now Sym entered. He wore a yellow, long-haired wig and nothing else except a loincloth.

Plainly he was Eve. Miles continued.

> *"Together, you'll govern all that is,*
> *Evermore in endless bliss.*
> *And now you're both in Paradise,*
> *I'll leave you here, in peace."*

Miles climbed down from his throne and left the stage again. Adam and Eve turned to each other. Jankin stood up now in full view at the front of the stage and spoke to the audience directly.

> *"Who'd have thought this time to have seen?*
> *That I who in such mirth have been,*
> *Should find myself suffering so much woe?*
> *Who'd have thought it could ever be so?*
> *But listen all to what I say*
> *I'll win back my joy one day.*
> *Now man is in Paradise –*
> *But he'll be gone, if I am wise."*

The stage was empty. The audience let out a collective sigh. Now for the next part, so well-known, yet so much wanted, of Eve tempted by Lucifer, of God calling to Adam in the Garden and then throwing them out of Paradise for ever. Joslin watched on, in a trance. He'd seen plays like this in France and loved them. Now he longed to reach Coventry and see them all.

Then, with no warning, everything changed.

Someone ran out of the crowd and vaulted on to the cart. "I'll have no more of this," he shouted. He faced the audience. He was a strange, even frightening-looking man. He was dressed in tunic and hose, ordinarily enough, and he was large and strongly built. But his head was what made Joslin gasp. It was monstrous, freakish, too big, it seemed, even for those broad shoulders. His lips were thick, nose bulbous, eyes big, bulging and black. Joslin had never seen such a repulsive human being. He was suddenly certain that *this man meant evil.*

"I'll not have it," the man shouted again. "I know this story through and through. Aye, and so do all of you. I hear priest and friar tell it so it comes out of my ears, I see it acted out every Corpus Christi and other times besides – and a lot better than this, as well, as you all know if you're honest with yourselves."

"That's right," someone shouted in the crowd.

Miles realized something was wrong. He jumped back on to the stage, still with gold paint on his face. "What's going on?" he demanded.

The monstrous-headed man shoved his broad face up close to Miles. "I'll tell you what's wrong. We don't want your rotten play that we've seen till we know it in our sleep. We want to laugh. We want to see great folks made fools of and poor folks levered up. Travelling players should give us that, and if they can't they should follow a trade and earn money honestly."

The crowd were angry now. He had won them over. "He's right. Give us what we want or get off." That was the mildest of many shouts.

Miles strode forward and raised a hand for silence. "Friends," he said. "I wish we could. But we are but five actors here when we should be six. It's hard enough to do Adam and Eve without making everybody take two parts. We'd willingly give you the interlude of the cheating butcher or the one about the bishop and the sexton's daughter. But the only actor who can do the funny roles so you wouldn't boo us off the stage isn't here. We're waiting for him to join us and until he does there's no plays from us except those we'd do on Corpus Christi Day."

"We don't want them," said monstrous head. "Have you got that?"

"Yes, have you got it? Have you got it?" The crowd turned the question into a chant which thundered through the air and deafened Joslin. "*Have you got it? Have you got it? Have you got it?*"

"Yes, I've got it," Miles replied and turned away again. Joslin muttered to Crispin. "They're in trouble. They need our help."

"You're right," Crispin answered. They pushed their way through the people struggling forward to get at the stage. Behind the curtain they found Alban, Sym and Lambert cowering and muttering prayers as if their last moments had come. Miles and Jankin were trying to rouse them into action. Molly and Peg were looking disgusted.

"Come on, you miserable crew," Molly was saying. "Behave like actors, not frightened chickens."

"We've been in worse straits than this when folk don't like us," said Peg.

"When?" Sym moaned.

"We have to do something," Miles urged. "They'll break our cart up and wreck our costumes."

"Such as they are," said Alban.

"Shall we let them burn our gear and hang us?" yelled Jankin. "There's plenty of good strong branches to string us up from."

Arnulf pushed through to the frightened actors. "I told you they wouldn't like it," he said.

"Who's that man with the big head?" asked Miles.

"No idea. Never seen him before," Arnulf replied.

"Yet they followed his word as if he was their leader."

"Perhaps he is. Perhaps he can rouse up any rabble." Arnulf looked gloomy. "I wish none of you had come."

"*Arnulf!*" A shout from the yard. "*We want you.*"

Arnulf clambered up on the cart and faced the crowd. Joslin heard what went on.

"Arnulf, we came here tonight to be entertained – have a bit of a laugh and a bit of a cry."

"And be entertained we will. Or we'll leave no ale in the place."

"And not much in the way of walls and roof either."

"*All right,*" Arnulf yelled. The noise stilled, as if the crowd had somehow made a mass decision to give Arnulf a chance. "I'll tell you what I've got in store. This is your lucky night. Not only do we have actors, but three minstrels from the courts of kings here to sing to you."

"What's he saying?" asked Lambert.

"Quiet," answered Crispin. "We'll just have to find out. Let him get on with it and don't say no when you hear what it is. This may be our only chance of getting out in one piece."

"Minstrels? That's lucky all right," shouted someone. "Especially as we won't pay a penny to listen to them."

"I know that. And they know that."

"Do we now?" Lambert said.

Crispin gripped his shoulder. "Quiet and listen," he hissed.

Arnulf went on. "I'll tell you what we'll do. We'll have a bit of sport. We'll make it interesting. This tavern hasn't got much in the way of beds for passing travellers. We don't get very many calling."

"They've all been killed off by Randall Stone before they get here," a harsh voice shouted and there was a burst of laughter.

"So having eight arrive at once is not very good for me. Or them." Lambert, Crispin and Joslin listened with trepidation. "I'll have to let the actors stay because they were here first. But as for the minstrels – I know, we'll have a competition. They'll sing to you. When they've finished, we'll find out which one you like best. He can sleep here and the other two will go out in the night and burrow down under leaves in the forest. And the best of luck to them. How's that for an idea?"

The roar showed they thought it was a good one.

"No fear," squealed Lambert. "I won't sing. I'm with the actors."

He jumped up to run round to the front and protest. Crispin pushed him down with a huge hand. "You'll stay there and do what he says. I want to leave here alive and I reckon this is the only way. There are times when we have to pocket our pride."

"You're right, Crispin," said Joslin. "It's sad to say, but you are."

Lambert grumbled to himself, but did not object again.

Arnulf came back. "Did you hear that?" he asked. "Then let the second part of the night's frolics begin."

"**N**obody's asked us," Miles roared.

"Nobody's going to," Arnulf retorted. "You've no credit here bar a night's shelter." He seemed to talk more for the crowd's benefit than Miles's. In answer, they cheered mockingly.

"I've not been so humiliated in thirty years on the road," said Miles. His face was old through the gold paint and his robe patched and grubby. He started to tear down the curtain. Arnulf pushed him off.

"Leave it," he shouted.

Joslin watched and did not like what he saw. He said so to Crispin.

"Let it be," Crispin answered. "Unless you want a cold night and likely worse before dawn comes."

Joslin knew Crispin spoke sense. Meanwhile, Arnulf was setting up his contest.

"The minstrels will draw straws for their playing order," he said. "Shortest straw goes first, longest last." He held out a clenched fist with three stalks projecting. "Each take one and don't look till I say."

Lambert took his and hid it without looking. Crispin

48

did the same, then Joslin. Lambert's straw was longest, then Joslin's. Crispin would go first. As Crispin prepared, Joslin looked out at the crowd. The torches still burned under a black, starless sky. Flickering light cast strange shadows and left patches of jettest darkness. Faces were fleetingly lit up, strangely bright but furrowed and creased with darkness. He remembered the panicked faces going down to Hell which Robin and Alys painted on the Doom in Stovenham church, which led to such pain, misery and death. Some faces leered, some gibbered like raving madmen. Eyes twinkled, glowered or lay hard like stones.

Crispin got ready to sing. Suddenly, Joslin shivered. A message was reaching the cart from somewhere in that press of people: menace – cold, frightening menace. Could they really sing through this?

Arnulf, Slad the brewer and two potboys were busy pouring beer into jugs for the jostling customers. Crispin regarded his audience with scarcely veiled contempt. Lambert, after his first sulking, was now at ease sitting on the cart. He saw Joslin and mouthed, "Don't worry. This lot will love us."

"They'll love one of us," Joslin replied. But he doubted it. He thought of the piles of leaves the losers would sleep on, branches creaking, wild boars rooting about, perhaps wolves, robbers on the lookout for prey. What could be worse? Then he had a strange, foreboding feeling. It could be a lot worse.

Arnulf left pouring beer to Slad and the potboys. He lifted an empty barrel and banged it on the floor of the cart. The crowd quietened.

"Forget the play," he shouted. "We know what's going to happen to Eve, don't we?" He crashed the barrel down again. "Now for a bit of sport. When these three have finished, you'll shout for each one. Loudest shout wins. I'll be the judge. Two go off into the night, the other beds down here in the dry. The big one sings first, the foreigner second, the little London louse last. He'd better be worth the wait."

Crispin stepped forward. His drum was slung over his shoulder, his flute in his hand. "I shall sing you the tale of Gamelyn," he said.

The very tale he'd teased the audience with in Warwick – the tale that would so anger them they'd burn every manor and hang every lord in the shire. Priests, bishops and lords wouldn't like it. "*But the folk will*," Crispin had said last night. "*It means a lot to me, does that story.*" To understand this strange person who seemed to be his friend, Joslin knew he had better listen very carefully.

"It's a long tale," said Crispin. The crowd groaned. "But I'll stop between each part for a rest. I'll call you to order each time I start again."

He gave a roll on the drums and a shrill fanfare on the flute. Then his deep, gravelly voice cut through the talking and everyone fell silent.

"Now shut up and listen and get this right.
You'll hear me tell of a doughty knight.
Sir John of the Borders: that was his name.
A tough man, a fair man who played a hard game.
Three sons the knight had from the seed he sowed.
The eldest was a villain, and this soon showed.
The others loved their father: and of their brother
    were aghast.
He deserved Sir John's curse and got it at the last.
That good knight, their father, had lived many
    years.

Now Death was approaching and with it death's
   fears.
The good knight cared deeply as sick there he lay
How his three sons should prosper when he'd had
   his day.
He'd been far and wide, no stay-at-home he,
And much land he'd come by: all his, legally.
He wanted it all divided up fair
So each of his sons would have his right share."

The eldest brother was called John after his father, the second was Otis, the youngest was Gamelyn. The old knight willed his lands to be shared equally between them. Otis and Gamelyn were happy about this, but John was angry because as the eldest he didn't get the lot. He plotted to cheat Gamelyn out of his share. Feigning friendship, he brought his young brother to live with him at his manor house – but then treated him like the meanest servant and let his share of the land go to rack and ruin. Powerless, Gamelyn vowed to have his rightful inheritance.

To prove his strength, he entered the local wrestling contest. He begged John for a horse to ride to the forest where the ring was set up. John agreed. But when Gamelyn was out of sight he locked the gates against him – "for ever" said the false elder brother.

Gamelyn came to the ring. There stood the huge champion – and near him, an old man crying.

"'Alas,' cried the old man, 'that ever I was born.
The champion here has wrestled and torn
My two fine sons to pieces and death,
The pride of my life while I drew breath.
I'd give ten whole pounds to hear him scream.

But no one can hurt him – it's just a wild dream.'
'Hold my horse,' said young Gamelyn. 'I'll make
    him pay.
Nobody here will forget me today.'"

Gamelyn strode up to the champion, hurled him to the ground and broke three ribs and an arm.

"*'Shall we call that a throw? Or do you want more?'"* said Gamelyn. No, the contest was over. Gamelyn was champion. The watchers went wild with delight and when they heard his story vowed to come back with him to help take his rightful inheritance. But the brother's gates were locked.

Crispin gave a roll on the drums, sat down and took up his tankard of ale. The folk were silent for a moment. The menace Joslin had feared seemed to have died away. Then they drank and talked again as if they weren't sure what was to come next.

Crispin drained his tankard and held it out for a refill. Then he gave another drum roll, a perky tune on the flute, and started again with a piercing shout.

"*NOW SHUT UP AND LISTEN, both young and*
    old
And you'll hear of good sport with Gamelyn the
    bold."

And they did shut up. A story may not be worth more than a quart of ale, but when both come together. . .

"*Gamelyn came back and knocked on the gate.*
It was locked fast against him with a bolt of great
    weight.
Gamelyn said, 'Porter, open it wide.

There are many good men here waiting outside.'
The porter soon answered, and swore by his
   beard,
'You'll never, young Gamelyn, come in this yard.'
'I will,' shouted Gamelyn. 'You'll not stop me, you
   dolt!'
He kicked at the wicket door, shattering the bolt.
The porter saw clearly that perhaps it might be
Best if he went quick. He started to flee.
'Oh, no,' said young Gamelyn. 'That'll do you no
   good.
I can run faster than you ever could.'
He soon caught the porter. Ignoring his groan,
He seized his fat neck and shattered the bone
And threw the limp body straight down the well –
Seven fathoms deep so I've heard tell.
Young Gamelyn now, had shown how he would
   play.
Armed men who'd been waiting crept quietly
   away.
They'd seen what he'd do. It scared them all
   right –
And so did the company he'd brought there to
   fight.
Gamelyn seized the gate and opened it wide.
His followers, unhindered, all rode inside.
'You're welcome,' cried Gamelyn, 'each one of
   you.
We're masters here now. We say what to do.
When I was last here, that brother of mine
Down in his cellar had barrels of wine. . .'"

   So they feasted and drank for seven whole days
and nights, while the eldest brother John fled and hid

in a turret wondering what to do. But on the eighth day, Gamelyn's guests came to him and said they must go. "So soon?" asked Gamelyn. "Yes," they answered, and Gamelyn was left on his own.

John saw his chance. He and his men came out of hiding. Straight away Gamelyn was taken, fettered to a chair and starved. Then John spread rumours about the country that Gamelyn was mad.

But Gamelyn had one friend – Adam, the steward. One night, when John was asleep, Adam took keys to unlock the fetters and gave Gamelyn food and drink to get his strength back. Then they waited for a great feast John was giving to all the holy men of the church.

Perfect. When all those bishops, abbots, monks and priests were sitting round the table feeding their faces and getting drunk, Gamelyn and Adam were among them with their staves, cracking heads, breaking legs, snapping arms. No matter the curses: once they had started, they wouldn't stop until all the holy men were nothing but hobbling wrecks and John could only watch in horror.

But the sheriff and his men were close by and a servant slipped out with a message to them. So the sheriff with his soldiers was soon banging on the door. "Keep them out for a moment," cried Gamelyn to Adam, "while I think of a plan."

The plan was simple. Gamelyn and Adam drank a last glass of wine, then crept silently away, as the sheriff burst in to the battered, groaning priests demanding they be helped before anything else.

The two made for the forest and the outlaws. The outlaw king welcomed them and soon Gamelyn and Adam were outlaws like the rest.

The time came when the outlaw king wanted to be

king no longer. There was, he thought, only one there to take his place. Gamelyn. No sooner was Gamelyn crowned in the forest than amazing news came. His brother John was made sheriff – and his first task, he had vowed, would be to get Gamelyn.

"Not if I get to him first," said Gamelyn. The day of John's first meeting in the assembly hall dawned. All the great men from round about were there to see John in all his glory. A judge and jury chosen by John alone were there to pronounce death on Gamelyn. But when they least expected it, Gamelyn and his outlaws burst in and the tables were turned.

"The judge and the sheriff were both hanged on
* high*
For their bodies to swing till their bones were
* picked dry.*
Gallows were built in the town, there and then,
Where the necks were all snapped of those false
* jurymen.*
Thus died Gamelyn's brother. Who's sorry at
* that?*
He'd spent his whole life as a cheat and a rat."

So Crispin ended Gamelyn's song and how he gained great fortune.

"Sir Otis, his brother, made Gamelyn his heir.
And Gamelyn wedded a maid good and fair
They lived long together in the joys that God gave
And then they were buried deep in the same grave.
And so might it be for us all, ere we die.
May God bring us all to that great joy on high."

In that last line, Crispin's voice rasped sarcastically. No "joy on high" would ever satisfy him.

The song was over and the folk seemed to have loved it. No, they hadn't rushed out to kill every lord in the shire. But as they cheered, Crispin looked at them and a strange expression crossed his face which Joslin could not understand.

So that was the song that meant so much to him. Why? Did it have something to do with Crispin's "unfinished business"? Was this the tale of Crispin Thurn as much as the tale of Gamelyn?

Joslin had a lot to think about as he tuned his harp ready for his own song. He looked over his audience. The feeling of menace came again – especially when he saw, in the middle of the crowd, that sinister figure with the monster's head. Arnulf jumped on the cart and banged the barrel on the floor again. "It's time for our little Frenchman to give us a song now. Don't ask me what foreign muck he'll sing us because I won't understand a word of it. If you don't like it, just remember what we did to his lot at Poitiers."

The audience was sullenly quiet. Joslin wondered if he really wanted to spend a night in this place. What should he sing? He'd been so busy listening to Crispin's *Gamelyn* that he'd not given it a thought. His mind had gone blank.

This was the minstrel's nightmare. He never thought he would find himself in it.

"**G**et on with it," came a voice.

What with? He remembered another song after a journey – the first night in London at Randolf Waygood's house. He'd sung that strange song, half-English, half-French, *Lay le Freine*, the song of the ash-tree. They'd loved it then. Would these?

He played a mournful introduction. Then:

> *"We sometimes read and often tell –*
> *And many minstrels know them well –*
> *Magical stories to plucked harp strings*
> *Full of enchantment, miraculous things:*
> *Some of war and some of woe,*
> *Some of joy and mirth also.*
> *In Brittany, in the olden time,*
> *This story happened – so says this rhyme.*
> *And of this story, made up long ago,*
> *I can sing most, though some I don't know."*

"Then why start?" yelled a voice and there was a burst of laughter round where it came from. Joslin gritted his teeth and carried on.

A great knight's lady gave birth to twin girls. She was worried. She knew what people would say. Two babies must mean two fathers. Why, she'd already accused another knight's wife of being unfaithful to her husband when she'd had twins. But she herself *hadn't*. What should she do?

"Learn a bit of sense," a voice shouted.

"He's not palming that old wives' tale off on us, is he?" bellowed another.

"Of course not," Joslin shouted back. "The song's hundreds of years old. They believed it then."

"Well, we don't believe it now."

"I bet they do in France. They're thick enough."

"Sing us a proper song or get off."

"Better still, just get off."

They liked that. "Off! Off! Off!" they shouted.

Crispin jumped on the cart and put an arm round Joslin's shoulders. "Best do as they say, lad," he whispered. He led him off the cart and behind the curtain. Joslin was shaking. Tears stung his eyes. "That's never happened to me before," he said.

"You're lucky," Crispin answered.

"If I had a penny for every time I've been shouted down I wouldn't need to do this daft job," said Lambert as he took Joslin's place on the cart.

Dimly, Joslin heard Arnulf's voice. "Forget him. We've got better here now. A proper Englishman, even if he does come from London. Let's see what our Cockney friend can do."

The noise for Lambert was not so hostile. "I'll give you the song of the blacksmiths," he said. "You join in when I tell you." At once he was in it, a rollicking tune that made you want to stamp and clap. Joslin saw that if he'd wanted to win he should have sung a song like it, noisy, simple, with no story. And he knew plenty. But then, he knew now he didn't want to win.

"Sooty, sooty blacksmiths, spattered all with smoke,
Such a row every night, it never stops, never.
They drive me to death with their desperate din,
It just goes on, for ever and ever."

He stopped. "That's the verse. Here's the chorus." Now he was shouting at the top of his voice.

"'Huff! Puff!' goes one, 'Haff! Paff!' goes another.
'Pick! Pack! Hick! Hack! Tick! Tack!' goes his
brother."

The words were like hammer blows on an anvil. They'd make anybody want to join in. Lambert stopped again. "Every time I get to those two lines, you come in with me," he said. "We'll have a great time."

He started again. The people loved it. At the end of each verse, in they came, shouting and stamping until the noise climbed into the sky, woke sleeping creatures, deafened hunting owls and questing badgers and made outlaws deep in the forest stand ready lest the king's soldiers were on the march for them.

"'Huff! Puff!' goes one, 'Haff! Paff!' goes another,
'Pick! Pack! Hick! Hack! Tick! Tack!' goes his
brother."

Time after time, as Lambert unwound each verse, the chorus crashed in until he hoarsely croaked, "Just one more time." And there it was, loud as ever, until it was lost in shouts of, "More! More!"

"No fear," said Lambert. "I want my beer."

He scrambled behind the curtain, grabbed his tankard, took a long swig and winked. "That should see me all right," he said.

Arnulf was in front of the crowd again. "Decision time," he shouted. "First – what did you think of Master Crispin and his story? I bet you never heard anything like that before." He was sarcastic again.

The air rang with hisses and boos. Crispin shrugged. "Pearls before swine," he said.

"No doubt there," said Arnulf. "What about the Frenchman?"

Silence, then a barely audible hiss.

"Well, at least you didn't want to tear him limb from limb," said Arnulf. "Now for our last little songbird. A bit different, wasn't he?"

Yells rang out. "Lam-*bert!* Lam-*bert!* Lam-*bert!* Lam-*bert!*"

"It's not hard to see who you like best," said Arnulf. "I'll tell him the good news."

He jumped down and joined the minstrels. "Lambert," he said. "Come up and take a bow." He turned to Crispin and Joslin. "That's it, then. The folk have spoken. Just get on your way."

Crispin turned the full force of his glare on Arnulf. "I wouldn't soil my feet on your floor or my hands on your blankets," he said.

In the dim light, Arnulf stepped backwards. A strange expression crossed his face. "You think I don't know you," he said. "Don't delude yourself. Who could forget? So you call yourself a minstrel now, do you? That's a laugh. Get out! *Get out! GET OUT!*"

"Don't worry," said Crispin. "I'm going."

Joslin and Crispin led the horses cautiously along the northward track. From the Tavern Where the Ways Meet, Lambert's blacksmiths' chorus could still be heard, faint and blowsy.

> "'*Huff! Puff!*' *goes one.* '*Haff! Haff!*' *goes another,*
> '*Pick! Pack! Hick! Hack! Tick! Tack!*' *goes his*
>   *brother.*"

Neither spoke until their eyes were used to the dark. Then Joslin said, "Shall we get as far away as we can?"

"I don't like riding in the dark through this place," Crispin replied. "Besides, like I said, I want to keep an eye on that tavern." They walked a few more paces. Then he said, "This will do." Thick-leaved branches hung low from two oak trees and the leaf-mould underneath was dry and springy. They tethered the horses. "Listen," said Joslin.

A crowd of leaving drinkers staggered towards them, still giving a slurred and breathy rendering of the blacksmiths' chorus. Joslin and Crispin waited until they passed and the racket dwindled into nothing.

"We're safe now," said Crispin. They made beds from fallen leaves and Joslin used his cloak as a blanket. There was, he thought, a lot he would like to know, and now seemed a good time to ask.

"How does Arnulf know you?" he asked. "Why weren't you a minstrel then?"

Crispin said nothing. Joslin tried again. "Why should the song of Gamelyn mean so much to you?" Still no answer. "Is Gamelyn's story like yours? I wish you'd tell it to me." No reply, but Joslin was sure he was near the truth. "What did Arnulf mean by saying he knew what lay behind that song?" No answer again. "Who *is* Gamelyn? Are *you*?"

"Ask no questions, hear no lies," Crispin replied. "Stay long enough and you might find out."

"One more," said Joslin. "Who's Randall Stone?"

Crispin laughed. "Him? Take no notice. A tale for mothers to frighten their children with." He paused. "Just be glad you're out of that place in one piece and never mind Randall Stone. There's evil afoot in there. Didn't you feel it in the air?"

"Yes," said Joslin. "That's why I thought we'd keep going tonight."

"There are dangers along the way as well. We'll stay where we are. Leaves for a mattress, panniers for pillows, cloaks for blankets? It's a fine night. What more do we want?" Crispin answered.

Joslin didn't argue. He realized how tired he was.

"We'll take it in turns to sleep," said Crispin. "The other keeps watch. We'll draw for who's first." He picked up a leaf, turned away and then held out two clenched fists. "If you pick the leaf, you choose."

Joslin touched Crispin's right fist. It held the leaf. What should he choose? He was tired. But his mind was too active for sleep. "I'll watch first," he said.

Crispin seemed content. "If nothing happens, wake me when the rising moon touches the treetops," he said. "But if it does and it's bad, rouse me at once." He unsheathed his sword and laid it on the ground. Then Joslin heard leaves rustle and, soon, snoring.

The night was still, the track deserted. He could not see the tavern though it was barely two hundred paces away. Only the forest's night noises and the horses' breathings and snortings disturbed his ears. His eyes kept closing, however much he wanted them not to. The moon stubbornly refused to climb near the treetops. He'd never keep awake. . .

With a jerk he opened his eyes. Had he dozed? Crispin still slept.

But something else was happening.

Even though he had won a roof to sleep under, Lambert was sorry to lose his new minstrel friends. They were in the same line of business and spoke the same language. Now, everybody was a stranger, even the actors. After all, he'd only met them in Cambridge, and if he hadn't turned up tonight they probably wouldn't have noticed. His bed was a pile of straw in a chamber shared by Alban, Hob and Sym. Behind a thin wall slept Miles, Molly, Jankin and Peg. "Bartholomew should be here," said Miles. "You can have his place." But Miles had a trumpeting snore, Sym an irritating sniffle, Alban a breathy gasp and Jankin a chesty rasp like a file on iron. Only Hob slept quietly, like a true Christian with no sins on his conscience.

Lambert stared up at bats flying round the rafters. He'd never sleep. He might be better off under the stars like the other minstrels.

The chorus of the sleepers, rising and falling like some strange plainsong, drowned every sound. That must have been why he never heard a new movement. Had the huge silent shadow suddenly over him come through the door? Or was it in the chamber all the time?

The shadow spoke. "You're the one. Come with me. There's something outside I want you to see. Make no sound. Let them sleep."

Lambert peered upwards. "Do I know you?" he asked.

The noise was nearer the tavern. A rustle of leaves, crack of twigs. Voices, indistinct, low yet occasionally raised to a sharp yelp.

Then one yelp became a cry, a shriek, a terrible scream of agony which dropped to a repulsive bubbling, then stopped short. Then silence, oppressive and complete. Then footsteps, slow, then faster, at first making more twigs crack and branches break, then clear as if running free, until they faded from Joslin's hearing.

For a moment he hardly breathed. That was no animal being killed. The cry was human. Crispin slept deeply. The moon was nowhere near shining through the treetops yet. He had to know what caused that scream – yet he couldn't leave Crispin unguarded.

He shook him by the shoulder. Crispin grunted.

"No, it's not time yet," said Joslin. "Something's happened. There was a scream. Someone may be hurt. Whoever did it may come for us. If someone's dead, we must find out who."

Crispin was fully awake. "You go," he said. "I'll stay on guard and watch after you. I'll be more use if someone's after our belongings. But I'll be there if anyone tries to harm you, never fear."

Joslin made sure he had his dagger. Then he set off to where the sound came from. It must have been off the path, because of the snapping twigs and branches. The escaper, though, had made no such noises. So he used the path – but away from Crispin and Joslin. Where to? Back to the tavern or deep into the forest?

The scream had come from some way down the path and off it among the trees. Joslin's minstrel's ears could distinguish well between sounds. Which side of the path? He was sure it was opposite.

He made eighty paces towards the tavern. Then he stepped off the path and into the forest. His eyes were used to the dark now and moonlight filtering through the leaves helped him. Even so, searching the forest floor was scrabbling round a black, shifting blanket of leaves, broken wood and leaf-mould made deep from years of autumns.

Then he tripped over a soft, heavy, yielding object. His hands landed in something soft, sticky and still warm. After these last months, he knew exactly what he had found.

He stood up. Here was someone newly dead and left for others to find or be buried in leaves, eaten by animals and never known at all. The open eyes glittered upwards. Greasy black hair, pointed, even rat-like, nose and chin. The bloodsoaked garment was a minstrel's tunic. Lambert of Shoreditch had come all the way from London to meet his end in the Forest of Arden.

Joslin squatted on his haunches and wanted to cry. He had met Lambert not twelve hours earlier, yet he felt he knew him like an old friend. Lambert made him laugh, had a voice fit to charm wild beasts, could turn an audience the way he wanted, shared the travelling way of life. It was like finding a long-lost brother and then losing him again.

There was nothing he could do for the dead minstrel. Lambert was stabbed through his heart. There was no doubt he saw his killer. At least this was not the secret shameful knifing in the back that poor Martin de Mawdsley had been dealt in Oxford. But why Lambert?

Shivering, Joslin looked for a landmark to know the place again. A large fallen tree-trunk sprawled nearby. He left Lambert, went back to Crispin and told him what he had found. Crispin was silent. Then he said, "Let me see for myself."

Joslin led him back to where Lambert lay. They looked down on him and Crispin moved the body slightly with his toe. Then he said, "Travelling actors and minstrels don't seem well-liked round here."

"What shall we do?" asked Joslin.

"Get out of here quick," Crispin replied.

Joslin shivered again. He put his cloak on for the cold night air. But he was not sure if Crispin was right.

"We daren't," he said. "When Lambert's found, we'll be blamed."

"They won't find us," said Crispin.

"What? Two minstrels without money? One young, one older? One local, one French? We wouldn't last a day," Joslin answered.

"If they accuse us, we'll deny it," said Crispin.

"What good will that do? I've been accused of things I didn't do ever since I came to England," said Joslin. "They'll be only too glad to put it all on a Frenchman." He looked at Crispin's dark shape. "No, we have to go back to the tavern and raise the alarm."

"Are you mad?" Crispin exclaimed. "We may as well say it was us."

"Not at all. If the killer went to the tavern he won't be expecting this. We'll have the advantage. If he didn't, then we see who's missing."

"What if it's one of last night's crowd?" said Crispin.

"We can't do much about that," Joslin replied.

Crispin thought a moment. Joslin wondered what went through his mind. Then he spoke. "I'm impressed, Joslin. You see clearly and think quickly. You've done better over this than I would."

Joslin added for himself what Crispin meant but didn't say. *You're not the young innocent I took you for. Perhaps you're worth staying with after all.* Because one thing was obvious – he had just been tested.

They went back to where they had slept, loaded up and led the horses down the path to the tavern. They tied them up outside, then each hammered on a door. "Get up! Murder! There's a killer loose!"

A door opened. Arnulf stood before Joslin, a lantern in his hand, supremely angry. "I thought I told you to go," he spluttered.

"Lambert's been murdered," Joslin answered.

"Nonsense. Lambert's curled up on the good sweet straw I gave him, sleeping like a baby."

"He's not, Arnulf," said a voice behind him. Miles. "All my actors are safe but Lambert's certainly not where he was when we first slept."

"Show me," said Arnulf.

Miles led the way. Sym, Hob and Alban were sitting up. "Is Lambert back?" asked Miles.

"No," Alban replied.

Light from Arnulf's lantern showed a dent in the thick straw.

"The straw's cold," said Sym. "He's been gone some time."

"Did none of you hear him?" asked Arnulf.

"We were tired. We were well asleep," said Hob.

"Everybody in this tavern must show themselves," said Arnulf. "I'll find who knows about this."

Soon, everybody gathered by the actors' cart in the yard. Dawn was breaking: Arnulf, two potboys, five actors, Molly, Peg and Slad stood like dim, grey ghosts. No, nothing was known, nothing seen or heard, not a moment of sleep disturbed.

"Nobody here did it, Arnulf," said Hob.

"If the killer came from outside, how did he get in?" asked Joslin.

"More to the point, how did he and Lambert get out?" growled Crispin. "And did Lambert want to go?"

"I can tell you one way he could get in and not wake anyone," said Slad. "He could climb over the gate into the yard where carts come in with malt and barley for the ale. He could get into the tavern through the hatch I push barrels down to the cellar."

"And would Lambert be fool enough to go with him?" said Arnulf.

"He might if it wasn't a him but a her," said Alban.

"Depends what she promised him outside," said Slad, and the potboys sniggered.

"Or perhaps you talk moonshine and there was a knife at Lambert's ribs," said Crispin.

"Let's see this hatch," said Joslin.

Slad's idea was possible. A barrel could roll easily down to the cellar and a man could scramble up.

"That must be it," said Crispin.

"But why should Lambert be worth breaking in for?" asked Miles.

"Someone with a score to settle from the past," Alban suggested.

Something occurred to Joslin. "Why are we so certain somebody broke in?" he said. "Perhaps the killer was here already one of last night's crowd. He might have stayed behind and hid."

"We certainly had a tavern full three times over," said Arnulf. "Drank us dry, they did."

Suddenly, Molly spoke. "It was the man with the huge monster's head which looked like it should topple off his shoulders. I *know* it."

"Why should you say that, my love?" asked Miles.

"Because he led the cries against you. If it weren't for him, you'd have finished the play and been loved for it."

"I saw him as well," said Peg. "He led the cheering for Lambert in the minstrels' contest. He belted out the choruses and egged everybody on. Without that Lambert might not have won. Crispin might have. But that man didn't want Crispin to win. I saw him whispering to people round him. His thoughts seemed to go through the crowd like a plague."

"You know everyone round about the forest, Arnulf," said Miles. "Who was this monstrous man?"

"He's not been here," said Arnulf quickly. "I've never seen him."

"Well, that's a pity," said Crispin. "If it's minstrels he doesn't like he could be after us next."

"But he doesn't seem to kill minstrels just because they're minstrels," said Joslin. "He was only after Lambert. But Lambert was a stranger here."

"That's what I said," Alban insisted. "He was followed here."

"Why go to such trouble?" said Joslin. "He could have killed him in the forest, covered his body with leaves and nobody would know. There's more to it."

"It was us that old big-head didn't like," said Sym.

"Lambert sang at the start of our play. He'd think

Lambert was one of us. Once we'd all met again, I suppose he was," said Miles.

"Miles, are you saying Lambert was killed because he was one of us actors?" Jankin demanded. "If that's true then I'm frightened."

"I wish Bartholomew was back from Coventry," said Miles. "This forest seems dangerous to me."

"We've been through dangerous places before where the folk didn't like us much. This is the same, isn't it?" Peg asked hopefully.

"Nobody's tried to kill us, though," said Jankin.

Everyone was quiet. Arnulf broke the silence. "We're forgetting our duties," he said. "Lambert's body's been found so we must bring him in, lay him out and fetch a priest. No man can lie unknown on a forest floor till animals and worms consume him and his soul is left to wander round purgatory like a waif. And we'd be damned for letting it happen."

He led them back into the tavern. Then he, Crispin, Miles and Jankin set out, with Joslin to show them where to go. The forest seemed different now it was full of colour and touched by the first sun of a fine day. Joslin confidently paced along the path. When he stopped he said, "The body's off the track, close to a fallen trunk. Now it's light, I should find it at once."

He led the way into the trees. Yes, there was the trunk. So over here must be Lambert's body.

"Here," he said.

But there was nothing but a hollow in the leaf-mould as if something heavy once rested there. Whatever it was had disappeared.

"So where is this murdered man, Joslin?" asked Arnulf in a dangerously quiet voice.

Crispin answered. "Take that suspicious look off your face, Arnulf Long. He was here and he was well murdered, you take it from me."

"There's blood on the leaves," said Sym.

"So someone dragged the body away," said Miles.

Arnulf wasn't finished with Crispin. "And I know who. *You* did, Crispin Thurn or whatever your name is. It wasn't Crispin Thurn when we met before, that I do know. You weren't a minstrel either."

"You're mistaken, Arnulf," Crispin replied. "Minstrels are born, not made. Once a minstrel, always a minstrel." He smiled. "If you think you know me, perhaps you'll tell these good people how."

Arnulf turned away and said nothing.

"I thought not," said Crispin.

The rest watched this exchange open-mouthed. Then Miles said, "Have you finished? This matters more than your old scores. Someone was killed here or, if not, he bled a lot. Where is he now?"

"Perhaps he wasn't dead and he limped off," said Alban.

"If that was so, we'd see a trail of blood and him dead very close," said Joslin. "If Lambert was still alive, he wouldn't have lasted more than a few moments. No, he was taken away. . ."

"By the murderer." Molly finished the sentence.

"But the murderer ran away," said Joslin. "I heard him pushing through the forest and running off."

"Which way?" asked Miles.

"Towards the tavern."

"Then he *did* come back in last night. It *could* be someone here," said Miles.

"But it could still be you," Arnulf said angrily to Crispin. "You waited a while before you roused us, to throw us off the scent."

"Leave it alone, Arnulf," said Miles. "Anyone can see it wasn't."

Crispin's face darkened, as if he would strike Arnulf, but Joslin whispered, "This isn't the time."

"It seems obvious," said Miles. "The murderer was in the tavern last night. He rode here. When he'd killed Lambert he came back for his horse, slung the body over it and took it away."

"Well, that settles it," said Arnulf. "The killer's gone, the dead man's gone and as far as I'm concerned, they were never here. And you can go as well and I don't want to see any of you again. Pay what you owe and get out of my sight. And if you go to Coventry after this, you're dafter than I thought you were."

"Arnulf, we've paid enough," said Miles. "We didn't get a penny for our play. Not one groat will you get from us. We'll come for our cart and be on our way."

Arnulf looked round. "Four of us," he said. "Me, Slad and my potboys. Five of you. Two of you don't look up to much and I don't count the women. If it comes to a fight, I'll get my money."

Crispin stood tall and spoke. "We're coming back with the actors, so you'll have us to fight with. I'll make sure all's done fairly."

An hour later, the sun was risen and the actors on their way. Crispin had altered the odds enough for Arnulf to forget his money.

"Besides, Arnulf," said Crispin. "Think of the profit you've got out of these poor folk with all that extra sour beer you sold."

"I don't brew sour beer," Slad protested.

"I don't doubt it, Slad. It's the careless way your master keeps it."

Arnulf's face darkened. "Last night never happened," he said. "I know nothing about a murder: there was no body in the forest and if you bring the law here I'll laugh in your faces."

Crispin shrugged. "He's right, you know," he said to the others. "We can't do a thing if he won't help."

Sym and Hob heaved on the shafts of the cart – "We had to sell our horse last winter," said Miles. Slad opened the gates and they passed through, on to the northward path. "If you go to Coventry you'll be sorry people," Arnulf shouted after them.

"I'm glad to be out of that place," said Hob.

"We'll be saying goodbye then," said Crispin.

"Yes," said Miles. But Joslin saw the actors' faces and knew what he would say next. "Or you could come with us to Coventry."

The offer of going with the actors was too good to turn down, Joslin thought – much better than going alone. And it wasn't just for the plays. He wanted to find out more about Lambert's death, yet already last night seemed unreal, like a dream. If he wanted to know more – well, Coventry was as good a place as anywhere to start. After all, Lambert was with the actors, and travelling actors didn't seem welcome in Coventry any more than they were here.

Margery ran as fast as her legs would carry her, up Little Park Street and Cow Lane until she was opposite Greyfriars, where the monks lived round their lovely church. Then she turned up Greyfriars Street, to the cottage where she lived with her parents. Her father was at the weaving trade – and so, most of the time, was her mother. They made fine cloth from wool which came to Coventry from the Wolds of Leicestershire and the hills of Shropshire and Wales. She could hear the loom's "clack–clack" even before she reached her house. *They haven't even noticed I was gone*, she thought.

She crept into the cottage. The room was deserted. The fire, damped down, smouldered and the tang of smoking wood stung her eyes. "Clack–clack" went the loom, louder now. Margery went to the outhouse. Her mother worked alone. She looked mildly at her child, without question.

"Where's Father?" asked Margery.

"He's with the Guild," her mother replied. "They're making their silly play for Corpus Christi. He's being a learned doctor. Robert Meriden and the friars should know better than to let good workmen waste their time with such foolery."

Margery knew about the learned doctors, the wise men Jesus argued with when he was little and made them look silly. She knew who Robert Meriden was –

the Mayor, Master of both the Corpus Christi Guild and Guild of Weavers and the most important man in the city. As for the Grey Friars. . .

"And all the other weavers are there, while their wives get on with the work to keep us all alive," her mother continued grumpily. "Why shouldn't I be in the play too? I'd be a good Mary." A "clack" from the loom sounded like an angry smack. "But, oh no, they won't let us women anywhere near their precious plays." As her mother grumbled on, Margery wondered whether she would ever stop to draw breath. So she said, "I've been down into Hell and saw a lost soul being carried away to burn for ever in its fires and I saw two devils and one of them spoke to me and then they let me go so I came home."

Her mother never even heard. "Plays, indeed," she sniffed. "What do they want to start doing *plays* for?"

"I was going to Coventry anyway," said Crispin.

"Come with us," said Sym. "Be our minstrels. Until we met Lambert, we hadn't got one. Now we could enter Coventry with two."

"Judging by what happened to Lambert, it strikes me there's not much future in being a minstrel with you," said Crispin.

"There's a difference between what goes on in a forest and a well set-up town," said Miles.

"The town of Lady Godiva," said Alban.

"And Peeping Tom," said Molly. "Not everything's good there."

"It's the city of Hock Monday, after Easter, when the men chase the women and tie them up and the women try to fight them off," said Hob.

"I wish we'd been there for that," said Jankin.

76

Peg slapped him round the ear and said, "I'd have made sure you were tied up before the day started."

"I only meant that I'd like to celebrate the day the people of Coventry defeated the Danes," said Jankin, pained. "That's how they remember it."

"Anyway," said Molly, "on Hock Tuesday the women chase the men. Some old scores get settled then, I shouldn't wonder."

"Coventry's a fine town," said Miles. "I've been there before with a band of actors and the folk received us well."

"It's a town that the plague ruined, that was left desolate and will never be the same," said Crispin. "And I'm told the Mayor and Council rule so harshly that there's much anger among the poorer folk."

"Even so, everybody watches the plays at Corpus Christi and we've always made good money, whether in Lincoln, Chester, Norwich, York or Wakefield," said Jankin. "I hope things never change."

"And I hope Coventry likes you more than Arden did," said Crispin.

"They will," said Miles. Then: "We've talked this over among ourselves and we're agreed. Will you both come with us?"

Joslin and Crispin looked at each other. "Yes," they said together.

Coventry was ten miles to the north-east. By straying into the forest, Joslin had gone past it, on a road leading south-west away from Warwick. He had entered the north-eastern fringes of the Forest and he might have wandered blindly south to the forest's dark heart and out the other side, going the wrong way altogether for Wales.

Coventry lay on a plain crossed by the River Sherbourne. From north, south and west, by road and river, pack horse, cart and barge, wool came for weaving and making cloth for the people of the Midlands and beyond, far across the sea. From London, Leicester, Gloucester and Worcester, travellers came, spent their money and went again. Coventry had grown rich. The weavers and tailors, shearmen and cardmakers formed powerful Guilds. They knew their worth and bowed to nobody. That was why the Hock days were celebrated, because the people of Coventry had years before put the Danish invaders to flight. It was also why they remembered Lady Godiva, because her naked ride through the town defied king and lord and upheld the rights of the folk. Yes, it had been a proud city – before the plague. Coventry was hit harder than many: the scars stayed. Yet the folk loved their plays and they travelled miles to see them. Coventry should still bring good profit.

But things were changing, in ways the actors would not like.

Crispin agreed to let his horse pull the cart and Joslin agreed that Herry would take its place halfway. They journeyed slowly. The trees thinned and the sun shone ever more clearly through until the forest was left behind. Joslin felt a weight leave his mind in the clear air. "So the tavern wasn't a mile from the edge," he said.

"I wish Bartholomew was back to lead us into Coventry," said Hob.

"We might see him coming to meet us," said Sym. "He'll have good news. I know he will."

"Who is this Bartholomew?" asked Joslin. "What's his news?"

"Ah, Bartholomew's a lovely man," said Peg.

"He can do any part in any play you mention," said Alban. "But chiefly he can be a clown and a jester. He can make an audience laugh just by raising an eyebrow."

"He may act the fool, but be sure he's not one himself," said Jankin.

"Bartholomew was trained to the law," said Miles. "He's kept his lawyer's mind even though a life with old books and dry arguments didn't appeal to him. We met him five years ago. We were trying to squeeze money out of the folk in a dim little town in Essex. They were glad to watch but didn't like paying. So we left sadder and wiser – but as we left, this young man ran after us, still in his black gown. 'I'm coming with you,' he shouted. 'A life on the road is better than one in that stinkhole.' And he's stayed ever since. He soon learnt the trade and his black gown does for a Pharisee when we play Christ's Passion."

"Ah, he's wonderful, is Bartholomew," said Jankin. "We can't do without him." He looked at Joslin. "Come to think of it," he continued, "he's like you. If you didn't sound French and Bartholomew didn't sound what he is, a man of Essex, you could be brothers."

"He can make people laugh, can Bartholomew," Peg repeated wistfully. "And never more than in the Judgement play."

"But the Day of Judgement isn't funny," said Joslin.

"It is when Bartholomew's in it," said Jankin. "He's worked out a way of being the Devil's porter at the gates of Hell. You won't find that in scripture. The priests hate it, but the folk roar their ribs out."

"And what's the news he's bringing back?" asked Joslin.

Miles told him. "Whenever a feast day approaches, we try to be near a big town. There's no feast day greater for the actors than Corpus Christi. All the plays based on the scriptures are done – from Creation right through to, well, to the Day of Judgement if they can stand it for so long. We like to have things cut and dried before we enter – what we'll act and where, how much we'll be paid. For these things we have to seek out the mayor and aldermen, so we become a proper part of the town's celebrations and not chased off as vagabonds. You need someone who can talk to these people properly. That's why Bartholomew's so important. He knows the law and he can argue with men who think they're so great. We send him on in front with his black gown so they'll know he understands the law, he makes the arrangements and comes back, then we enter the town in style."

"Not this time, though," said Hob.

"He's come back in good time before," said Molly.

"He'll be back," said Jankin. "He always is."

"But if he doesn't, we'll enter Coventry not knowing what's agreed for us," said Miles. "I don't like that. Especially when Molly and I are the only ones here who've been to Coventry before, the rest of you being new in the troupe."

"He'll meet us," said Alban. "This is the only road he can take."

"We must just hope," said Miles.

But the road stretched on and there was never a sign of Bartholomew.

At midday they came to Coventry. For some time across the plain they saw church towers. Miles pointed them out. "There's St John's at Bablake nearest to us and the one just to its right is Greyfriars. And in the middle of the town are Holy Trinity and St Michael's. If you look carefully, you can see the great Cross, where Broadgate meets Cross Cheaping. Yes, it's a fine set-up Christian town, is Coventry."

The sun had reached its highest point as they came to the city walls and through Spon Gate in the ward of Coventry called Bablake. As they passed underneath, Alban suddenly said, "Listen. What's that?"

"I heard nothing," said Miles.

"I did," said Peg. "Like a horn blowing. Listen again."

They stopped and listened. Yes, clearly, though from some way off, came a long blast on a horn.

"There must be a hunt passing nearby," said Jankin.

The long note broke up into three short notes. Then it continued without interruption until it suddenly ceased. "It's stopped. He fell off his horse," said Sym.

They laughed and continued into the town. Once through the gate they saw St John's church close by. In the space between the church and Hill Street was great activity. A huge cart was being built, so wide that if it were pulled through the streets, not even a dog could walk past it. On the cart, wooden structures were being made: men were swarming all over them whacking nails in.

Joslin knew what it was. So, judging by their quiet, did Miles and the actors. "A pageant wagon," said Miles bitterly. "It's true. They're building their own, far better than our little cart. They don't want us here now."

"Cheer up, Master Miles," Hob replied. "They can't do the plays without proper actors. There'll be a place for us here."

"Then why hasn't Bartholomew come to tell us?" said Miles.

"Perhaps he's waiting with the mayor to welcome us," said Alban.

"Look on the bright side, my love," said Molly.

But Miles's grim face showed he could do no such thing. A depressed silence settled over them all.

"What shall we do, Miles?" asked Peg at last.

"We go to St Mary's Hall," Miles answered. "The mayor might be there, or an alderman or two, or at least a clerk. Someone must know where Bartholomew is and they must know the chances for us as well."

"Ah, but what if they don't, Miles?" said Jankin.

"Then if there's nothing for us here, we should look for pickings somewhere else. But if they can't say where Bartholomew is then I won't leave Coventry until we find him."

There was a grim quiet at those words.

"So let's find out," said Molly.

A man on the pageant saw them. "Hey, you," he called. "No call for your sort round here. We've sent four troupes like you packing already." There was a ragged laugh from the few who looked up. "You may as well go now," called one. "Or you could if you had homes to go to," shouted another. They laughed louder. Then someone on the pageant wagon said words which stopped them. "I knew something bad would come to Coventry when I heard that horn blow."

"Time was when they would have rung bells as we came though the city gates," said Miles bitterly.

They trudged on through Coventry, Herry pulling the cart and Crispin leading his own horse. First came Fleet Street, which soon gave way to Smithford Street. They saw fine houses, fine shops – but also gaping windows and ruined roofs and knew the marks of the plague had not left the city. They passed the Bull tavern. Opposite was another pageant wagon, but those on it were too busy to notice them. Then they came to High Street. To their left they could see the great Cross where the market in Cross Cheaping started and hard by were the two churches of Holy Trinity and St Michael's. Close was St Mary's Hall, its fine proportions showing the pride of a city which thought well of itself. Joslin knew the actors' hearts shrivelled with hopelessness at the sight.

"The mayor and aldermen will be in there," said Miles. "We'll wait and ask when they come out."

"Just because the council meets here doesn't mean they live here," said Jankin. "They'll be passing their laws or sentencing their prisoners or whatever they do to keep the folk under their heel."

"Anyway, what do you think they'd tell us?" said Hob. "They'd say what those fellows on the pageant said, only a bit more fancy."

Molly linked her arm in her husband's. "Let Miles think," she said.

"Actors had friends here before," said Miles. "They spoke up for us. We got work and we were appreciated. They can't have forgotten."

"Then hammer on the door and demand those friends see you," Crispin urged impatiently. "I didn't join you for this nonsense."

"No," said Miles. "It's plain that things have changed. We're here as suppliants, not the welcome guests we used to be."

"Maybe Bartholomew's arguing in there now," said Sym hopefully.

"I doubt it," said Jankin.

At that moment, the door of St Mary's Hall opened and a man emerged. He was tall with a neat black beard and his short coat was trimmed with fur. He looked prosperous and pleased with himself.

"I know him," muttered Miles. "He's an alderman and a master weaver. For all I know he's mayor now. Let me talk."

"Why, Miles," the man said genially. "What brings you here?"

"The same as brings all actors to town at Corpus Christi, Robert Meriden. Though it seems they're not welcome any more."

Robert Meriden laughed. "Now, Miles, you can't blame us. Why give the city's hard-earned money to packs of vagabonds when we can do the job better and please the Church at the same time?"

Miles did not answer at once. Then he said, "We're

actors, not vagabonds. Ours is an ancient craft as good as any of yours in the city."

"Miles, I meant no slur," Robert Meriden said quickly.

"But you said it," Miles replied. "I see Bartholomew argued in vain. We'd better find him and go."

"Bartholomew? Who's Bartholomew?" asked Robert Meriden.

"The messenger we sent to sort out what you wanted from us," Miles answered. "He'd have got here three days ago. He was to meet the aldermen and council. Young fellow, he is, quick of tongue. He brought his lawyer's black gown to wear when he disputed with you."

"I don't know who you mean," said Robert Meriden. "No Bartholomew has spoken to me or to any alderman or Guild man."

Jankin broke in. "We want our friend. Where is he?"

Miles looked furiously at him. But Robert said, "Forgive me. I was too hasty. You have the right to look for your Bartholomew and you should not be cut off so cruelly. You actors have done this city good service in the past. You can stay until you find him."

Miles seemed grateful. "Half a loaf is better than no bread," he said. "Thank you, Robert."

"For nothing," Jankin muttered. Peg elbowed him in the ribs.

"Find lodgings in the Bull Inn before it fills up. Tell them I sent you."

"If you say so, Robert," Miles replied. Joslin was amazed at how meek he sounded.

"But before you go. . ." Robert began, then paused.

"Yes?" said Miles. Robert was staring at Crispin. Then he turned back to Miles. "Oh, nothing. You do as I say now." He turned away and walked briskly up Earl Street.

Joslin, too, looked at Crispin. "Do you know him?" he whispered.

Crispin's face never flickered. "Why should I?" he said.

"Well, if he says go to the Bull, that's what we'll do," said Miles. "It's better lodging than most we get." He walked on heavily, as if he had been dealt a blow. The rest followed, silently except for Jankin, who was talking angrily to anyone who cared to listen. "We shouldn't let that man patronize us. We should find Bartholomew and get out of here."

"I think you do know him. How?" Joslin persisted with Crispin.

"Ask no questions," Crispin replied.

That was his usual answer and Joslin was getting tired of it. First Arnulf, now Robert Meriden – people who had past dealings with Crispin which he wouldn't talk about.

Then Joslin remembered Arnulf. "*It wasn't Crispin Thurn when we met before . . . and you weren't a minstrel either.*" So who and what was he? Joslin again recalled other strange things: the night visitor at Warwick, the figure with Crispin's voice in the forest, Lew and Mab knowing him so well, the story of Gamelyn. Yet, in spite of these doubts, Joslin stayed on Crispin's side. He hadn't liked Arnulf Long. And he was pretty sure he didn't like Robert Meriden either.

They plodded back, through High Street and Smithford Street to a large, tall building, the wattle and daub between the timber framing smart with new whitewash. A sign hung above the door: "*The Bull*".

Joslin noticed Crispin was hanging back. *He thinks someone will recognize him. If that worries him why did he come here?* He regarded the tall minstrel doubtfully for a moment, then decided. *I'll have a long talk with Master Crispin. I'm getting worried.*

"We'll enter the Bull together," said Miles.

"Wait," Alban exclaimed. "Look at the pageant."

They turned. The pageant they had taken no notice of before stood opposite the Bull, where guests could watch from the windows. A play was in rehearsal. This time Miles and the others watched. A friar in a grey habit also watched intently, standing gravely and silently. On the cart were three men in black gowns before the altar at the temple. A young boy stood in front of them. To one side were a boy in a blue woman's gown and a man in a brown smock.

Hob knew what they were doing. "It's the play of Mary, Joseph and Jesus, how when Jesus was a young boy, he ran away and Mary and Joseph went to look for him and found him in the temple beating the great doctors of law in argument. But they've got three doctors here while we can only manage one. That's always Bartholomew."

"I'm always Jesus," said Sym proudly.

They watched. Miles winced. "Useless," he said. "They don't know the gestures, what shows suspense, what pleasure, what suspicion. Every feeling has a gesture proper to it and every actor knows them. If not, who can tell the meaning behind the words?"

"This lot certainly need gestures," said Jankin contemptuously. "I can't make out a word they're saying."

Joslin was not impressed either. The characters stood like sticks, merely mouthing their words. Mary and Joseph were watching the boy Jesus talking to the learned doctors. Joseph spoke.

> *"Mary, tell them your tale first,*
> *For you're the best to do that deed.*
> *I would do it if I durst,*
> *But I'll wait here. Now God you speed."*

Mary went up to the altar.

> *"Ah, Jesus, Jesus, son so sweet,*
> *Why did you leave so suddenly?*
> *You made us both to wail and weep*
> *With bitter tears, abundantly."*

Jesus answered.

> *"Mother, why do you seek me still?*
> *The angels have often said to you*
> *My Father's will I must fulfil*
> *In every way, for well or woe."*

Miles watched, too shocked to speak. "I never thought to see the day. . ." he finally managed. The first doctor spoke again.

> *"In truth, lady, you must know*
> *That such a brilliant son as he*
> *Must soon from both his parents go.*
> *How long, pray, has he been away?"*

Miles could stand it no longer. He hauled himself up on to the cart. "*No!*" he roared. He seized the first doctor by the shoulders. "Can't you see? You're telling

Mary something she doesn't want to hear though she knows it's got to happen, you're amazed at the boy's cleverness and then you're asking her a question. All that at once. You sound as if you're measuring a piece of cloth. *Think* about what you're saying. *Show* us. Use your voice, your arms, your face. Like *this*." He declaimed the doctor's verse again, with big gestures and facial expressions to fit. Now people at the top windows of the Bull and far down the street could hear and, if they couldn't, would have a good idea just by watching.

Everyone on the pageant seemed turned to stone. Miles finished and drew breath. Then he turned to Jesus, Mary and Joseph. "As for you three. . ." he started. But he got no further. The monk in the grey habit himself climbed up on the cart and started talking quietly to Miles.

Joslin was as surprised as the rest. But he sympathized with Miles. As well, he thought, have Gyb from Banbury put down his stonemason's chisel, pick up the harp and sing, as expect these craftsmen suddenly to be good actors. But as he mused thus, he felt something pluck at his sleeve. He looked down. There stood a little girl, no more than seven years old. She looked up at him with big, blue eyes.

"Please," she said. "Why was that man shouting at my father?"

Before he could even wonder how to answer, Molly cried out, "Look at the learned doctor Miles has just tried to correct."

"What about him?" said Jankin.

"That gown he's wearing. It's Bartholomew's."

For Margery to see a stranger nearly strangling her father when he was only doing his best was no more strange than everything else lately.

Yesterday, she had come home from Hell-mouth and found her mother complaining. Father arrived home in the evening and Mother tried to make him guilty by showing the cloth she had woven on her own. But he didn't feel guilty. "You don't understand our plays, woman," he shouted. "You'll be sorry you spoke so."

Margery's mother was a woman of spirit. She was taller than her husband and she could make him cower. Blue eyes blazing, fists clenched, she stood a handspan over him. She did not shout. She spoke in a firm, level voice. "A wife only owes duty to her husband when he does his duty in return. Weaving cloth and making a living is your duty. Prancing around in borrowed clothes on a cart is not."

She had hit home. He was speechless. He should have an answer ready, because Robert Meriden and Father Anselm of the Greyfriars had told him why the pageants were so important, but he'd forgotten it.

Ah, now he remembered. "It's for the good of the Weavers' Guild, the glory of Coventry and the greater glory of God that folk may know of His plan for the world better than from any sermon or scripture."

"I'd say that was all right," said his wife, "if women took their part in them. While they can't, then to me it's just prancing round on a cart."

Now he *had* something to say to shut her up. "No woman ever sets foot on a stage. It's God's will."

"So is it His will that your wife keeps on weaving when the real weaver and Guild man is out fooling around?" she said tartly.

While he searched for an answer, she picked up a ladle, hit him round the head with it and stalked out. He gingerly felt where it landed and swore softly. Margery pretended she didn't hear. After all, he might be more interested in her news than her mother was.

"Father," she said. "I've been down into Hell and saw a lost soul being carried away to burn for ever and I saw two devils and one of them spoke to me and then they let me go so I came home."

Her father looked at her sadly. It was plain he hadn't listened. "Corpus Christi's but two days away," he said. "Things will get worse before they get better."

As she lay that night in her little bed, Margery wondered what he meant. What would get worse?

Next morning, she was sure. Perhaps he had listened after all. He must mean that before Corpus Christi, *everyone in Coventry* would be taken down into Hell to burn in its fires. That meant everyone in Coventry was very wicked. Including her parents? Well, they had been angry with each other and it wasn't the first time either. Was that enough?

Then she remembered what they had told her. Once, before she was born, when her father was young and her mother a little girl, a terrible plague with nasty black boils had taken away every other person in Coventry. What did that mean, "every *other. . . ?*" Father said, it meant that if there were four children, two died of the plague. If there was a mother and a father, one stayed alive. This made Margery shiver. If it was true, that of four children in a family, two died, what would happen to her? There was only one of her in her family. Would half die, so her head and arms stayed in Coventry and her legs went down to Hell? What would that be like?

She might find out. If half the folk had gone already, that meant the other half would follow. Some people said God sent the plague because he wanted to punish the people. Others said the devil sent it because he wanted more souls down in Hell. Which was it? Oh, everything was so hard to understand.

The sun rose and the day started. Margery soon saw that her father would do no weaving that day. "I must go to the pageant," he said. "Robert Meriden commands it. The Weavers' Pageant has to be the very best when Corpus Christi comes."

"Why don't you get apprentices like other weavers?" said his wife. "It's not fair to expect me to go on with all your work."

"I've told you. I won't be bothered with apprentices. Margery will marry a good man who'll take the business over after I die. I'll make sure of that." Then he left. Mother, muttering, sat at the loom.

For an hour Margery fetched wool for the loom and tried to help. But her mother said, "Oh, please, girl, clear off out of my sight. I'd rather be on my own."

So Margery went outside. What should she do? Follow Father? She knew where the pageant was. But once in Greyfriars Street, she felt her feet walking as if they had a will of their own. They wanted to go to Hell-mouth again. They made for Cow Lane and she felt she was following them into Little Park Street, Dead Lane and the alley at the end and she could no more have made them turn round than fly.

Hell-mouth was still there. Now her feet told her they didn't want to go down into Hell again so they made her crouch round the corner of a wall where she could see but not be seen.

She looked at Hell-mouth. What a terrible, frightening place. Those teeth, that evil red glow from inside, those wafts of smoke coming from its depths. There were the devils again: one with his huge horned devil's head, his red body and his sharp, wicked tail, the other smaller but just as frightening. The big one held something. What was it? A trumpet?

The devil raised the horn to his lips and blew a long blast. The actors as they entered Coventry through Spon Gate heard and thought nothing of it. So did others in Coventry. Yet others said to themselves, "Ah, we've been waiting for that." The note carried on: Margery wondered how anybody could have so much breath in his body. But a devil had all the breath he wanted.

Two unexpected people ran out of Cow Lane and past Margery to Hell-mouth. They wore long, grey habits tied with rope girdles and she knew them at once. They were monks from Greyfriars. She should be pleased to see them, but she was always frightened by the swirls of grey cloth which hid their feet, sleeves which made them look as if they had no hands and hoods hiding their faces so you couldn't be sure if a death's head was where a proper face should be always. She felt cold when one passed in the street. And when from Greyfriars church she heard their voices raised in chanting, she shivered again because they sounded like voices from the dead singing far away.

Now they were angry. "Stop!" the leader cried. "What blasphemy is this? Only God blows a horn on a pageant, and only on the proper Judgement Day."

"Go away, brothers." The devil's voice came out as a snarl. "Or your turn will come."

Suddenly, Margery was stirred with deep, churning fear. She turned and ran, up Little Park Street and all the way to her father's pageant – just in time to see some strange man trying to strangle him.

"Bartholomew's gown? Are you sure?" said Peg.

"Of course I am," said Molly. "Look, there's a tear in the front. I said I'd stitch it up and he said he'd give it to me but he never did."

"I'll tear it off that clown's back," roared Jankin. "I'll make him tell me where Bartholomew is."

He tried to break away and join Miles on the pageant. Peg and Molly held him back. "Wait," Molly urged. People were looking at them. "We don't want people against us from the start. Miles is doing quite enough on his own for that. Wait until this is over."

Jankin shook her off. "All right," he said unwillingly. "For now."

Miles and the Grey Friar had gone to the side of the pageant, still talking. Then the friar placed his hand companionably on Miles's shoulder, they nodded to each other and Miles jumped down from the pageant back to the ground. To their surprise, he was smiling.

"I've done us a good turn," he said. "The friars are fine people."

"That fool pretending he's a doctor is wearing Bartholomew's gown," muttered Jankin.

Miles looked back to the pageant. His eyes narrowed. "Are you sure?" he said.

"Of course," said Molly and Jankin together.

"All the more reason to stay here," said Miles. "It makes what that friar just said to me the first stroke of luck we've had for weeks."

All this while, Margery was holding Joslin's sleeve, her question still unanswered, thinking the whole world had gone mad. At last Joslin could tell her something. "Here's Miles. He's the one to ask."

So she did. "Please, why were you shouting at my father?"

Miles looked at her for the first time.

"So that was your father, was it?" said Jankin. "Why was he wearing our Bartholomew's gown?" Margery looked at him blankly.

The play was finishing. Margery's father was speaking. He had not learnt from Miles's instructions.

> *"For all good souls I hope you'll pray
> And so we take our leave at last."*

"About time too," Jankin shouted. Joslin thought that Jankin wasn't so pleased the night before when folk shouted much the same at him.

"That play was *awful*," said Hob.

Margery was determined to get her question answered. She tugged at Miles's sleeve. "Please, why were you shouting at my father?"

Miles looked down and smiled. "I was shouting at

your father, child, because though he's trying as hard as he can, he's not very good at acting yet. I only want him to be better. Sometimes, to help people do things properly, you have to shout at them."

Margery stared up at him, eyes wide. She said nothing, but her face said that her father must be the best at acting in the whole world. Miles understood. "If he listens to me," he said, "perhaps one day he may be the best, and I wouldn't be surprised if he was the best weaver in the world already."

Now Margery smiled. "Oh, he is. And so's my mother."

"So they'd both shout if I tried to do weaving," said Miles. "With good reason, because I wouldn't know the first thing about what to do."

"Why did your father wear Bartholomew's gown?" Jankin persisted.

Miles turned away from Margery. "Listen," he said. "There's much to tell you. We'll do as Robert Meriden said and go into the Bull. Then we start the search for Bartholomew."

They left and Margery watched them go.

Even though the Bull looked a fine set up building outside, inside all was dark dinginess. The host was a short, miserable-looking man. A first taste showed his beer was sour and thin. Suddenly, Robert Meriden's promise did not seem so inviting. Miles remembered the host's name as Godric Chase. "If Robert says so," he replied to Miles's request. "But as far as payment goes, I'll expect it in full and on time."

A surly potboy showed them upstairs to two rooms, both lined with dirty pallets and straw mattresses. When they came downstairs again, they bought ale and sat together in a corner. Crispin and

Joslin saw the horses well stabled and then sat with the actors, listening, but somehow not part of them.

"What did that Grey Friar want?" Alban demanded.

"Only our good," said Miles. "He made me an offer."

"What offer can a Grey Friar make except a relic or two, probably a sheep's ankle-bone, and a few prayers?" Jankin scoffed. "Why don't we follow that man wearing Bartholomew's gown?"

"We'll have time for that," said Miles. "A Grey Friar can offer more than you think. I'll ask you a question. The plays that we do, how did they come about? How is it that we know all the words we speak?

"We put most together ourselves," said Alban.

"Sometimes we make them up as we go along," said Hob.

"Or we hear plays done by other actors and take bits," said Sym. "When we do plays for Corpus Christi, we make them up from what we know of the scriptures and sermons we've heard from priests."

"That's why we need Bartholomew back," said Molly. "He knew Latin and could read scripture, so we didn't need to listen to priests."

"So in the end they were *our* plays, nobody else's," said Miles.

"How can they be?" growled Crispin. "Those people who drove you off your stage at Arnulf Long's tavern knew your play well enough."

"They knew what happened in our play," said Miles patiently. "No one can change that. But they didn't know *our* play. Don't tell me a story you sing would be exactly what another minstrel would do – or the same twice running when you do it."

"That's different," said Crispin.

"No, it's not," said Joslin. He knew what Miles

meant. "I'm always changing things and making new bits up. I think of new ideas as I sing. My father did as well. Don't all minstrels?"

Crispin grunted. "Go on, Miles," he said.

"We're in a town like a lot of other towns now. They want to do their own plays and cut us out. But where do their plays come from?"

"They see and hear them and learn from them, like us," said Alban.

"How can they? They're weavers, tailors, nail-makers, carpenters. They're not actors. They heard the plays once a year, when a band like us came through and they thought it was wonderful. It's nothing to us: it's miraculous to them, like making nails is to me. You know how our plays work. To them these things are really happening. I often wonder what would happen if just once the stories in the plays didn't work out the way they're supposed to."

"What do you mean?" asked Joslin. What Miles said was intriguing.

"Well, what if one year someone meddled with the plays so Herod managed to slaughter the infant Christ along with all the other innocents? Or if Abraham was about to sacrifice Isaac but no angel came to stop him so Isaac had to die when we all know he didn't? What would the people do?"

"That's daft talk," said Jankin. "How could that happen?"

"But if it did?" Miles persisted.

"They would die themselves," said Alban. "They wouldn't know what to think any more. Everything would be taken away from them."

"Rubbish," said Jankin. "Where do these people get plays from?"

"The Grey Friars," said Miles.

There was silence. Joslin looked round the tavern. He saw surly faces and heard indistinct murmur. A voice near by sounded clear in his ear.

"We shall never have our rights until we have struck off three or four heads of the churls that rule us."

Where did that voice come from? There was no telling. Heads were lowered, voices carried on. Then another voice spoke. *"True. Yet it was even worse in the old time, in the days of. . ."* The voice was drowned in someone's tipsy shouting at the other end of the room.

So all was not well in Coventry. That might be worth knowing. He listened again to Miles.

"For the friars to make these plays is good sense," he was saying. "When they leave their friaries, they travel the land preaching, befriending the people. I know some abuse their position and cheat folk with false relics and prayers, but others are loved because they're good men, better than many priests. To make plays for the people is another way of doing what they always do."

"So," said Jankin. "We have rivals. But what can they offer us?"

"The friars and us, we're all travellers," said Miles. "We perform to the folk and they flock to see us. So do the friars and the people flock to hear them. We couldn't do what they do. They couldn't do what we do. The Church may say we're vagabonds and the lowest of the low, but the friars are part of the Church and they respect us for what we do."

"All right, I'll believe you," said Jankin. "So?"

"The friars can tell the people what words to say

and get carpenters and wheelwrights to make pageant wagons and weavers and dyers to make drapes better than any that we could have – but they can't tell them *how* to do the plays. You saw that."

"That's right," said Alban. "They were really bad."

"So that friar wants us to tell them." Miles sounded triumphant, as if he had sealed a wonderful deal.

There was silence. Then Jankin burst out: "Why should we do ourselves out of work? Let the friars tell them if they're so clever."

"What exactly do you mean, 'tell them'?" Alban asked.

"I mean that each one of us would work with the actors on a separate play. Father Anselm said that he'd persuade the Guilds to pay us. We'd teach them about voices and movements and all the things we've learnt over many years about acting."

"Oh, so it's Father Anselm and Master Miles already, is it?" Jankin muttered.

"Are you sure we'd be paid?" asked Molly.

"Father Anselm said he'd make sure we were," Miles answered.

Jankin looked at the rest. "Well, I say it's a bad idea and if you say yes, you're mad. Would any Guild craftsman tell us how to do his job?"

Miles spoke firmly. "Look, Jankin, this may be our only chance to stay together. Times are changing. The Church wants the Guilds to take the Corpus Christi plays over. Not just here but all over the land. There'll soon be no place for us. But if we do this, and come back every year to help new actors with new plays and make old ones better, we'd still be wanted."

Jankin was not happy. "It's not right that the towns should take the bread from our mouths like this."

"You can't blame them," Miles answered. "Look around you. Half the town's busy and thriving, getting back on its feet, but look at all the empty houses, the ruined walls, the gaping windows. Coventry was hit hard by the plague. It's never got back to what it was. A lot of people don't care any more. They say, 'What's the point? The plague will come back and ruin us again.' But if the town comes together with its own plays every year and the Guilds show what they can do and the folk say, 'These plays are ours and nobody else's', then the town gets its pride back and, says the Church, the folk get their faith back as well."

"Isn't it grand for the town," said Jankin. "Who said that rubbish?"

"Father Anselm."

"He told you a lot in a short time."

"Miles," said Alban. "What would we be letting ourselves in for?"

"Right," said Miles. "There are nine plays done here. Creation and Fall, Cain and Abel, Noah and the Ark, Abraham and Isaac, John the Baptist, Birth of Christ and Slaughter of the Innocents – that's with the shepherds, three wise men and King Herod – Simeon and the Doctors, Christ's Crucifixion, and the Resurrection."

"What about the Day of Judgement?" said Hob.

"Give me a chance to finish," said Miles. "Each play is done by a Guild. On Corpus Christi Day, Creation's done where its pageant is now and then it moves off to the next station. Cain and Abel is wheeled along to the same place and done and every pageant follows it. Meanwhile, Creation's gone to the next place so in the end each play is done nine times in a different place. They finish up in St Michael's Green and there the bishop gives a great sermon about Judgement, which it's all led up to. Anselm wants each one of us to go to a different pageant tomorrow and help get the actors performing better. If we come next year we'd have longer, so in the end they'll be really good."

"Do you mean there's no Judgement play here?" said Hob.

"That's right," said Miles.

"Then they need one," Hob replied. "What good is some bishop prating away when they could *see* it happening with their own eyes?"

"That's right. It could be our play," said Jankin. "So we have to find Bartholomew. That comes before everything else."

"Miles is right," said Alban. "I say we do as he says."

"You'll be silly if you don't agree, Jankin," said Peg. "This way we can stay in the town and look for Bartholomew."

Jankin's face was pale with anger. "This is ridiculous, gabbling on about Father Anselm. Nobody seems to care about Bartholomew except me. Nobody took that learned doctor by the throat and squeezed it until he told us where he'd got Bartholomew's gown from. No, as soon as you get the chance of a bit of money and a quiet life, you forget our good friend who we sent on alone to fend for himself. Well, I'm not having it. If you aren't interested any more, *I am*." With that, he got up and stalked out of the Bull.

Peg stood, put her hand to her mouth and gasped, "I'm sorry. Miles. I'll go after him and bring him back."

"You stay here, Peg," Miles replied firmly. "I'm not

letting any more of you out of my sight. We're in enough trouble as it is. "

Father Anselm stayed on the pageant watching his actors and thinking that in future it might be better. These actors – they could do so much for the Guilds, for Coventry, for the plays.

For these plays could do so much – and if the folk really felt the power of the stories they were telling – ah, but that could cut both ways. For suddenly he remembered the nightmare he'd had so often lately, of plays set before the people where what should happen did not, where the stories changed so the opposite happened – and especially a Judgement play which turned into a *real Hell*, with a *real Satan* having vanquished God and condemning all the trembling folk to torments eternal.

No, he should forget it. Such thoughts were blasphemy. But if it did happen. . .

Robert Meriden shivered. That tall man – he brought bad times back.

After the strange man who shouted at her father to make him do better had gone with his friends into the Bull, Margery stood thinking. She wouldn't follow them. Her mother and father didn't like her going where big, rough men spent hours drinking ale. Father said that Godric Chase was not a nice man and the Bull was not what it used to be. She looked at the big solid building and wondered what it used to be. A church? A tree? A *real* bull?

She couldn't imagine it being different. So she turned to the pageant cart. This was a thing of wonder. She loved the little wooden houses on it, brightly painted and draped with coloured cloths. Yes, they were just made of wood here in Coventry, yet they also really were the temple in Jerusalem where Simeon first saw the baby Jesus and where the boy Jesus showed all the wise men he was cleverer than they were. She was so proud that her father was a learned doctor. When he was on the pageant in his gown, he wasn't her father any more, and the boy before him, whom she knew well, had become Jesus.

Yet she knew that one man was really just one man. One girl like her was just one girl. If you saw one devil, what else was it but one devil?

One devil. But she'd seen two devils and two brave friars running at them as if to fight them. A cold shiver spread up her spine and wrapped itself round her stomach. Then she wondered, why was she so afraid, just standing here in front of the lovely pageant and close to her father?

Because she realized what she'd seen. It hadn't struck her before. *Real devils.* Not many people had seen one. Everyone knew they were there, of course, waiting to trap them. Those who'd been wicked would see them when they were dead. BUT SHE HAD SEEN THEM NOW. This was deadly serious.

She still felt faint. So she walked away from the pageant, to the corner of Greyfriars Lane. There she sat on the ground and pondered.

They were real devils. The friars ran at them as if for a fight. Well, friars were men of God, so perhaps only they could. But what could friars do to devils? Throttle them with their girdles? Slap them to death with their sandals? If it were so easy there'd be no devils left to trouble us. No, the devils would breathe fire on them or sting them and that would be the end. The friars wouldn't have a chance.

She'd have to ask someone about it. Who? Someone nice, who'd listen, who wouldn't laugh either. But she didn't know anyone like that. Only . . . she remembered the young man she asked about the stranger shouting at her father. He was the one. She just knew, from his gentle face, that he wouldn't tell her to run away. How could she could find him again? For now, he was in the Bull. She'd go back to the pageant and wait for him to come out.

All the weavers, including her father, were on the cart, listening to Father Anselm and Robert Meriden. Margery kept quiet: she was a little bit afraid of both. She didn't understand what they said, but her father was nodding so it must be right. At last it was over and the weavers came off the pageant. Her father saw her. "We'll go home, Margery," he said. "Perhaps Mother will find something for us to eat."

Yes, I'm hungry. I'll look for the nice man afterwards, she thought.

"Is that man who shouted at you going to make you better, Father?" she asked.

Her father sniffed. "He can try," he answered.

When they got home, Mother wasn't too pleased to see them. But she found bread, cheese and a piece of cold mutton to keep the hunger pains away. But hardly had Father supped his first pot of ale when there was a hammering on the door. A strange voice shouted, "Open up, Thomas Dollimore. I want to talk to you."

Miles led them out of the Bull. The pageant wagon was deserted. He climbed up and called: "Anselm." The friar appeared from behind a drape. "Well met again," he said. "I'm glad you're all happy to help us."

"How do you know? I've only just spoken to my companions."

"But the long-haired one is with you, isn't he? He just asked me where he could find the doctor you corrected when he was in full flow."

"Jankin. Did he say why?" said Alban.

"Of course. To start helping him straight away. I was impressed with his enthusiasm. I told him his name, Thomas Dollimore."

"Where is this Thomas Dollimore?" asked Miles.

"Gone home. His house is third on the right in Greyfriars Lane."

"Thank you," said Miles. He turned and loped off down Smithford Street, the others following. Joslin and Crispin looked at each other. Crispin shrugged his shoulders and they set off as well.

"But I thought we'd talk," Father Anselm called.

"Later," Miles shouted over his shoulder. "We have a job to do."

The house was easy to find. Miles knocked on the door and Thomas Dollimore, without Bartholomew's gown on, opened it.

"Not more of you," he groaned. "I've got work to catch up with."

"So Jankin's been here," said Miles.

"The long-haired one? Yes, he has. And now he's gone again and we were glad to see the back of him. There's no use asking me the same questions, because I'll give you the same answers."

"They'll be new to us," said Alban. "We don't know where he is."

Thomas Dollimore looked at them. "You'd better come in," he said.

Inside, Joslin saw Thomas's wife and the girl he hadn't answered properly. When she saw him, her face lit up. He had to talk to her.

"Where did Jankin go?" asked Miles mildly.

"Him?" Thomas replied. "He bursts in here, shouts something about the gown I was wearing, demands to know where I got it and as soon as I tell him he flails again as if demons are chasing him. The man had a demon inside him already if you ask me."

"So where *did* you get it from?" asked Hob.

107

"From Father Anselm of course," Thomas replied. "Now I suppose you'll rush off as well, because there's nothing else I can tell you."

As the others dashed out, Joslin lingered. The girl saw him and came outside. "Please," she said. "I saw devils. They came from Hell and took me back there. I saw a soul which was just dead. I was right down in Hell but they let me go again. I wanted to tell you because you look nice. Nobody listens to me."

"What's your name?" asked Joslin.

"Margery."

"Well, Margery, wasn't it just a dream?"

"No. I saw Hell-mouth in Dead Lane where no one goes any more, where the souls go when they die. It was there again this morning, but it wasn't there before I saw it. I know it wasn't. The devils brought it."

Joslin looked at her. She looked back, earnestness all over her face. Well, she thought it was true, even if he didn't. Unless she'd seen a pageant built for a Judgement play. That would explain it.

"Of course you saw all that," he said. "But it was part of a play. The devils were actors dressed up."

Margery's face twisted up into tears. Nobody believed her, not even this young man.

"They weren't actors," she screamed. "They weren't. One had a big head like a goat and that's what devils have. I saw a real lost soul because he was dead. I saw him dead."

She turned and ran back to her house. When she was nearly there, she remembered that she hadn't told him about the friars. Well, she wouldn't now. She'd thought he would listen to her and believe her, but he was as bad as the rest. So who could she tell?

Not her parents: they never listened anyway and would be angry if they did. She'd tell Father Anselm if she saw him in the street: she'd never dare go to Greyfriars. No, she'd just have to keep what she'd seen to herself and try to find the friars on her own.

Joslin watched her go, feeling sorry. Then he thought on what she had said. "*I saw him dead.*" Who had she seen?

At once, a fearful thought crashed into his mind. "*Please don't let it be Bartholomew,*" he cried aloud.

"I reckon foul play's been done to Bartholomew," said Hob when they were outside. "And this Father Anselm must know about it."

"You've no reason to say that," said Molly. "Thomas only told us Father Anselm gave him the gown. What's wrong with that?"

"A lot if he tore it off his dead body," Hob replied.

"You'll have to ask Father Anselm yourself, Miles," said Alban.

"I will," said Miles. "I'll find him now. We've a lot to discuss anyway. But we won't all go. I'll take Molly with me to see fair play. The rest of you split into pairs and scour the city for Jankin and Bartholomew. Crispin and Joslin, are you with us in this?"

They both nodded. Joslin wondered whether to tell them what Margery said, then decided against it.

"Then I suggest Peg goes with Hob since he needs someone to give him a bit of sense, Sym goes with Crispin and Alban goes with Joslin. If you find Jankin or Bartholomew, bring them here to the Bull and wait. Otherwise, keep looking until you hear St Michael's bells ring for evening mass, then come here."

They spent a moment working out where each pair

would go. Then they went their separate ways.

Joslin and Alban left Miles and Molly at the pageant in front of the Bull and wandered into Cross Cheaping. There, by the cross, was another pageant. They saw or heard no trace of Jankin, let alone Bartholomew.

"Why did Jankin rush off?" said Alban bitterly. "Now two of us have met foul play. I know it."

Joslin didn't answer. He wouldn't tell Alban alone about what Margery told him. He was looking at the pageant. That the play was about Christmas was obvious. One house, lined with fleeces and covered in straw, was plainly the inn and stable. The other house was bigger, draped in the greens, reds and deep blues for which the dyers of Coventry were famous. Gold crowns were sewn into the cloth. This was a royal palace. At the front stood three impressive robed figures. They were bidding each other farewell: one was ending his last speech.

> "Now we know we all must go
> For fear of Herod so full of wrath
> Who wants to kill this child we know.
> And so I sadly leave you both."

They bowed to each other, then went their ways.

"The three kings," said Alban.

A great and gaudy procession entered through the royal palace: soldiers, then musicians beating drums and playing raucously on pipes and horns. Joslin winced and wanted to cover his ears. After them came the courtiers: then, unmistakably, Herod himself. His garish gown jangled with baubles and trinkets and he brandished a huge sword. On his head was a turban such as a Saracen would wear. But he was not noble, as a Saracen would be. The turban was too big. He looked grotesque as if he could hardly balance.

The courtiers told him the three kings had gone without saying where they found the infant king. Herod was beside himself with rage.

> *"Have those false traitors cheated me?*
> *I'm ranting, raving, running mad.*
> *If I could get those wretches here*
> *I'd hang them, burn them, see them dead."*

He hurled himself off the pageant and strode up and down the street, swishing his sword so those nearby had to dodge for their lives. Alban and Joslin did too. They could not tell how real his rage was.

> *"That little clown in Bethlehem,*
> *His parents too, I'll see to them."*

"At least someone can act," said Alban. "Even though they've made his head too big for his body."

Joslin wasn't listening. He had remembered the huge-headed man at the Tavern Where the Ways Meet and that feeling that here was evil. Like Herod, also with a huge head. And the devil. "*A big head like a goat and that's what devils have,*" Margery said.

Alban was looking at him as well. "That King Herod's like in the old Mummer's play," he said.

"What do you mean?" asked Joslin.

"Don't you know? I thought everyone did. '*Here come I, Beelzebub. Big head and little wit.*'"

Joslin stared at him. "What?" he said.

"Beelzebub," Alban replied. "The devil second only

111

to Satan himself. Some say he *is* Satan by another name. He's in the old Mummers' play and that's what he says. He's always got a big head and the folk just laugh at him."

Herod screamed into the soldiers' faces.

> *"Here comes the best thing I've ever said.*
> *All tiny children will have to be DEAD,*
> *Slain by your swords."*

"They wouldn't laugh at Herod," said Joslin.

"Deep down they don't laugh at Beelzebub. They're afraid, even in a Mummers' play," Alban replied. "They may know the actor, but they're not quite sure Beelzebub couldn't harm them."

Big head. Beelzebub. Herod. The man at the tavern.

"Alban," Joslin said. "Listen. I can't prove what I'm saying now but I know deep in my bones that I'm right. Lambert's murder wasn't a stroke of blind fate by someone from the forest. There was a reason behind it. It's connected with Bartholomew's disappearance. I have a bad feeling about Bartholomew. I think he's dead. Perhaps Jankin is too, though he's been gone hardly an hour. The man with the huge head will be here in Coventry. The whole truth is in this city, very close to us. It's up to us to find it, because nobody else will."

Alban was hardly listening. "I can't forget what Miles said in the Bull. What would happen, what would the folk do, if the infant Christ was one of the babies that were slaughtered?" Then he seemed to come out of a dream. He looked at Joslin and cried, "*What* did you say?"

Sym was not happy with Crispin. He was afraid of the tall minstrel with a face like an axe-blade and he couldn't keep up with his huge strides. They had set off up Smithford Street as far as Greyfriars Lane. Here Crispin stopped.

"We've been down here already," said Sym.

"I know that," Crispin answered. "I was just thinking."

"Why not carry on and go down the next street?" Sym suggested.

"That's what I was going to do," Crispin answered. He set off again and Sym stumbled after. Soon they reached Little Park Street. Crispin stopped again. "Down here," he said.

Little Park Street stretched to the city walls and Park Street Gate. Crispin strode down it. "Have you been here before?" Sym asked.

"Yes," said Crispin. "Near the end is Dead Lane. You know what they say about Dead Lane?"

"No. What?"

"Everybody living in it died in the plague. Coventry

113

folk believe that since then the devil lines up the damned of Coventry in Dead Lane to take them to Hell. No one goes there, not for a year's wages."

"So we needn't either," said Sym in a quavery voice. "Not to a place where everybody died."

"Maybe we have to," said Crispin. "Especially to a place where everybody died."

Sym followed him down Dead Lane. Their footsteps echoed dully from the broken buildings. To Sym, the stillness was unnerving. They saw nothing but ruin until they reached an alleyway which led to the right and fetched up against the city walls.

Sym took a few timid steps up it, then peered round a crumbling wall. "*Look at that,*" he whispered, awestruck.

In front of them stood the Mouth of Hell.

Father Anselm was little help to Miles and Molly. "John Crowe the tailor gave me the gown," he said

"So where did he get it from?" asked Miles.

"You must ask him. As a tailor he finds costumes for the plays."

"Where can we find him?" asked Molly. "How will we know him?"

"He'll be in his shop in Gosford Street. As to how you'll know him, there's little I can tell you. He's a man like any other."

"The tailors have a Guild," said Miles. "Don't they do a play?"

"Of course. The Shearmen and Tailors together. The Birth of Christ and Slaughter of the Innocents. John Crowe won't play in it, though. He's too shy to stand on a pageant. He's happier finding costumes."

"Miles, we must speak to this John Crowe," said Molly.

"I'm sorry," said Father Anselm. "I know you're worried about your missing friends, but please give me a little time. We have important business together." So, as Miles chafed with impatience, Father Anselm explained how he wanted the actors to turn the Guild plays into things worth watching.

Joslin now had Alban's strange question to think about. Alban was looking amazed at Joslin. "*What* did you say?" he repeated.

"I'm right," Joslin answered. "I know I am."

"I can't believe it," said Alban.

On the pageant, three actors playing women held babies. They sang a poor, tuneless song in cracked voices. Joslin longed to jump up and sing something better. Now he knew what Miles felt like listening to Thomas Dollimore mouthing good words as if ordering a bale of wool. But the song ended violently. Herod's soldiers burst in, seized the babies and cut them to bits with their swords.

"On Corpus Christi Day those dolls will be filled with pig's blood," said Alban. "It will anger the folk. They'll remember stories about Danes and Normans slicing up babies."

The women cried and ran off. Herod appeared and the soldiers strutted up to him as if they had won a great victory.

"*Look, King Herod, here you see*
How many enemies we have slain," said one.
"*Your will is law. It has to be.*
No one can threaten you again," said another.

But Herod's triumph did not last. A messenger

entered to say that Mary, Joseph and Jesus had escaped to Egypt. Herod left the stage waving his sword and screaming for vengeance.

"Herod's good," said Alban. "He doesn't need much help from us. And if you're going to upset me like that, do we need help from you?"

"I'm not joking," said Joslin. He told Alban about his father, his flight from France and quest to Wales, what happened in Stovenham, in London, in Oxford. He talked for a long time as the pageant quietened, a friar spoke approving words to the actors and Herod – now without his turban and looking normal – Joseph and two soldiers sauntered off down Broadgate, towards the Bull.

"So you see," Joslin ended. "I've been through enough these last months to know that even when things look impossible, they've probably happened, or if they haven't, they will soon. Never ignore anything: always consider everything. That's what I believe now."

Alban didn't answer for a moment. Then he said, "How do I know you've not told me a pack of lies? And what's it to do with Coventry?"

"I've said the truth," Joslin replied. "You have to believe me."

"I still don't see why Herod with a turban, someone in a Mummers' play and a man with a big head makes you think the answers to Lambert and Bartholomew are here," Alban replied.

"Herod's evil. The devil's evil. The man with the big head drove you off the stage at the tavern. He made sure Lambert won the minstrels' contest so he knew where he'd be during the night. It's likely he murdered him. So he's evil too. He's probably in

Coventry now. If Bartholomew's dead, he knows why."

"Do you really think having a big head makes you a murderer?" said Alban derisively. "You must do better than that, Joslin."

"I *know* I'm right. There are devils in plays here, aren't there?"

"Even if there's no Day of Judgement play here, they'll be around somewhere," said Alban.

"Then we must find the pageant where they are," said Joslin.

"We'll ask the friar," said Alban.

But the friar was no help. "My son, we have no Judgement play and there are no devils anywhere else."

"We can do a Judgement play for you," said Alban brightly. Then his face fell. "Or we could if we found Bartholomew."

"But our Corpus Christi Day has no need of one," the friar replied. "Ralph Breville, our bishop, comes here on Corpus Christi Day and tells us enough of devils and condemned souls in his sermon on St Michael's Green when the pageants are ended. Surely Judgement Day's awful message is better in the words of a Prince of the Church than the mouthings of common men?" With that he left.

Joslin remembered something. "Then why did Margery, Thomas Dollimore's daughter, tell me about seeing devils and lost souls at Hell-mouth at the end of Dead Lane if he says there aren't any?"

Alban said nothing.

"Where's Dead Lane?" said Joslin.

Sym had never seen anything like this. It was as well he knew it could only be a pageant wagon, or he might really think it was the place where souls found wanting at the Day of Judgement were herded together and whipped down by demons into the everlasting fires. He saw sharp, bloodstained teeth, a cavernous and stomach-churning mouth, fearful red interior, wafts of smoke from somewhere far away inside and thought, *This is really how it must be.*

Then he saw something odd. If this was a Judgement Day pageant, where would the judging be? There should be steps up to a level where heaven was, arching over the pageant. He knew how the world was and how stages should be. Our place was in the middle, Hell was beneath and Heaven over our heads. Why was there no place for God to sit on a throne waiting for the chosen souls to arrive? Why, they even managed that on their little cart. This big pageant was only half-built.

Or else – and now a strange thought came – in Coventry, *no souls at all would be fit for Heaven and everyone was to be condemned.*

That made no sense. Stages were not set out accidentally. If there was a Hell, there must be a Heaven. As in scripture, so on the stage. But on this pageant there was an inescapable message. Everyone was marked for Hell.

He said so to Crispin. "Don't be a fool, Sym," was the answer. "Truth can't be changed to suit a play. The pageant's not finished yet. Heaven will be put on top next, you mark my words."

"But Corpus Christi's only two days off. There's no time, Crispin," said Sym. If a Heaven were half as striking as this Hell-mouth it would be huge. This pageant would tower over the others, so big that it would overbalance, no horses could pull it through the streets, shop signs and inn signs would be torn off as it passed – if it could pass.

No. This Hell-mouth was complete. There was no way of building any more. Might Heaven be on a separate pageant? Could you do one play on two pageants? "What Guild does this play?" he said.

"How should I know?" Crispin answered.

There was no sign of life round Hell-mouth, except for the smoke.

"I wonder what's inside?" Sym said.

"I don't know and I don't care. We're here to find people, not pageants," Crispin replied.

But Sym wanted to know. He hauled himself up and picked his way through the teeth, passed the red drapes which from outside looked as if they were soaked in blood and reached a room where devils' costumes hung and near-dead fires in two braziers explained the smoke.

Sym examined the costumes. Goat-faced masks with horns, red and scaly bodies, tails with sharp barbs. Yes, these were real devils – or the people inside would feel like them once the costumes were on. These were far better than the little shifty things their own company possessed. What would it be like to wear them? Would you actually become a devil? Sometimes he felt himself *being* the person he was acting. But to be a devil as terrible as those costumes would make you – he couldn't take it in. Though he was the youngest actor, he took on many parts and even when he felt the character he played somehow became him, he knew it wasn't really so and in a few minutes he would be eating, drinking and laughing with Miles and the rest. But to someone not used to it like these Coventry folk... Sym walked quickly through, down a wooden ramp and into the dark and dusty space between the pageant and the city wall. What he'd seen disturbed him. Though he was only a moment in the pageant, he felt when he came back to Crispin as if he had been undergound for hours.

"This is a dead end. We have to go back," Crispin called. "Turn left and it's Little Park Street Gate."

Sym shivered. "Let's go through the gate," he said. "We'll look outside the city walls."

Crispin shrugged his shoulders. They walked back along Dead Lane, passed under the gate and crossed a causeway over the town ditch. They saw open land crossed by unkempt footpaths. To their right, the wall turned away round a corner. To their left, it stretched straight for about three hundred paces. Here it seemed to end abruptly, but the London road beyond showed where it sharply changed direction to the main city gate. The wall was only completed during this King Edward's reign: the stonework was new. The town ditch stretched round it, a filthy moat. The scene was desolate, empty but for distant serfs on such fields as were cleared. Straggly trees and bushes ran riot. It would not have looked like that before the plague.

"Come back, Sym," said Crispin. "This is a waste of time."

Sym sighed and turned. But then he looked into the ditch. Half-stagnant water hardly moved. Much of the city's rubbish had been thrown into it. A strong, unpleasant smell rose up.

"Crispin," Sym said in a strange, half-strangled voice.

"What's the matter now?" said Crispin.

"Crispin, I think I've found Bartholomew."

At last Miles and Molly had managed to leave Anselm. They had agreed that next day each actor would work on a different play and Crispin and Joslin – if they wanted – would help with the music. Now they walked along High Street, Earl Street and Jordan Well into Gosford Street.

The sign saying "John Crowe, tailor" was hard to find. Inside the small, gloomy shop Miles and Molly blinked after the sunshine. When they asked the tiny man with weak red eyes who said he was John Crowe how he came by Bartholomew's gown, he was not helpful.

"So much comes to me," he said. "New clothes to finish, old clothes still wearable, garments of no use to anyone which I put aside for the plays."

"Then you must remember a black lawyer's gown," said Miles.

"I can't say I do," John replied.

"But you can't get many," said Molly. "Especially one with with a big tear in the front which I'd said I'd sew up but never got a chance to."

"Means nothing to me," said John stubbornly.

121

"Well, it means something to Father Anselm, for he told us you gave it to him," Miles said grimly. "What do you say to that?"

"Nothing," John answered.

"I don't believe you." Miles was angry now. "That gown belonged to our friend and we can't find him."

A brief look of guilt and fear crossed John Crowe's face. He spoke agitatedly. "What is there to know? The gown was in a pile of old clothes. Some are from the newly dead. Some are given by those who don't need them."

"And which was the gown from?" said Miles. "Someone newly dead?"

"I don't know. I've no more to say."

Miles stepped towards him. "I warn you. . ." he began.

John cowered. "Stop there or I call the watch," he stuttered. Miles checked himself and John turned spiteful. "They'll throw you out of Coventry so you can whistle for your lost friend and his gown."

But Molly smiled and said, "Take no notice of him, John. He's half-mad with worry. You see how it is, don't you? This isn't our town and we fear we might have suffered a grievous loss."

"I *know* we have," Miles muttered.

Molly looked into John's face with her deep grey eyes. "You'd help us, wouldn't you, John? If you had your own way, you'd help us?"

Her words had an effect. John's face shrieked out guilt. "Yes," he said. "I lied to you. It's not right. Mind you, there's not much I can tell."

"Anything's better than not knowing," said Miles. "Go on, John."

"It was two days ago," said John. "I was in my shop.

Business was poor: I hoped for better things when Coventry fills up for Corpus Christi Day. Then a man came in. I didn't know him, though something seemed familiar. He gave me the gown. Nothing else: no other clothes with it. 'Take this to Father Anselm,' he said. 'He'll know what to do with it. It's ideal for his play.' Well, it seemed a poor enough piece of cloth to me. 'Is it worth the giving?' I asked. 'To me it is,' said the man. 'Some might get a nasty shock if they saw it. Enough to pack their bags and get out.' "

Miles and Molly looked at each other. "This man," said Miles. "You said he seemed familiar. There's no chance he'd be familiar to me, but I'd like to hear what he looked like so I might know him if I saw him."

"I remember he had rough brown hair to his shoulders and a cast in one eye," said John. "That eye rang a bell in my mind."

Miles was thoughtful. "It rings a bell in mine as well," he said.

"Before he went, this fellow threatened me. He said, 'Tell no one who gave it to you, or we'll find out and you'll be sorry.' So I put it with a pile of others and gave them to Anselm. There, now I've told what I swore I wouldn't and already my knees are trembling with fear for it."

Miles laid a hand on his shoulder. "Don't worry, John," he said. "We'll look out for you."

Outside, Molly said, "So a bell rang in your mind?"

"Yes," Miles replied. "Though I can't think why."

"I can," said Molly. "If I didn't know he was far away in his tavern, I'd think John described Arnulf Long."

Peg and Hob had turned a different way, over the river and to St John's Church and Spon Gate where they entered the city. The pageant there was deserted. Past the church along Hill Street was Bablake Gate and the city wall. Through the gate a road stretched away westwards.

"We've come to the end," said Hob. "There's no more of Coventry after this. What shall we do?"

"There's no point in going back," said Peg.

"We should have stopped people and asked if they knew where Bartholomew was," said Hob. "Unless Jankin's found him already and they're at the Bull waiting for us."

"It's Jankin I fear for most," said Peg.

"Why should you? He's only just gone. He can't be far away."

"So you'd think," Peg answered. "But he's vanished into thin air. I'll tell you, Hob, the ache in me for him is greater than that I feel for Bartholomew. Bad things are happening here."

"So why aren't we asking anyone?" said Hob.

"First we look," said Peg. "Asking comes later." She looked up at the wall. "We'll walk the length of this. I can see a path. It will lead to another street coming into the town."

The wall stretched northward about four hundred paces over empty, marshy ground. Another little river wound through it. Beyond, low wooded hills rose and at their foot were houses and shops along a street and another road out, leading north-westward. The path was difficult and they had well wetted feet by the time they crossed the river. Cattle drank from it, thin and unhappy. One was dead: its carcase lay rotting, buzzing with flies, half in, half out of the water. Two men, smocks wet and filthy with mud and worse, were trying to drag it to a cart half stuck in wet earth. One looked up.

"See what we've come to?" he shouted to his companion. "Has Meriden as Mayor brought us to this? Were things better under Ragnal Stow?"

"You've a short memory if you think that," said the other. "Nothing could be worse than those days." They heaved again on the dead animal. Peg and Hob walked on.

"Coventry's a dead-and-alive sort of place," said Hob.

They reached Well Street, quiet and away from the centre. Empty, ruined houses alternated with others smart and lived-in.

"Dead-and-alive indeed," said Peg. "Coventry doesn't seem to know whether to be happy or sad. A strange place."

"It makes me wonder whether it's worth staying in," said Hob gloomily. You can't say we've had a wonderful welcome."

"I know," said Peg. "Maybe we should just find Bartholomew and Jankin, pack our bags and be on our way."

The shop was quiet after Miles and Molly had gone. The afternoon passed slowly. Three customers came in but left without buying. John counted yet again the few coins earned that day, sighed, then wondered whether he had done right to talk to strangers.

He did not have to wonder for long. The door opened. John looked up. Perhaps he had a customer. What a surprise. It was someone he'd known well years ago and never thought to see again.

"Why, Seth Broad," John said. "It's so long since I saw you. I thought you'd left Coventry for ever. And what can I do for you?"

"No, John," the new arrival replied. "The question should be, 'What should I do for you?'"

"What do you mean?" Thomas asked.

"John, you had visitors this afternoon, I believe."

"Yes," John answered. Something like dread touched him.

"And I should imagine they asked a lot of questions."

The dread was suddenly greater, a black blob he could somehow see as well as feel. "Whatever could they find to ask me?" he muttered.

"You tell me, John. Though I know what the answer would be."

"It was about. . ." John began haltingly.

". . .About the black gown, wasn't it?" The voice was harsh now.

"I told them nothing, nothing at all. I swear it."

"Now John, you and I know that people who've said nothing never look frightened, because they have nothing to be frightened about. Yet you're very frightened. I believe you've done what my friend asked you not to do. And since I can't be sure that you're telling the truth, I have to treat you as though I know you aren't. A pity, John: you've been a good tradesman in Coventry. You'll be missed."

And John Crowe stared down at the bright flash of the sharp blade in the dark shop and could not even cry out as the wicked stab felled him and blood soaked the clothes he was sorting.

Sym stared at the body of his good friend Bartholomew. That familiar face floated on the stagnant, foul water, its eyes fixed open, saying accusingly, "Sym, why didn't you come sooner and save me from this?"

He answered. "I'm sorry, Bartholomew. We shouldn't have sent you on alone. Forgive us." He sobbed. Crispin put an arm round his shoulders but there was no calming him.

"He can't stay there," Crispin said. "We'll bring him out to see how he died. Then he'll be buried properly and the right things done to save his soul."

Sym threw himself on the ground. His shoulders heaved in his grief. Crispin lowered himself slowly, his head over the ditch, looking down into Bartholomew's dead face. He clamped his feet hard into the ground so he didn't slide in, reached down into the foul water and hooked his arms under Bartholomew's shoulders. He grunted with effort because he had little purchase on the body. "Sym, shape yourself and grip hold of my ankles, or you'll have to get us both out," he shouted.

Sym stirred himself enough for that at least. Gradually Crispin pushed his legs backwards while his arms clung to Bartholomew's body. After a long struggle, Bartholomew lay on the ground, eyes staring. His top clothes had been stripped off: he wore a skimpy, sodden shift. Decay had set in: he brought the smell of the ditch and worse with him.

But what made Crispin gasp was the ragged wound, not the gash a knife made but a hole, like a well sunk for maggots to crawl down. He turned Bartholomew over. Another wide hole. What pierced him came from behind and went through his body.

"He could have been run through by a lance," he said aloud. "He was impaled on its end like an insect."

Sym stopped sobbing. "A lance? Was he killed by a knight?"

Crispin sniffed. "I wouldn't put it past some knights to seize him off the road and use him as a human target for tournament practice," he said. "But no, I don't think so. Not if he ends up in a ditch here. They'd have better ways of losing his body."

Sym burst into tears again. Crispin stood up and looked round warily. "Not a soul in sight," he said. "Who could have done this thing?"

He squatted on his haunches. "And yet the hole is too big for a lance," he said. "Besides, not even knights would lance him through the back." His fingers played round the wretched torn skin. "A fly on a thorn. It's as if some huge hawk such as even travellers have never told, swooped, scooped him up and impaled him on a thorn from Hell itself." He stood again. "The answer must be close by," he said.

He looked round. Someone answered him at once.

Alban and Joslin came through Little Park Gate, saw them and hailed them.

They had found Dead Lane easily. Alban merely asked the friar who was talking to the actors on the pageant where Herod had stalked. He never noticed that the friar looked at him strangely and the actors stopped talking and drew back, one or two making the sign of the cross. They left Cross Cheaping, came down Little Park Street and turned into Dead Lane. They found the alleyway and the wall with Hell behind it. They saw the sharp teeth, red depths, and wisps of smoke, with the high city wall brooding above. They shuddered: the sight oppressed their minds. Then Alban collected his wits and made the same comments as Sym – why was it all Hell with no Heaven and no Earth? Joslin said, "Now I know what Margery saw. But if this isn't a play pageant, what is it?" They walked up and down Dead Lane again. Then they came through Little Park Gate and saw Sym, Crispin and Bartholomew's body.

Alban sobbed like Sym and made Sym start again. They clung howling to each other. Appalled though Joslin was, he saw there was no sense to be got out of either. He turned to Crispin. "Well?" he said.

"Impaled on something," Crispin answered.

Joslin looked at the dead man's face. He remembered Jankin: "You could be taken for brothers." But days of lying dead in the water had taken its toll. The young face was sadly ravaged: Joslin shivered, thinking how often in the last months his own face was near to being in the same state. But he was used to such sights now. He looked lower and saw the wicked hole. And, suddenly, he was sure.

"A tooth," he said. "The huge, wicked tooth that I've just seen. He was pushed down hard on one of the teeth of Hell-mouth."

"Why so sure?" Crispin asked.

"I don't know," Joslin replied. "But I am sure. One thing I've learnt to do these last months is to trust my own intuitions."

Crispin continued his searching gaze. "I see," he said, half-admiringly. "I was right to save you from death when your intuitions didn't work so well."

"Bartholomew was sent here," Joslin continued. "We find him dead, impaled on one of Hell's teeth. A Hell with no Heaven. The place of devils. Beelzebub is one of them – second only to Satan."

"So?" said Crispin.

"Beelzebub. A devil with a huge head. Like the man we saw last night – the man who got the play howled off the stage and us minstrels made to look fools. Lambert dead. We found him this very day, just as it was dawning. They're all part of the same thing. Put them all together, Crispin. What do you get?"

"You tell me," said Crispin.

"I don't know," said Joslin. "But I know I'm right."

"We'll see," Crispin said. There was a strange look on his face. *He's testing me again,* thought Joslin.

Alban had recovered enough to speak. "We must bring the others here. Miles will decide what comes next."

"You can find the others," said Crispin. "Joslin and I will keep watch over Bartholomew's body."

When he heard that, Joslin thought he might at last find out more about this strange man and the puzzles which surrounded him.

Peg and Hob were back in the Bull. They sat downstairs alone. Coventry was at work or rehearsing its plays and Godric Chase would not serve them with ale to slake their parched throats.

"Your sort aren't wanted here any more," he said.

They sat miserably. "I fear the worst for my Jankin," moaned Peg. "Where Bartholomew's gone, he's gone."

"Bartholomew's not gone far," said Hob. "He's not been harmed and nor has Jankin. Nobody here would dare. You believe me, Peg."

But Peg had the stricken look of one who knew better and wouldn't be shaken until it was proved otherwise. Miles and Molly came in. Miles spoke to Godric, received a stony stare for answer, shrugged his shoulders and sat down beside Hob.

"Nothing," said Hob. "We found nothing."

Strangely, Miles took no notice. "Now, both of you," he said. "Think hard. Try to remember everything you can about Arnulf Long."

"*Why?*" Peg cried. "It's now we care about."

Miles looked stern. "Do it," he said firmly. "It was

131

he who gave Bartholomew's cloak to Father Anselm."

Joslin and Crispin sat by the ditch. Nearby, Bartholomew stared until Crispin gently closed his eyes and covered them with a dock leaf. Neither spoke for some time. Joslin broke the silence. "Crispin, there's a lot I don't know about you," he said.

"Be patient," Crispin replied. "You will in the end."

"But we're in danger," Joslin cried. "Two are dead: we may be next. We have to trust each other – and for that we have to know about each other."

"You can trust me," Crispin replied.

"But I saw you that night in the tavern in Warwick. Someone brought you a message."

Crispin started. "Did you now?" he said.

"What was that about?" Joslin demanded.

"I'm sorry. I can't tell you," Crispin replied.

"Lew and Mab know you well. They won't hear a word against you. But when outlaws attacked the woodmen, you were with them."

"Why should you think that?" Crispin said.

"I saw you. I *know* it was you."

"Do you? Well, suppose I was? What did I do?"

"You called them off."

"There you are then. Did Lew see me?"

"He didn't say."

"No, he wouldn't." This said with a smile.

Joslin was getting nowhere. "All the while I was with Lew and Mab, you were in the forest. What were you doing there?" he said.

"You'd better ask Lew and Mab," he said.

"And you know the forest as if you'd spent a long time there."

"Just as well for you that I had."

"Arnulf Long knew you. Why was that?"

"A travelling minstrel meets many people. You should know that."

"But Arnulf said you weren't a minstrel then. And you weren't called Crispin Thurn, either."

"Perhaps Arnulf has a poor memory. Once a minstrel, always a minstrel, Joslin."

"I'm sure Robert Meriden knew you as well."

"Whatever makes you think that?" said Crispin.

"Because I watch people's faces. If I didn't, I might not have got this far through England."

"Arnulf Long, Robert Meriden – you'll be telling me the Bishop and Father Anselm are my friends."

"Don't mock me," said Joslin. "You test me, then you mock me."

"How do you mean, I test you?"

"You always do it. You tell me things and ask me questions which lead to the easy way and you're happy when I give the difficult, right answer. Once you said I'd done better than you would have. But I don't try for the answer you'd like. I say what I think."

"I know you do, Joslin," Crispin replied gravely. "That's why I respect you." Joslin wondered if more tests were coming. He had to know more about this man whose destiny strangely joined his. But if Crispin wouldn't say, how could he trust him?

Crispin seemed to know what he felt. "Joslin," he said. "I'm sorry I've not answered your questions. I can't. Not yet. But this I'll tell you. I'm not just in Coventry for the plays. I have dangerous work here. The actors' plight may well be part of it. In fact, now I'm sure it is. And, yes, I know more about the forest and the people in it than I've told you. That's connected with my work in Coventry as well. But I still

133

don't know how. I think you'll find out at the same time that I do. Does that help you?"

Joslin considered this. "Not much," he answered.

"Well, it's all I'm going to say for now. You must trust me. I mean no harm to you or the actors. I'm a friend to you all. Take my word." He paused. Then he said, "I know I'm not being fair to you."

Joslin asked another question. "About the song of Gamelyn. Why is it so important to you?"

"When this is over, you'll know why."

"Why not before?"

"Because it won't help you in Coventry." He paused. "You're good at putting evidence together, Joslin. So think on this. *He who has ears to hear, let him hear.* And when you've worked that out, keep it to yourself, or we might all be killed."

The grief-stricken actors wandered blindly into the Bull. "Any news?" Miles asked. Without need for them to say a word, he knew they had.

They gathered over Bartholomew's body. It seemed only Miles could think. "There's but one place we can go now," he said. "Greyfriars. Father Anselm must answer our question. Did he tell us all he knows about Bartholomew's gown? And Bartholomew must be buried properly. Who else but Father Anselm can do it? Because I'll ask no parish priest in this town when every hand and voice but his seems turned against us."

18

The grieving actors and Joslin blundered into the friary. An old friar stopped them at the gatehouse. "We seek Father Anselm," said Miles.

"He's at prayers in the chapel," the old friar said.

Friars working in the garden looked up as they passed. They came to a great court ringed by cloisters: the church's tower cast a shadow across it. In one corner was a chapel: gingerly they entered. They could almost touch the quiet. Eight friars knelt. At the squeak of the door's hinges, one rose, with a look of annoyance.

"We want Father Anselm," whispered Miles. "Our friend is dead."

"You need your parish priest, not us," the friar whispered back.

"We have no parish, nor priest," Miles replied. "We're travellers on the road like the friars: they are our priests. Tell Anselm that Miles must speak with him. If it wasn't important, we wouldn't be here."

"Wait," said the friar. He knelt again. Hob impatiently whispered, "This is no good. Let's go."

135

But Miles motioned him to stay still. At last the friar rose, made the sign of the cross and joined them. "Come outside," he said. He fetched Anselm and Miles told why they were there. "Of course we'll bury Bartholomew," he said. "Take me to him."

They walked down the road leading away from Greyfriars, called Chylesmoor, to the hardly used Park Gate. Like nearby Little Park Gate, only seldom-used footpaths led from it. Once into the wild land, they saw Crispin a hundred paces away, with Bartholomew's body.

"This is a mournful sight," said Father Anselm, moving aside the ruined shift to see the dreadful hole.

"Made by the teeth of Hell," howled Hob.

Father Anselm looked at him sharply. "If you think you speak true," he said, "that would be blasphemy. The soul which feels such sharpness cannot come back to tell us unless God sends him."

"But I *do* speak true," Hob answered, nearly hysterically. Molly put her arm round his thin shoulders. "We'll show you."

"You'll show me after Bartholomew lies in a place more worthy of a man whose soul is meeting God," said Father Anselm. Miles, Crispin, Alban and the two Brothers gently lifted Bartholomew and bore him back to the friary. Father Anselm led them. "Nobody will begrudge him the privilege of lying in our chapel until a grave is dug," he said.

When Bartholomew, coffined decently, lay on a trestle table before the altar, Father Anselm said, "We'll give him proper burial when Corpus Christi is over. *Now* show me the teeth of Hell."

Even Father Anselm seemed cowed as they walked

the dismal Dead Lane. "You know what Coventry people say of this place?" he said. When he saw Hell-mouth, he caught his breath. Then he said, "We must be calm. This is men's work, not devils'."

"We *know* that," said Hob scornfully. Miles looked at him furiously. "Hob means," he said quickly, "that an actor can see it's a sort of pageant. But a pageant stage is threefold, with Heaven and Earth as well. To see Hell on its own gives us both thought and fear."

"I understand," said Father Anselm. "I took no offence from Hob. And I know what you mean by fear. Seeing this makes me remember my bad dream. For several nights now I've dreamt that we do have a Judgement play, but that Satan himself, not an actor, takes the leading role and everyone in the town is damned because there's no choice for them. I see a monstrous Hell-mouth in front of us and know the flames come from the real torment and I know that the folk cannot say, 'This is wrong,' because it is in one of the plays and the plays are never wrong. That's the folk's faith, because the priest's words and the plays' action are all they know of scripture, and if one is wrong then their worlds crumble round them."

He stopped and they saw sudden sweat on his forehead. But he collected himself and spoke briskly. "I agree that this seems some sort of pageant. It's well fit to join the others in the Corpus Christi procession. Hell is for a Judgement play but our day ends with the bishop's homily. If we wanted a play we could make one or borrow one. There are Judgement plays at Chester and York. But who in Coventry would make this but keep it hidden?"

"We could act a Judgement play," said Miles.

"No, Miles. You agreed to what we want," Anselm

replied. "I still ask: who made this fearful thing?"

They climbed on the stage, felt the sharp teeth and fancied they could see Bartholomew's blood on them. Crispin went towards the depths behind but Anselm called him back. "Not yet. This may not be devils' work, but it's not God's either. Why are the teeth sharpened? There's no need for that in any play. No, we'll consider things first."

They did so, at a loss, not knowing what they should be considering. Joslin spoke first, with a conviction which settled like lead.

"Evil's been done here," he said. "The place reeks with it. This Hell may be wood and paint but there's wickedness in every nail and brush stroke, and it's human evil. Though Hell-mouth seems deserted, I know it's watched and every move we make is seen."

"Then why won't this evil claim us like Bartholomew?" said Miles.

"It bides its time. It can take us when it likes and it's mired us round since we entered Arnulf's tavern. I'm certain of that now."

"Come back to Greyfriars," said Anselm. "Light may dawn there."

But as they entered the friary, the old friar shuffled agitatedly out of the gatehouse. "Anselm, have you found Brother Fulk and Brother Micah?"

"Why?" enquired Anselm. "Have you lost them?"

"They aren't here. After you left again, they were missed. They were seen leaving the friary at midday and nobody's seen them since."

"They're young novices and they don't know the discipline yet," Anselm replied. "I was a novice once and used to slip out when nobody was looking. So, I've no doubt, did you."

"This is different," said the old friar. "When that horn blew at noon they ran out at once. 'It's a passing hunt,' I shouted. 'Put such trifles behind you.' 'We want to know why that horn is blowing,' Micah answered. Then they were gone."

"But we heard a horn as well, as we came through the city gates," said Alban. "It seemed like the start of a Judgement play. Which you don't do."

"Many said they heard it," said Anselm. "But no hunt passed by. Others say the hearers had supped too much of Godric Chase's ale."

Crispin laughed grimly. "Don't tell me people think Herne the Hunter's come out of the forest," he said.

"No," Anselm answered. "They think about Dead Lane where Hell-bound souls meet, and Judgement Day's terrible summons."

"This is strange," said Miles. "If there were a Judgement play here, a horn would be blown to summon all souls to their reckoning."

"But there isn't," said Molly. "So why did that horn blow?"

"It was like some warning," said Joslin.

"Was it warning that two good young men who will adorn our order would disappear?" said Anselm.

Peg spoke wildly. "They're with my Jankin. Find one, find all."

"We must go back to Hell-mouth," said Crispin.

"Yes, that's right." "So we should." The actors' cries made Anselm raise his hand to stop them.

"I know how you feel and in part so do I," he said. "But Fulk and Micah know why they became Grey Friars. They're pledged to follow God's will and if God's will is to take them when they're young, then so be it. As for Jankin, I don't see that for you to swarm mob-handed over a painted show you know nothing about will help him."

"Perhaps you're right, Anselm," said Miles. "But I have a question. I saw John Crowe this afternoon. He told us he gave you a pile of clothes with Bartholomew's gown among them because you'd know what to do with them."

"Of course I knew. I'd see if any could be used in the plays. The rest I'd give to the poor."

"But you didn't know Bartholomew's gown was among them?"

"Miles, of course I didn't."

"And you don't know who gave Crowe the clothes?"

"No. John didn't tell me."

"You've heard of Arnulf Long?"

Crispin looked up, surprised. "Arnulf? Are you sure?"

Miles turned to him. "I don't wonder you're surprised. We've not told you what we found on our search through Coventry."

"I've no idea who Arnulf Long is," said Anselm.

"How many of those clothes did you use in the plays?" asked Miles.

"Just the one. The rest was poor stuff. A lawyer's black gown was an odd item, I thought, in such a rag-bag. But it had its uses."

"On Thomas Dollimore's back as a learned doctor," said Miles. "And you had no idea it belonged to our Bartholomew?"

Father Anselm stared at the ground as if in shame. Then he straightened, looked Miles in the face and said, "Miles, I did not. And right sorry I am. If I knew where it came from I'd have flung it back in the faces of those who stole it off his poor body."

Joslin regarded the friar carefully. His hood hung

free and his head was bare. Since he had been in England, Joslin's experiences with friars had not been good. But Anselm had an earnest, broad face as clear as day. "So who did steal it?" Joslin asked.

Father Anselm spread his hands helplessly. "I wish I knew."

"Someone must," said Hob, still looking suspiciously at Anselm.

"John Crowe described a man we think is Arnulf," said Molly.

"But does he know more than he told?" said Miles.

"There's one way to find out," said Crispin. "Force it out of him."

"That's no use," said Molly. "Try to beat it out of him and he'll dig his heels in. I've seen stubborn little men like John Crowe before."

"Perhaps he'd tell you, Anselm," said Miles.

Anselm considered a moment. Then he said, "Yes, he may. I'll see him. But you must come with me."

Shadows lengthened as they walked to John Crowe's shop in Gosford Street. But before they reached it, they knew something was wrong. A crowd was outside, silent, watching the doorway. Then four men came out with their sad load, followed by a chanting priest.

"Dear God," said Father Anselm.

For the load the men bore was the limp, scrawny body of John Crowe, his frayed tunic soaked with blood from the knife wielded by a man he knew and had presumed was his friend.

They were back in the Bull. They could do nothing at the shop. Father Anselm was not needed: a priest from St Michael's was there. A bystander told them what he knew: a customer had found John dead in the shop and raised the alarm.

"I must go back to the friary," said Father Anselm. Then, with real anguish, "I should never have taken those clothes or used that gown. I sinned without knowing what I did and a good man is dead. I shall find my confessor and seek absolution."

They walked back without speaking. Before he left them, Father Anselm said, "This alters nothing about tomorrow. We made an arrangement and we'll keep it. The plays go on."

Then he left. In the Bull, Godric sold them a wretched meal of stale bread, turnip and stinking fish with quart pots of his thin brew. They were so hungry that even those repulsive lumps slid down and made them feel slightly better. Miles leant back, belched slightly and said, "So what can we make of such a business as this?"

"Nothing," said Alban. "We shouldn't have come and we certainly should never have sent dear Bartholomew on ahead."

"But we did," said Molly. "So we must make the best of what we have. Grief shouldn't stop us looking out for ourselves."

"One thing worries me," said Miles. "The coroner will want to see everyone who went to John's shop this afternoon."

"We must say nothing, Miles," said Molly.

"Let's leave this dreadful city." said Hob. "We could creep out tonight and nobody would know."

"We have a bargain with Anselm," Miles said.

"You never asked us," said Hob.

"I don't have to. If you don't accept my word you must join another band of actors," said Miles. "Remember this. You can see how the land lies. Every town worth going to at Corpus Christi thinks the same. They want to give the plays to the Guilds, cut real actors out and keep the wealth and pride the pageants bring for themselves. Where will that leave us? Scratching for scraps in miserable villages and hostile taverns, starving and freezing in winter, sweating and starving in summer, losing out to jugglers and tumblers. But if we do Anselm's bidding we've steady jobs for ever. There'll always be new plays to do and new actors to train. We can make the actors worth watching and these plays the way we want them. We'll earn thanks, respect and regular money. We'll be back every year until they can't do without us. When did we have that before? Tell me, Hob."

"All right," Hob muttered. "Have it your way."

"I'm not leaving Coventry until I've got my Jankin back," said Peg.

"There you are, Hob," said Miles. "Argue with Peg if you dare."

Hob's face showed that he didn't.

"That's settled, then," said Miles. "Now, about this afternoon. You know what happened to Molly and me. We spoke to John Crowe and now he's dead. He might still be alive if we hadn't. But he described a man with long hair and a cast in one eye who reminded us of Arnulf Long. We know what happened to Crispin and Sym and what they found. It was worse than we could have seen in the most terrible of dreams. Alban and Joslin, what about you?"

"We saw a play and then joined Sym and Crispin," said Alban.

"Nothing else?" Miles asked.

Alban looked at Joslin, who said nothing. He didn't know how to start. But Alban started for him. "Well, Joslin came out with some daft ideas which don't mean anything. You won't want to hear them."

"Wrong, Alban," said Miles. "Tell us, Joslin."

"Well," he said. "It started when Margery, Thomas Dollimore's daughter, told me she'd seen devils at Hell-mouth. She said one had a big head. I thought it was a little girl's fancies until I saw Herod in the play. He wore a turban big enough to make his head look as if it would fall off. It made me remember the man in the tavern. Just then, Alban said, 'Here come I, Beelzebub. Big head and little wit.' "

"From the Mummers' play," said Miles. "Where does this lead us?"

"Herod – and then Beelzebub, the worst devil after Satan. I thought of what Margery said. And I remembered last night's man with the huge head stirring everybody up, and then finding Lambert dead. I believe those are connected. That man was pure evil. I believe he murdered Lambert. And after what Margery said, I believe he's in Coventry. We know Arnulf is. He visited John Crowe and now John Crowe's dead. The man with the big head, Lambert murdered, Jankin and Bartholomew disappearing – it's all of a piece with what's happening today. I don't think Alban believed me. Then I saw Hell-mouth in Dead Lane and Bartholomew dead. Margery's devil had a big head: I *know* Bartholomew was killed on the teeth of Hell – that devil killed him and that devil is the man from last night."

"Then I fear for Jankin," said Alban.

"If you're right, Joslin," said Miles slowly, "what does it all mean?"

Joslin thought for some time before he spoke. Then he said, "I know I'm right about *what* happened. But I don't know *who*, nor *why*." He looked at Crispin, whose face remained completely expressionless.

The actors seemed speechless. Then Alban said, "Why should we speak about this Hell-mouth when we're mired in the real Hell now?"

Miles turned to Peg and Hob. "You've not told us about your search this afternoon. What did you find?"

"Nothing," said Hob.

"Come on, Hob, there must be *something*."

"Hob's right, Miles," said Peg. "We really found nothing. We just walked round the town, seeing what sort of a place it was. Dead-and-alive. That's what you called it, Hob. We hardly saw a soul," said Peg.

"Except two serfs pulling a dead cow out of the water," said Hob.

"They were talking," said Peg. "We didn't know what they meant."

"Tell us," said Miles. "Perhaps we might."

"They weren't very happy," said Hob. "One asked if this was what they had come to now Robert Meriden was mayor. Had things been better under some man called Ragnal Stow?"

"And the other one said he must have a short memory if that's what he thought."

But Crispin had sat bolt upright and nearly choked on his beer. "By God above, I thought you said Randall Stone," he spluttered.

"Who's Ragnal Stow?" asked Alban.

"I've heard the name," Miles replied. "It's in my mind that it's something to do with – oh, anyone here will tell us. What about Godric?"

Crispin spoke scornfully. "I wouldn't ask anyone here for the time of day," he said. "Except that friar. Ask him tomorrow."

Then Joslin remembered what he had heard in the Bull that very day, when they first came there. "*We shall never have our rights until we have struck off three or four heads of the churls that rule us.*" He told them. "There's a lot of angry people in Coventry. Aren't we in enough trouble without getting mixed up in the town's problems?"

"You're right, Joslin," said Miles. "We must keep out of their troubles and think of our own. So what more is there to say?" He looked round. The actors looked back blankly. "There's only one answer," he went on. "Nothing. We had little sleep last night. The last two days have been harder that any I can remember. We've seen a new friend and an old friend both cruelly dead, we've lost another who may have gone the same way, we've been made an offer which may change our lives and tomorrow we must work hard to

repay the trust we're shown. So I want to forget everything tonight and sleep as well as Godric's lumpy
mattress will allow." He rose stiffly, looking very old.
So did Molly, then Peg and Sym. Alban and Hob
stayed where they were looking mutinous, but Miles
glared at them. "Nothing more. Not tonight. I don't
give many orders, but that's one of them."

Unwillingly, the two rose and left. Joslin wanted to
follow. His last proper night's sleep had been with
Lew and Mab. But he couldn't. Crispin stayed on the
bench. When the others had gone, Joslin said, "I
haven't forgotten what you said – *he who has ears to
hear, let him hear.* You mean – hear Gamelyn's story,
don't you? Well, he suffered a great wrong. But he
righted it. I believe you've suffered a great wrong that
you haven't righted. But as for the rest, the wrestling
match, becoming king of the outlaws, well, I'm not
sure about that yet."

Crispin made no answer.

"So tell me about Randall Stone," said Joslin. "I
thought he was just a name to frighten children with."

"So he is," Crispin replied. "But that's not all
Randall Stone is."

"Then who is he?"

"Look, Joslin, when you said I know the forest well,
you were right. And I know the name Randall Stone
and what he stands for nowadays. Another Herne the
Hunter, that's what he's supposed to be. But he doesn't
hunt ghostly stags like Herne. He hunts real ones and
real people too. Find bodies of travellers in the forest,
robbed, stripped and left for dead – 'Randall Stone's
been here,' they say. Find a fine stag dead, with rats
and crows eating the scraps – 'Randall Stone's been
hunting again,' is the cry. But it wasn't always like that."

"I remember Lew and Mab telling me about him," said Joslin. "Will-o'-the-wisp, Lew said."

"Lew was right. Soldiers not wanted after the wars were over, felons in hiding, that's who does those things. They sully the brave name of Randall Stone which stood for good things for so many years."

"So what about '*Randall Stone shall come into his own*'?"

Crispin stared. "Where did you hear that?"

"In the forest, when the foresters were attacked."

"Take no notice," said Crispin. "It means nothing."

Joslin did not press him further, though he remembered how thinking he heard Randall Stone's name mentioned had nearly made Crispin choke. Instead, he asked, "Then who's Ragnal Stow?"

"Ragnal Stow was once mayor of Coventry. There was a bitter fight for the city between him and the likes of Robert Meriden. That was years ago. Ragnal fled and wasn't heard of here again."

"But the names are so similar. Could they be the same person?"

"How can a mayor of Coventry be the same man as an outlaw king in the forest?"

"How indeed," Joslin murmured. He remembered the song of Gamelyn last night, put one or two things together and wondered whether the fog surrounding Crispin might be lifting a little.

"So tell me. What should we do next?" said Crispin.

That was easy. It had been on his mind for some time. "Talk to Margery again," he answered. "I'm convinced she saw Bartholomew being killed."

Smithford Street was quiet. Next evening it would fill up, as folk from miles around arrived for Corpus Christi Day. But now, though it was not yet curfew, most Coventry folk were law-abidingly behind their doors.

"It's dead for a city like this," said Joslin.

"Citizens here are on a tight rein," Crispin replied. "Meriden and his like want things their own way."

"'*We shall never have our rights until we've struck off three or four heads*'," said Joslin again. "Crispin, would things have been better under Ragnal Stow?"

Crispin laughed scornfully. "Things are neither better nor worse under such jumped-up churls. Give people power and they use it. At least barons are born to power. Meriden and Stow schemed their way to it and when they got it, made everyone suffer."

"Some say things are worse now," said Joslin. "Peg and Hob's peasant with the dead cow for one."

"Believe me, he's wrong. His friend who said his memory was short was right. By God, some people hardly know their own names."

"Does it seem to you that this place is near rebellion?" said Joslin. "Perhaps a few heads of churls who rule the folk *might* get struck off."

"And who's to lead this rebellion?" said Crispin scornfully.

Joslin tried an answer. "Ragnal Stow?" he said.

Now Crispin laughed out loud. "The man who was mayor would be hung from the nearest tree if he even looked through the gates," he said.

"Ah," said Joslin. "But would the man whose name sounds the same, who makes men tremble and children stay awake at night?"

Crispin looked hard at Joslin and then was enigmatically silent.

Margery had gone to bed, a little pallet in a corner of her parents' room. She knew from the bells of St John's and St Michael's that there were four hours to midnight. She had so much to think about. She'd seen real devils in Dead Lane. The friars had gone to fight them. She shouldn't have run away but stayed and helped the friars. God would want her to. That's why he'd let her get away from those devils even though she'd gone into the very depths of Hell.

Should she have told her parents? But they never listened to her. What should she do? The friars might need her. She knew how to get out of Hell. Perhaps the friars didn't, even though they were friars.

She slipped out of bed, plumped up the mattress so it seemed she still slept, put a shawl round her shoulders and tiptoed to the window. A sharp breeze chilled her. "Stay where you are, Margery," it seemed to say. No, that was the devil's voice. She *would* go.

She climbed on to the rough sill. It was a long way

down. But if she wanted to help friars against devils, then surely God was with her. She climbed over and hung on by her finger-tips. Then she thought of something nasty. If she went back to Hell-mouth, the devil might keep her there. She tried to pull herself back to the sill. But her scrabbling fingers couldn't find better holds. Then they lost the ones she had. She was falling free. Now she'd fall for ever, never stopping until she was on the floor of Hell and Satan would meet her there and laugh.

But – *bump!* – she was on the ground, nowhere but in Greyfriars Street, outside her cottage and not hurt except for a few little bruises. So God had looked after her. This was a sign. She gathered her shawl round her and set off for Dead Lane.

Joslin and Crispin were outside Thomas Dollimore's cottage in Greyfriars Street. Joslin knocked on the door. Thomas opened it. "Well?" he said.

"We need to speak to Margery," Joslin said. "It's important to us."

"Is it now? Well, my Margery's asleep and there she'll stay. I don't know why you want to see her and I don't care, because you won't. I bid you good night." He shut the door in their faces.

"No matter," said Crispin. "We'll find out more ourselves if we look round that Hell place."

Hell-mouth at night. Joslin shivered. Was he afeared of whoever pushed Bartholomew's body on that wicked tooth? Or the real Satan and Beelzebub? He didn't know. But Crispin was right.

"Yes," he said. "We'll go."

The night air made Margery's teeth chatter. She

wished she was back inside. But she couldn't climb up and she daren't knock on the door and say, "I fell out." Who was she most frightened of, Satan or her father? She thought, then said out loud, "My father."

In her mind she saw the poor friars, bound and burning in Hell. "Margery, we need you," they cried. Dead Lane smothered her in a shroud of thick air, as if the dead beneath were pulling her down with them. But a voice inside her said, "Margery, you must finish what you started." The rising moon showed her the ruined houses like rotting teeth. She walked slower, until she reached the alley where Hell-mouth was and saw those other, knife-sharp teeth which did not rot.

In front of Hell, she couldn't take another step. Voices whispered: "*Go home, Margery, or harm will come to you.*" Satan was watching beyond those teeth, down in that chasm, a place of unimaginable darkness without even a glimmer of Hell's furnaces.

But in there were the friars. Did they need her now?

Yes. What she had to do was clear. She clambered up to the floor of Hell-mouth, pushed past the teeth and cautiously crept beyond. She felt under her feet first wood, then stone. She stumbled and nearly fell. She reached out for a handhold. There was nothing. She lowered herself until she rested on her hands, Then she pushed her right foot forward. Now she remembered, from when the devils hustled her blind-folded out of Hell, that she was on a stone stairway.

She sat on the cold steps and went down them on her bottom. They seemed never-ending. It was so dark that she might as well be blind. At last she reached the floor. It was bitterly cold. She listened. Nothing except a drip of water somewhere. What should she do now?

Drip. . . Drip. . . Drip. Was there a spring or a well nearby? The silence made the drip almost deafening. She strained her ears further.

The drips were not the only noise. She held her breath. Someone else was breathing – jerky, shallow breaths.

Dare she speak? If she didn't, why had she come down here?

"Who's there?" she whispered.

Joslin and Crispin had reached Hell-mouth. Away from those teeth, darkness smothered them.

"I have tinder," Crispin whispered. "And a candle."

"Dare we show a light?" Joslin whispered back.

"We'll break our necks if we don't," Crispin answered.

The bright flash and the candle's glow somehow let them talk more normally. They passed the devils' costumes, and down a wooden ramp. Crispin held the candle forward.

"Steps down," he said. "They lead to some sort of cellar."

At the foot of the steps, the cold hit them. Joslin spoke. His voice echoed. "A cellar?" he said. "More like a vault."

Crispin shaded the candle, then lifted it up. The light spread a pitifully short way. But what he saw made him catch his breath and when Joslin saw as well, he felt fear snatch at him. They were surrounded by stone coffins: scores of them on the ground and stacked on top of each other. Crispin bent to the nearest. It had no lid. Inside was a skull, stark ribs, spine and limbs and a few rags of clothes.

"You know what we're in?" he said.

153

Joslin did. "At least these plague deaths were given coffins," he said. "They weren't just shoved in a lime pit and covered over."

"Listen," said Crispin. Water dripped. To the right, something stirred. Crispin held the candle towards it. Now Joslin felt the hairs on the back of his neck rise. In the dim light a human shape sat up in a coffin. Next to it rose another. What devil's sorcery was this?

But these shapes were alive. The smaller one spoke. "It's all right. It's the man who asked me about the devils."

"Margery," said Joslin, disbelieving yet relieved.

"Don't you worry about these two, little girl," said the other. He knew that voice well enough by now. It was Jankin.

"This man's hurt himself," said Margery. Then, as Joslin and Crispin bent to Jankin and held the candle close, she added, "I'm here to help the friars."

Jankin tried to move, but groaned with pain. "I got away from them," he muttered hoarsely. "But I fell and now my leg won't work. I hid in this coffin."

Friars and *Them*. Joslin wondered which to get clear first. As Crispin touched Jankin's right knee and Jankin bit back an agonized shout, he asked Margery, "What friars?"

"The two who came when the devil blew his horn," she answered. "They shouted at him and I was frightened. So I ran away. Then I saw you at my father's pageant. I came to look for them tonight because I shouldn't have been frightened. I've been down in Hell before."

Joslin looked at Crispin. "Fulk and Micah," he said. Then, to Margery, "Do you mean you *saw* a devil blow the horn at midday?"

"Yes. He stood in Hell-mouth and blew it there. The friars shouted that angels blew a horn to summon people to Judgement, not devils."

This was strange. Father Anselm said many people had heard the horn. They must have known that it came from within the city. But then, it was from Dead Lane, and nobody came near this cursed place. Whoever blew the horn knew they'd not be found – just as they knew that no one would find them building their pageant except perhaps a little girl nobody would believe. So why blow it at all?

He thought of an answer. Was it a signal? Who to? Before he could ponder on this, Crispin called him. He had torn a strip of cloth away from Jankin's tunic and bound it tightly round his knee. "Best I can do for now," he said. "A herb poultice later, perhaps. We'll find an apothecary tomorrow. Help me sit him up, Joslin." When they had made Jankin comfortable, Crispin said, "We'll get you out of here."

"Wait a while," said Jankin. "This leg hurts even now you've bound it. Let me rest a moment."

He leaned back and winced. Then he asked the question which must have been torturing him. "Have you found Bartholomew?"

Crispin answered. "Yes. Dead. Killed on that Hell pageant."

Jankin passed a hand over his eyes so they wouldn't see him cry. "I knew wicked things would be done on that place," he said.

"Jankin, who was it you said you got away from?" said Joslin.

"The devils," Jankin answered.

"You saw them too?" cried Margery excitedly.

"What happened after you ran off and saw Thomas Dollimore?" said Crispin.

"Him? He was no help. I wondered what to try next. I could see Greyfriars tower and I thought I'd go there. When I found it I wondered who I could see. Perhaps I'd be better off looking for Bartholomew myself. So I saw a street leading towards the city walls. . ."

"Chylesmoor," said Crispin.

". . .and I came to a gate in the wall. I couldn't go any further, so I went through. Well, it was just scroggy ground. Nothing there, I could see that."

"You were wrong," said Crispin. "That's where we found Bartholomew, in the ditch over the causeway, west of Little Park Gate."

Jankin groaned. "I reckon if I'd gone a little further, I could have saved myself all this," he said. "But I walked along the ditch until I came to another gate which was probably that very one. I must have been so close to Bartholomew then. I went through the gate. I could see one way led back to where I'd come from. I took the other way to my right. That was a terrible place. Ruined, deathly quiet, it made me quake in my shoes. As if all the dead souls were whispering to me to go away. Still, I thought, Bartholomew might be dead with them and this is where his body might be dumped."

He stopped, tried to move his leg and winced. In the candlelight they saw sweat on his forehead, even in this cold vault.

"I walked on, looking in those broken places, piles of stone, lumps of rotting wood. It was as if an army had looted the place and laid it waste and I'd find the folk left for dead. I felt the shrivelling of death. This was a place of ill-omen such as I'd not thought possible. I was sure this was doom – that this street wouldn't join another or peter out at the city walls but truly be the way the dead must travel. Well, you know what I saw. A high, crumbling wall – and then, when I looked round it, the place we're in now. It was everything I'd ever feared about the end of the road we all travel. I was at the very portals of Satan's home."

Another wince. Margery, who had been listening wide-eyed, leant across and wiped Jankin's brow with her sleeve. "That's what Mother does for me when I'm sick," she said.

Jankin went on. "But this Hell-mouth was just a boarded stage and the teeth sharpened poles of wood. The cavernous walls were draped cloth. I was on a pageant wagon. Ah, but such a pageant in such a place: it chilled my soul. Then I heard a voice from the bowels of this Hell. But not a devil's – it was an ordinary man's, saying an ordinary thing. 'That's one of them. He tried to frighten us by being Lucifer.' And *I knew the voice*. Then another voice, harsh and deep which chilled me because it could have been the devil's and yet was still a voice I knew, said, 'Then fortune's with us. We have the two we want the most. We've despatched the worse of the two but this one has his dangers as well.' Even then, I wondered if he meant Bartholomew."

"If you knew the voices, whose were they?" asked Joslin.

"The first was like Arnulf Long's. The second was like that man with the huge head. But I must have been wrong. What were they doing there, talking riddles in voices like Satan's?"

"How did you get here now?" said Crispin. "We searched Hell-mouth this afternoon."

"They threw a sack over my head. I couldn't see,"

Jankin replied. "And then they pushed me down steps and along a stone floor. Then up steps again and into clear air. I felt the sun on me."

"Back into Dead Lane?" Crispin asked.

"No, not Dead Lane. There was grass under my feet and my hands were scratched with briars and thorns. I was outside the walls."

"So this vault has another way in," said Crispin. "No wonder they could build their Hell-mouth with nobody knowing. They had a perfect way of bringing everything in."

"They pushed me on to a cart. It rumbled along a track for a while. I heard horse's hooves and a driver calling to peasants. Then we stopped. I was pulled out. The next I knew I was shoved sprawling on the ground. I heard talking. 'What shall we do with him?' said a voice. 'Get rid, like we did the other?' That made me quake, I'll tell you. They must mean Bartholomew, I thought. Then that terrible Satan again. 'Not yet. Keeping him alive may suit us better.' I wondered if it might be better to be despatched then than to stay alive with him around. He might be only a man, but I reckon I'd rather meet the devil than him."

"Well, they didn't despatch you," said Crispin. "So what happened?"

"I heard the devil's voice again. 'Jankin,' it said. 'You'll be of service to us. Tell your friends this. They should not have come to Coventry, yet now they're here and they think the city wants them here. But they aren't wanted, Jankin. They possess something which mustn't come to Coventry and if they don't leave now their mortal bodies never will, though their souls certainly will. You're to tell them that, Jankin. Those who cross us only go one way. Do you understand that, Jankin?'

"Of course I did. Except for one thing. 'What is it that we possess?' I asked. 'Work it out for yourselves,' said the voice. 'If I tell you, you'd know too much. But it could mean the deaths of all of you.' 'Why not kill us now and have done with it?' I cried. 'You'll see,' said the voice.

"Then he shut up. I racked my brains to think what he meant. Nobody could possibly want the meagre scraps we own, surely? And what did he mean by 'You'll see'? Then he said, 'We're taking you further, Jankin.' They dragged me up and pushed me across open ground. I could feel thistles and burrs scratch me. Then they threw me down again. They tied my wrists together and then my legs so I was like a trussed chicken. 'We're taking the sack off your head now,' said the voice. 'But you won't try to roll over and look up. You'll stay down until we're well away. Can you count?' 'Up to ten, like all men,' I answered. 'That's no use. I know – the other night you never finished your Creation play. Now you can play it for yourself, all the way through. Stay where you are, don't look up and shout the words from beginning to end so we can hear you. When you've finished you'll have to get yourself free. And when you've managed that, you must go back to Coventry and persuade your actor friends to leave. Don't worry about those minstrels. Leave them here. Do it well, Jankin, or Coventry will be the last place you'll ever see. And do it quickly, or we may be there before you.' Then the sack was pulled off and I felt a foot pressing my head down. 'Start the Creation, Jankin,' came the voice. So I did – '*I am the Lord enthroned, I am the first, I am the last.*' I was shouting: if they could hear me, they wouldn't come back, I thought. I kept on until God said, '*Now man is fallen, set to roam thoughout the world, with no place home.*' Then I stopped and sat up. I was in a wilderness, an empty village deserted after the plague. Its misery settled in my soul. I saw Coventry more than a mile away. I shouted until I thought my throat would burst. It seemed hopeless. Then, miracle of miracles, people came. Two peasants were looking at me over the ruined wall of a barn. They made the sign of the cross and were about to run away. But I called out to them, 'Help me. I'm not an evil spirit out of the ground. I'm a man like you.' So they stayed: they untied my knots and then ran away as if they still weren't sure. Then I walked towards the walls. The wasteland was trackless and the city seemed no nearer. I started to run. At last the city gate was close and I ran faster, blindly, desperately. Then I fell. My leg twisted under me. Oh, the pain of it! I couldn't get up. I sobbed with frustration. But I could just about drag myself along until I pulled myself into the shade of a clump of bushes.

"But then everything became even worse. I slipped: I was falling again, then I was sliding, I couldn't stop, down another flight of steps hidden by the bushes. When I reached the bottom I tried to pull myself up again but I couldn't. So I was in the dark again. When my eyes grew used to it, I tried to see where I was. Now my heart really froze. I was surrounded by stone coffins. I had somehow come into a huge vault."

"Jankin," said Crispin. "You'd come back to where you started."

"So I thought. It meant I could get out through Hell-mouth. I pulled myself along again, hanging on to the sides of the coffins. But I couldn't carry on. I was exhausted. Some coffins, I saw, were lidless and empty. When I could go no further, I thought that even beds like those would be better than nothing. So I pulled myself into one, lay back and straight away I must have fallen into a deep sleep."

"Then I came and woke you up," said Margery.

"And we followed," said Crispin. "Jankin, you had a long slumber. It's well two hours past darkness by now."

Even by the candle's weak light they saw Jankin's pale face go paler. He tried to struggle up. "Oh, my Lord," he said. "I haven't done what I should have done. Who can trust these devils? My friends may be dead by now. And my dear Peg with them."

Margery suddenly spoke. "Are your friends the same as the friends of the man who was the lost soul on the pageant?"

"She must mean Bartholomew," Joslin muttered to Crispin.

"He said they were in a tavern. He asked me to tell them they mustn't come to Coventry. But I'm not allowed to go in taverns."

Joslin stared at her. Then he said, "Margery, if only you'd told us that before. Now I know that everything I've suspected is true." Then he remembered something Jankin had said. "Why do they want you and me left here?" he asked Crispin.

Crispin's mouth set angrily and he did not answer.

It seemed that the air in the vault turned even colder and misty shapes swirled in the darkness beyond the reach of the candle's light.

"You must see to my friends," cried Jankin. "Leave me here."

"That we won't," said Crispin. He reached into the coffin. "Joslin, take his shoulders. I'll lift his legs. Margery, hold the candle."

Margery did so and saw Jankin's face twist with pain as they raised him up. "What about the friars?" she asked in a small voice.

"I'm sorry, Margery, but we must do one thing at a time, and the first is to get Jankin back," said Crispin.

Margery said nothing, but she felt her lip quiver. She'd gone through all this for the friars and now these two wouldn't help her.

"We'll get you home," said Joslin.

"Come on," said Crispin when he and Joslin were grasping Jankin round the shoulders so he could put weight on his good leg. "Margery, hold the candle and light the way ahead."

Now she saw how the steps came out at a little door in a wall at the back of the pageant and that the same red curtain which draped Hell-mouth was pinned above so it could drop down and hide it. They climbed the wooden ramp to the back of Hell-mouth, then across, past those teeth, truly menacing, ready to bite. She jumped down and helped the others hand Jankin to the ground without hurting him. Then the little procession moved slowly down Dead Lane.

Five minutes later they were outside Margery's cottage. It was dark and quiet. Nobody could have missed her.

"We'll have to wake them up, I fear, Margery," said Crispin.

"*No!*" squeaked Margery. That was a dreadful idea. "I can get in the way I got out. They won't hear me. *Please!*"

"All right," Crispin said unwillingly. "But be sure you do."

"I promise," said Margery, crossing her fingers behind her back. "They'll be too deep asleep to find out."

She watched the three disappear up Greyfriars Street. There was good reason for her to cross her fingers. She had come out to find the friars and find the friars she would. When the others were gone, she turned round and crept back the way she had just come.

High Street was deserted, with only a few lights. Joslin, Crispin and Jankin went carefully, to avoid constables on the prowl for curfew breakers to put in the lock-up. There were lights in the Bull. Coventry was filling up with visitors for Corpus Christi. A few, let through Spon Gate and New Gate, where main roads entered and night watchmen stood guard, still came, on horse and foot. As Joslin and Crispin guided Jankin and looked for a way round the back, the front door opened to admit two men with loaded scrips.

"Quick," said Joslin. "We could get in with them."

With a few silent strides, almost lifting Jankin off the ground altogether, they were with the new arrivals and inside. The bleary doorman blinked: then roared at them, "Who are you? I'm only letting these two in because I was told about them."

"We lodge here already," said Crispin quietly.

"We're with the actors," said Joslin.

"Our friend hurt his leg. We want water to soothe it," said Crispin.

"Then you'll have to want on," said the doorman.

"I hope that's not the fate of all here," said one of the guests and in his friend's laughter and the doorman's distraction, Crispin relit his candle from a lamp by the doorway and they gently eased Jankin to the chamber where they had left the others.

Crispin held the candle high. Joslin counted the sleeping forms. Alban, Sym, Hob – all there, together with four new guests. No pallets were left: even their own had sleeping, snoring bodies in them. He looked round the wall into the next room. Miles, Molly and Peg were there and other new ones as well. Jankin's place with Peg was still safe.

"All here," he whispered to Crispin.

"Is it likely our devilish friends would swarm into the city and break into the Bull at dead of night when their aim is to keep secret?" said Crispin. "No, there's something cleverer than that afoot."

"If only we knew what the actors possess

that these people want so much," said Joslin.

"I tell you," Jankin muttered between teeth clenched with pain. "*Nothing*. We possess *nothing*. Ask the others. They'll say the same."

"We'll ask tomorrow," said Joslin. "Let them sleep now. They'll wake up to joy when they see who's come back."

With difficulty, they eased Jankin's leggings off and saw where his knee was swollen. "That's a bad sprain," said Crispin. He felt it carefully. "But there's no break. Time will heal it."

Jankin closed his eyes. "Thank you, friends," he murmured. Almost at once, he slept. "His best cure," said Crispin. "He needs it."

"So do we," said Joslin. "Where, now our pallets are taken?"

"In the loft, of course," said Crispin. They climbed the ladder, piled straw into makeshift beds and Crispin said, "We'd better make sure we keep these. By tomorrow the loft will be full as well."

Sleep did not come to Joslin. Questions swarmed round his brain. What was so special that the actors possessed? Why did Bartholomew's killers want it kept out of Coventry? Miles and his band had no money, no secret messages from kings to great lords, not even a horse to steal. They had a cart, a few shabby props – and themselves.

Themselves. That gave Joslin a jolt. What did *he* possess but himself? What was he? A minstrel, that's what he was, possessing a harp, a talent and a memory packed with songs and stories.

What did actors have? A cart full of props, talents and memories packed with plays. Were these so valuable and dangerous?

Something evil was brewing up: that was obvious. Was it a rebellion? Why was that Hell-mouth, like yet unlike a pageant, built in the one place nobody would ever go? Why a Hell-mouth, when the Guilds didn't even have a Judgement play?

What about Crispin? He was sure Gamelyn was the key. But perhaps there were more urgent things than worrying about Crispin.

Arnulf Long. What about him? He was more than just an innkeeper in the forest. It seemed he'd been in Coventry, giving clothes to John Crowe, who was murdered for his pains. Arnulf was deep in it.

He was getting sleepy. Why not leave it until the morning?

Dead Lane was even more fearful now Margery was on her own. The dead seemed to crowd round her, their dark shapes touching her face and dry voices whispering, "It's too soon for you to join us." Many times she nearly turned back. But the memory of those friars vainly fighting devils while she ran away drove her on. Crossing Hell-mouth and finding the steps down was almost familiar now. The vault's darkness though, was a black, smothering pall. Without Crispin's candle she was blind. Still, she felt her way along the coffins, fearing any moment to find a dead friar's rough serge habit, rope belt or leather sandal.

On she crept: coffin after coffin. The world was a never-ending line of coffins. But most had heavy stone lids: she'd never find friars in them. When the line ended and she barked her shin against a stone step it was like a little death in itself. She felt for the step, sat on it, cleared her head of imaginings and listened. No sound but water dripping. She whispered. "Friars?" But no friar answered.

Should she feel her way up these steps? Jankin, she remembered, came down them, from bushes beyond the walls. But she'd never find friars out there. So she stood and felt her way to the other side of the vault. She expected another line of coffins to lead her back. But she found none. Instead, she clattered into something hard and metal. She stooped and put out her hands to see what thing she had stumbled on.

Her fingers made out the shape of a huge hammer lying on the ground, with a long haft and a heavy iron head. Next to it, she found another. And another, and another. *Great sledgehammers were laid out in a row on the floor of the vault.* What was this strange store? Who knew what, if she groped further, she might find?

Would she find the friars? But if she did, they would be dead, put in a coffin down here. She suddenly knew, with a force which made her feel sick, that that was not how she could bear to find them.

She wouldn't grope further. This was all too much for her all alone, merely a little girl. She stepped blind across the floor again until she found the coffins which led her there and, hand over hand on their sides, found her way back.

Clouds covered stars and moon: outside was nearly as dark as in. But she knew the way home. The dead seemed to have gone back where they belonged. She found her cottage, still quiet. Nobody had woken. She somehow pulled her way up and through her window and fell into a deep sleep as dawn was breaking.

Throughout the reaches of the night, Father Anselm lay sleepless in his narrow, hard bed. There was much to think on. The plays were his responsibility to make good. Corpus Christi was close and there was much still to do. For Miles and his people to turn up was providential: the friars could have real, knowledgeable help, even if little and late.

And insulting to the actors. Actors were for acting – everyone knew that. Except the Princes of the Church, to whom they were dregs, scum, devils' spawn. Anselm believed none of it. He knew, when he preached on a village green as actors travelled through and did a miracle play in the tavern yard, who it was the people flocked to see. He moaned aloud: "I only *tell* the scriptures. The plays *are* the scriptures, writ large. The folk *believe* through these plays."

Yes, against the power of a play, where the people *saw* God, *saw* Christ, the crucifixion, everything which would otherwise be faint pictures in fogbound minds, the mere words of friars and priests were as nothing. That was why seeing an actor dead, horribly murdered in *this city,* was so profound a shock.

But the worse shock had been how young Bartholomew was murdered. For the vision which he'd tried to suppress, to say didn't matter because it was only painted wood and dyed cloth, rose up, flooded his being, made him want to spit foul liquid from the inmost channels and chambers of his body because he knew that was the Hell-mouth he'd dreamed about. Why was it here? Who brought it and left it in the cursed, doomed part of Coventry? *What was it for?*

It is a dreadful Judgement. It was as if someone spoke the words in his ear. What was Hell but the place of dreadful, final judgement? His nightmare returned. Had he seen a vision of what was to be – the fate rounding off existence for humanity, in reality as well as every Corpus Christi Day? Another strong, awful vision swept in front of his eyes. He saw the bishop from his canopied throne outside his church exhorting the folk of Coventry after they had seen every pageant bar a Judgement play roll through the city. The people listened awestruck. But – even as this great bishop and lord of the Church pronounced the Church's judgement – that very Hell of which he spoke, that evil, slavering mouth, those jaws with jagged teeth, opened up in front of him. Satan appeared, the folk fell before his gaze. The bishop's words were puny and worthless. Oh, what a sight from the damned that would be. Where would Coventry be then? He could not imagine. But he knew that the folk would be putty in Satan's hands.

Father Anselm groaned aloud. At last a tortured sleep came, but not before one last waking thought. If only Coventry had its own Judgement play, as York, Chester and Wakefield had theirs. Then there would be no need for strange Hell-mouths built in secret.

Ralph Breville, Bishop of Coventry and Lichfield, slept on a wider, softer bed than Father Anselm's, with a rich canopy over his head. It befitted a great Lord of the Church. He never groaned aloud, nor were his thoughts terrifying or his sleep tortured.

He was pleased. The obscene laxity which once allowed vagabond actors, children of demons, to mouth the scriptures in vain show every year was gone. He had said it would be so: Robert Meriden and the Guilds had agreed and the Grey Friars would do the rest. If there must be plays, let the simple common folk act them, without guile or evil and in obedience to their Church. Let the plays be done so he and the Church could tame them, keep an eye on them. Vainglorious spectacles of the world should be turned into simple acts of piety. Then he could watch them benevolently and patronizingly, as beneath him but at the simple level of the ignorant multitude.

For the plays would pale into nothing beside his words to round off the day. His homily would make clear and terrible the great final Judgement all folk would come to, would draw the lessons to be learnt from it, make them leave afraid and cowed when they considered what would happen to those who strayed.

The bishop's sleep was untroubled. Tomorrow he would make a good breakfast and then see his throne set up in St Michael's Green ready for Corpus Christi Day. The folk must realize that, after Pope and Archbishop, he was three places away from God Himself.

As light came, Joslin woke after a mere three hours' sleep. What had roused him? He listened.

Nothing but snores rumbling all round.

What woke him? A thought. *See Slad.*

Why? What had Arnulf's brewer to do with it? Easy. He knew Arnulf, when he came to the tavern, where from, why. There wasn't much love lost between them. Slad could safely be asked about Arnulf, the one known link between Coventry and the murders.

He sat up. What about Crispin? The minstrel slept, composed and peaceful. Joslin decided he would go alone. But Crispin should know where he was. Joslin shook his shoulder. Crispin opened one eye, just as when Joslin woke him in the forest.

"I'm going to the tavern to see Slad," said Joslin.

"Are you now?" Crispin replied.

"He'll tell me about Arnulf."

"So he will." Crispin closed his eye and slept again.

Joslin quietly descended the ladder and went downstairs to the yard and stables. A stable boy woke up and helped him saddle Herry, then opened the gate. Herry clopped out into Smithford Street and soon they were passing through Spon Gate as daylight grew stronger and the sun made its first bright mark on the horizon.

He had better not be long away. Too much was to happen that day. He reckoned that if it took a morning to walk from the tavern to Coventry he and Herry should manage it in an hour at a canter. He spurred Herry on: the willing little horse soon moved at a smooth, regular, easy pace. On the way, he thought hard.

What about this *thing* the actors possessed? He knew the answer was very close: some *one thing* in particular, not just their talent or their props or their stock of plays. What did he hope to learn from Slad? Perhaps nothing. Was it worth coming? Yes, it was.

171

The ominous barrier of trees showed before him. Herry's canter slowed. There might be danger here. But they soon came to the clearing where the tavern stood, low to the ground like a giant beetle.

Joslin smelt hops and yeast long before he saw the tavern and knew Slad would be early in the brewhouse. The tavern looked quiet as he tied Herry to a tree close but out of sight. Arnulf, if he was there, scullions, potboys and guests were still asleep. He climbed over the double gates into the yard and ran to the brewhouse. Slad was inside, stirring at a huge vat over a fire, sweating with effort and heat.

"Slad," Joslin called softly.

Slad showed no surprise. He went on stirring, then said, "That'll do for a while," and turned to Joslin. "You here? What do you want?"

"To ask about Arnulf," Joslin replied.

"What do you want to know about him for?"

"We're in deep trouble, and I think Arnulf has got something to do with it. And if you won't tell me, I'll just have to go back. And don't tell Arnulf I was here."

"No, that's all right," said Slad. "You ask on. I'm not that fond of Arnulf that I wouldn't want to see him suffer a bit."

"How long has he been landlord here?" asked Joslin.

"Not long," Slad replied. "About a year. He came after old Walter died." He spat, then said, "I thought Walter wanted me to take the tavern on. But Arnulf turned up. There were people stronger than me – aye, and Walter too – who wanted him here."

"Who were they?" asked Joslin.

"I wish I knew. If I did, I might have done something about it."

"Where did he come from?"

"He never told me. I heard he was from Coventry and used to work in the Bull, but I never believed it. Who'd come here from a place like the Bull?"

As Joslin was taking in this news, Slad asked questions of his own. "Did you go with the actors to Coventry? Did they find Bartholomew?"

"Yes," Joslin replied. "They found him dead. Murdered."

"Oh," Slad replied. For a moment he didn't speak. Then he said, "I'm sorry. I liked Bartholomew. He made me laugh."

This was a puzzle. "Where did you see him?" Joslin asked.

"Here, on his way to Coventry. The others sent him on ahead."

"Yes, but. . ." Now Joslin knew what was wrong. "Arnulf didn't seem to know anything about Bartholomew. 'Not another one of you?' he said when Miles talked about Bartholomew coming back to join them in the tavern. What do you make of that?"

"I don't know why Arnulf should say such a thing. He'd remember Bartholomew all right. Bartholomew had us in stitches acting some of his parts in the plays. I'll tell you what I liked best – the bits out of the Judgement play. I never thought a Judgement play could be funny. He played a little devil who shows all the souls the quickest way to Hell. Like a porter carrying their luggage. The things he said! Oh, that was good, it really was." He laughed again at the memory of it. Then he stopped and his face fell. "I can't take in yet, what's happened to him."

"Does Arnulf ever leave the tavern?" Joslin asked.

"Oh, yes," Slad answered. "He's always going off. I

don't know where. I have to look after things till he gets back."

"When was the last time?"

"The day after Bartholomew left for Coventry. He was only back an hour before you all arrived. He went again last night. He's not back yet. You mind he doesn't see you if you pass him on the way."

"Thanks Slad," said Joslin. "I'm very grateful. I'll be off now."

"I won't tell him you were here," said Slad. "Trust me. He's not that good a master that I don't keep secrets from him."

Herry cantered easily through the forest, past where they found Lambert's body. Joslin let him find his own way as he sat thinking.

No wonder Crispin was surprised to see Arnulf if he'd only been there a year. And Arnulf came there from Coventry. Why? The news that Bartholomew had been there before, Arnulf had seen him and known he was funny – that held a key, which, if only he could turn it. . .

"I never knew the Judgement play was supposed to be funny," Slad said. No more it was: there wasn't much humour in it. Yet the Judgement play Miles and his actors brought *was* funny. That's why they couldn't do it at the tavern: Bartholomew wasn't there to provide the funny bit. What did Jankin tell them his captors said? 'We've despatched the worse of the two but this one has his dangers as well.' Bartholomew was the worst for them. But why did Jankin have his dangers as well?

Could it be that Bartholomew was dangerous because he was funny in the Judgement Play? If so, why was Jankin next worst? In the Creation he'd been Lucifer, who was the devil. So, in the Judgement play he'd be – THE DEVIL HIMSELF.

Not, though, a very frightening devil. Not like the ones Margery saw on Hell-mouth, who left Bartholomew spiked on one of its teeth.

Hell-mouth. Like but unlike a pageant. But what if it was a pageant, ready to be used? Then a Judgement play would be acted on it with no fun in it – and no light or hope either.

What was it, then, which the actors possessed which mustn't come into Coventry? Why – *it was a Judgement play which made people laugh*.

And if that was true, then Bartholomew wasn't murdered because he was trying to get work for the actors on Corpus Christi Day. *He was murdered because he was funny in the Judgement play*.

Why? *Why, why?* What vipers' nest had he strayed into now? None of it made the slightest sense.

He spurred Herry on into a gallop. The road was almost deserted. He overtook only one thing of note. A mile out of the forest, two men led a team of four black horses. Joslin had never seen anything like them. Their coats were sleek and shiny: muscles rippled in their bodies and the massive legs and hindquarters quivered with strength. They moved slowly, with a heavy tread which seemed to shake the earth round them. They looked bigger, stronger and more terrifying than even the largest destrier any knight ever rode into battle. What extraordinary task could they have waiting for them, he wondered.

Less than an hour later, as the sun rose over St Michael's tower, he passed under Spon Gate and headed for the Bull.

Margery woke up. She thought of her adventures the night before. When she was up and dressed, she remembered that she hadn't done what she'd set out for. She'd not found the friars. Poor friars: she feared they were gone for ever.

"Why are you crying, Margery?" asked her mother.

"The friars," she sniffed. "They're lost."

"God will take care of them," said her father.

"You're a strange girl," said her mother. "Worry about yourself and your family, not strangers in grey."

You don't understand, Margery thought and dried her eyes. Nobody listened to her, not even the nice man.

"So I'm weaving alone, am I?" said her mother.

"Yes," her father replied. "It's a big day on the pageants, now this Miles fellow and his friends are putting us right for tomorrow."

"When Corpus Christi's gone I'll make you sweat," said her mother.

Her father sniffed and stalked out of the house.

"As for you, my girl," said her mother, "it's a day of helping me get on with the real work."

Jankin had been to the apothecary. Crispin took him. When they came back, Crispin seemed very thoughtful. Jankin had got back his good spirits. "Smitten, were you, Crispin?" he said.

"What do you mean?" Joslin asked.

"The apothecary's fair daughter Eleanor. She made a big impression on Master Crispin."

"Be quiet, Jankin," said Crispin. Joslin never thought to see him embarrassed.

Jankin's leg was splinted, dressed and bandaged. Now he told everyone his story, with Peg looking fondly at him. Then Joslin talked urgently. "It changes everything," he said. "Arnulf is a Coventry man and what's more, he knew what Bartholomew did in the Judgement play. Bartholomew was killed for his part in it. I believe Arnulf came to Coventry to warn these people about Bartholomew and what he did in the Judgement play. Somehow that's important to them. So Arnulf's deep in the murders."

"But I can't see any reason for murdering Lambert," said Alban. "Nobody knew him."

"How do you know?" said Hob. "Perhaps someone with a grudge followed him up from London."

"Then it took him a long time to do anything about it," Alban retorted.

"Maybe nobody knowing him is the point," said Joslin thoughtfully.

"That's stupid," said Sym. "You don't kill people just because you don't know them."

"I don't know so much," said Joslin. "I reckon I may be right, though I don't know why."

"So we know something about Arnulf," said

Molly. "What about the man with the big head?"

"He was the leader last night," said Jankin.

They were quiet. To know they had seen their enemies was an uncomfortable thing.

"Do you know what I feel?" said Jankin at last. "If they're so worried about our Judgement play, we should do it, just to spite them."

"It would do more than spite them," said Joslin. "It's exactly what they don't want."

"But we have no Bartholomew any more and you're no good on a pageant with that leg," Miles protested.

"But we *must*," Jankin insisted.

"We don't have a devil or a porter," Miles repeated.

"I'd manage," said Jankin.

"A limping devil won't fill folk with fear," said Hob.

"Crispin would make a good devil," said Molly.

"And would he be ready by tomorrow morning, with everything else we have to do?" said Miles. "Hopeless."

"Joslin could do Bartholomew's part," said Jankin. "Didn't I say they could be brothers?"

"*There isn't time*," Miles insisted. "Not with everything we've said we'd do for Father Anselm."

"Oh, there's time well enough," said Crispin. "Joslin and I, we've minstrel's memories. If we hear something once, it's with us for ever."

"That's right," said Joslin. "But I couldn't be funny like Bartholomew."

"You might surprise yourself, Joslin," said Sym.

"Father Anselm doesn't want us to act," said Miles.

"Neither do our enemies," said Jankin.

"What good would it do?" Miles was not yet convinced.

Molly gave him the answer. Once she spoke, they all knew they would be getting the play of Judgement ready for tomorrow. "We won't know what good it does until we do it," she said.

Father Anselm kept watch in the chapel after the third hour of the morning. From the moment he saw Bartholomew's body, he knew this Corpus Christi Day would be a time of destiny and he must be strong to meet it. The sun was rising when he left Greyfriars and made for the city. As soon as he felt the sun on his face he felt better and by the end of the day he was more content than he had thought possible.

Yes, the plays were in good hands. His colleagues from Greyfriars, at his direction, knew well what they were to do: the untaught Guild men acting the plays already moved with regular discipline. Now Miles's actors throughout the day would go from play to play to cajole, threaten, shout, plead, declaim speeches and give extravagant gestures until they became exhausted. Only Will Woolman of the Shearmen and Tailors who played King Herod would not need them. Gradually the Coventry workmen would take the point. Performances would come to life, guild men understand what they were doing and be proud of their new powers. Father Anselm's heart swelled with pleasure when he thought how, with actors like Miles to help, the Coventry Miracle Plays would be known and admired the length and breadth of England.

The memory of Bartholomew and Fulk's and Micah's absence faded. So did his fears of the night. All would be well. Corpus Christi Day would do what it should – make God's purposes clear to the folk and restore the glories of the city of Coventry.

Margery was being no use at all. Her mind wasn't on

it. "I swear you're more trouble than you're worth this morning," said her mother. "Oh, go on, get out. I'd rather have your room than your company."

So Margery ran outside. In the street she stopped to consider. Which way? Hell-mouth again or into the city for the last play rehearsals? Just thinking of the choice decided her. Not for anyone would she go down Dead Lane again. She'd never find the friars now: God would have to look after them. She ran the other way, to her father's pageant, wanting to see him first. Then she'd go round every pageant looking for the nice man. Perhaps, at last, she could make him listen to *everything* she said.

Before they left the Bull for the pageants, the actors took Joslin and Crispin into the yard beside the stables. Hob and Sym dragged the cart out and there, in morning sunshine, they did their Judgement Play.

They just ran through words and movements, with no costumes or props. First, Hob as an evil man and Miles as a good man came on stage. Hob boasted of his misdeeds and dared God to send him to Hell: Miles protested his own unworthiness and was sure he deserved to go there. But then Sym appeared at the back of the cart. "I'm an angel," he said by way of explanation. "I should blow a horn now, but it's packed away so you'll have to imagine it."

But the effect on Hob as the evildoer was great. How that imaginary blast on the horn frightened him. How he cursed and swore, because now he knew what his fate would be. Yet Miles was calm: he'd wait patiently for what was to be dealt out to him because he knew it would be right. Sym as angel now said why some would go to Hell and others to Heaven. Then who should enter but Alban as Jesus.

> "When I was starving, who fed me first?
> When I was parched, who slaked my thirst?
> When I was naked, who covered me
> And when imprisoned, who set me free?"

> "Lord, when did you have such great need
> That I could help you? When did I feed
> You when you starved? Yet if I could,
> I swear to you, I know I would," said Miles.

> "Every time you did your best
> For someone hungry, captive, pressed
> Around with sorrow, anguish, poverty,
> You never knew that one was me," said Jesus.

> "I don't believe that. When I saw
> Someone all wretched, scabbed and poor,
> I slapped them and kicked them to make it worse,
> As they deserved. I made sure my purse
> Stayed shut. But Lord, believe this too –
> I'd have done different if I'd known it was you!"

That wasn't good enough. Hob was consigned to Hell. Sym led Miles out one way: Hob waited, then turned to Joslin. "This is where Bartholomew entered," he said. "He was supposed to take me down to Hell, but he didn't, not straight away, anyway. He started on the audience and it's that which made them laugh. And he made them a bit uncomfortable as well. I'll do what he said."

"Go on, then," said Joslin. "I'll listen."

So Hob started on Bartholomew's speeches as the porter at Hell-mouth. The more he spoke, the more

Joslin's heart sank. He'd remember it all right, but he was sure he'd never even raise a smile. Bartholomew must have had a huge talent to get away with it.

At last Bartholomew's part ended. Peg helped Jankin on the cart and he sat with his leg splinted and bandaged, looking like anything but the devil. He welcomed Hob to his home for all eternity and told him what was in store for him. Hob went down moaning and railing against his fate. Well, Jankin with his bad leg wasn't very frightening now, but Joslin knew straight away that Crispin, with his hard, axe-shaped face and deep, carrying voice, might be.

Hob and Jankin left. Miles and Alban appeared. Miles ended the play – and the whole cycle – with a speech of praise which made it clear that all the plays which had gone before had led up to this. And Joslin stood more worried than he had ever been, before even his most difficult performance as a minstrel.

He wasn't up to this – not if they wanted another Bartholomew. But he had this thought which wouldn't go away. *Be ready.*

By the end of the day, Margery was frustrated and unhappy. She'd gone to every pageant in turn looking for the nice man. On her father's pageant in Smithford Street she'd seen the old actor and Father Anselm. In Cross Cheaping, where Joseph and Mary and King Herod were they hadn't seen him. The mothers whose babies were about to be slaughtered were trying to sing their out-of-tune lullaby. "We're waiting for the young minstrel to help with this," said the friar looking after the pageant. "Joslin's gone with Hob to the pageant at Newgate," said Alban.

Off she went to Newgate, but he'd just gone. So she

went to Jordan Well, Gosford Gate, back to Mill Lane, then Well Street, Hill Street in Bablake and finally to St Michael's Green where the Bishop's Throne was being set up for the bishop's final homily.

By the end of the day she had trudged to every station in the city. The nice man had either just gone or they were waiting for him to help with the music. Now she was tired, dusty and footsore. She wouldn't go a step further. He could find out about those sledgehammers alone. They probably didn't matter anyway. It wasn't as if she'd found swords or bows and arrows. She wandered back to her father's pageant. Everything had finished. Father Anselm and that old actor must be pleased: they'd let her father go home. So, then, should she. But not yet.

She sat on the edge of the pageant, swinging her legs. Those hammers. She couldn't forget them. The nice man should know. She looked at the Bull opposite the pageant. Perhaps he would be there. Well, her parents didn't like her going in, but perhaps this once. . . So she jumped off the pageant, crossed the street and entered the Bull.

"Please, is the nice man here?" she asked Godric.

"What nice man might that be?" he answered.

"The one with the harp who talks funny."

"You mean the young Frenchman? He's not here. He must be on a pageant. He'll be in later."

"Please tell him I want to see him. I want to tell him about the big hammers in the vault."

"Do you now, young Margery," said Godric, looking at her keenly. "Well, how could I not pass on a message like that?"

"Oh, good," said Margery and ran home with a light heart after all.

While Godric was making his promise to Margery, Joslin was in the Bull yard. They were running through the Judgement play again. Crispin and Joslin tested their memories to see whether they had remembered their new parts. They had. "Like I told you," said Crispin. "Once heard, never forgotten for a minstrel."

"So we're ready," said Miles. "Though when we'll do it with that bishop is something I can't quite see."

"Nothing here like you expect it," said Crispin.

Back in the Bull, Godric called Joslin over. "Frenchman," he said. "A little friend of yours wants to see you. Says she's found some hammers in the vault. What might that mean, I wonder?"

Hammers in the vault? It didn't make sense.

"I imagine she's at Thomas Dollimore's house," Godric continued.

"Thanks," Joslin answered. "I'll go."

He told the others where he was going and why, and insisted he'd go on his own – "I don't want

Margery frightened by a lot of strangers," he said – and would be back soon.

He ran down a still busy Smithford Street into Greyfriars Lane. Thomas Dollimore's house was fifty paces away. But that was as near as he got. Two shapes hidden in a doorway stepped out: his journey ended suddenly, violently and in complete darkness.

With Joslin gone, the actors discussed their day. "We've done well," said Miles. "We're wanted and respected for what we do best. Every man on the pageants does his part better than when he started and it's because of the work we've done. Just think of how much better we'll make them in years to come."

"But it's not our real work," said Hob. "I don't like giving my skills to those who weren't born to them."

"Times change," said Sym. "Perhaps we need some time off the road and a bit of comfort instead."

"You've got tomorrow to get through before you can talk of comfort and time off the road," Crispin growled warningly. "Perhaps by nightfall the open road and shelter in a ditch outside Coventry may look like Heaven itself."

"I wish we'd never come here at all," said Alban.

Perhaps the sack thrown over his head was the same that had nearly suffocated Margery and Jankin before. The rope binding his wrists hurt unbearably and it was unnerving to be pushed along so fast without being able to see. "Shut up. Don't dare make a sound," a voice snarled. Several times he lurched and was hauled up roughly. "Stand straight, can't you, Frenchman?" The same voice.

He must have stumbled three hundred paces

before he was stopped, hauled upwards and felt wood under his feet. He knew where he was. All these people's roads led to Hell-mouth. Staggering down a slope with wood again underfoot told him he went down the ramp. He braced himself to be hurled down the steps, But he was guided carefully. No harm was to come to him after all. He was back in the vault, helpless, listening to indistinct voices.

Why had they brought him here? Did Margery really bring a message to Godric Chase? That strange news about hammers in the vault suggested she had and the landlord had betrayed him. He couldn't dismiss what Margery said. When did she find them? She must have gone back to the vault to look for them. Instead she'd found hammers. What would the friars want with hammers?

The voices ceased. Footsteps approached. Then came a voice which must be the one Jankin described. Yes, it had to be the man with the huge head – and, yes, if you tried to imagine the devil's voice it would be like this: deep, cold, powerful, menacing.

"Joslin de Lay, minstrel turned actor," it said.

Joslin said nothing.

"And what an actor. He takes on a part for which one man has met a terrible end: does he want the same end for himself? Do these Frenchmen never learn?"

Again, Joslin didn't answer. But he wondered: *How does he know?*

"Speak to me, damn you." The voice was raised in anger. Joslin stayed resolutely quiet.

The voice was quiet again. "Why should you speak to me anyway? What part should a Frenchman play in our little English drama? What happens in Coventry tomorrow has nothing to do with you: nothing to do with anybody except Coventry folk."

"Why not make him feel Hell's tooth now?" said another voice.

Joslin remembered Bartholomew's body lying in Greyfriars chapel with the wicked rent through it.

"Yes," said the devil's voice. "Why not?"

He was hauled to his feet. "Up the steps," commanded the first voice. They were too strong to resist. His shins were bruised and bleeding against the steps by the time they reached the ramp. More hustled steps across the pageant: then – "Push him down," ordered the devil's voice. "Let him feel what it will be like. But wait till I say."

Two sets of strong arms both pushed and pulled his shoulders down at once. Again he tried to fight. He arched his back: his spine seemed about to crack. Then he felt something out of nightmare: the sharpness of the tooth fined to a needle point against his spine. Those strong arms could push him down, work his body from side to side, make the terrible tooth enter, drive its way through so he would end in the ditch like Bartholomew – and at one word from whoever spoke with the devil's voice, they would.

But for now they held themselves back. The time before the devil's voice spoke again seemed as long as the whole of his previous life. "Joslin de Lay, there's one way to save yourself. Are you listening?"

"Yes," Joslin croaked.

"I can't hear. Your voice is muffled. Speak louder."

"*Yes*," Joslin shouted.

"There's one with you. You think he's your friend. Well, believe me, he's nothing of the sort. We want him dead. We don't want him to outlive tomorrow.

Now there's no chance that he will anyway: in the reckoning to come, he's marked down with many others. But I don't believe you'd want to join that group of unhappy people. And I want a special death for him. So you'll deliver him to me before the great procession starts. You'll bring him to Hell-mouth at the tenth hour tomorrow. But you'll live and be free to carry on your way. If you don't do this, though, you'll die with him at the end, that same special death. You'll feel the sharpest tooth of Hell *and worse,* and your friend along with you. If you don't bring him here, we won't come looking for him or for you. We have too much to do tomorrow. But it means that you've condemned yourself to the most miserable fate I can think of, in full view of Coventry folk as a fitting end to their Corpus Christi festival. And your friend will die beside you."

Joslin still made no answer.

"By then, Joslin, you'll know exactly what the hammers are for."

A thought crossed his mind. *If he knows I'm taking Bartholomew's part and that I left the Bull to find out about the hammers then Godric must have told him. There's nobody else. So they have supporters waiting in the town. And that explains the horn at midday. It was to let those supporters know this devils' work was starting. Whatever it is.*

"If you think you can escape this, then think again. Nothing and no one can avert tomorrow's end. Nothing stops us coming into our own." The words dropped into Joslin's brain with a dull thud. "But of course, you know which friend I mean, don't you?"

Again no answer.

"It is the man who calls himself Crispin Thurn."

Margery was tired of waiting. He wasn't a nice man after all but as bad as the rest of them. She didn't know what the hammers were for and now, if the nice man wasn't interested, she didn't care either. When her mother made her go to bed, saying, "Tomorrow you'll see the procession and your father being a learned doctor on the pageant and everything will be wonderful," Margery felt contented. Devils, coffins, hammers and dark vaults didn't matter a scrap really. Her mother was at last being nice about her father's pageant and that was what really counted.

So she didn't care any more about that not-very-nice-after-all man. And now she was so tired. . .

"What do you say to that, Joslin?" said the devil's voice.

"What about the friars?" he gasped.

"Them!" The devil's voice laughed mirthlessly. "Don't worry. You'll see them again. And if you don't do as I say, they'll live longer than you. Now, your answer."

"I'll do as you say," Joslin shouted.

"All right. You can go. Bring Thurn to Hell-mouth at the tenth hour of the morning. If you don't, that's your death warrant." To the men with the strong arms which held him excruciatingly, "Lift him up."

He was pushed down and hustled along Dead Lane. Then they stopped. "We're taking the hood off," said the devil's voice. "Don't look behind. You know what happened to your friend Jankin. Well, you don't have to recite a play. Instead, you'll look to the front and shout out that ballad you made a fool of yourself with in the tavern two nights ago. You'll finish it and

189

you'll be listened to. You won't see who by, but they'll know if you stop. Start your story, Joslin."

His wrists were freed: the sack pulled off. Dead Lane was deserted. Feeling foolish, he started:

> *"We sometimes read and often tell –*
> *And many minstrels know them well –*
> *Magical stories to plucked harp strings*
> *Full of enchantment. . ."*

He kept on to the end. Then he looked round. Dusk spread thick gloom. He could be the only person left in the world. He slowly started towards the Bull, his mind full of many things. Now it was proved. Their scourges were the two from the tavern.

In St Michael's, Ralph, Bishop of Coventry, celebrated mass and Robert Meriden came up first to receive the host. They smiled slightly at each other, for next day would bring them both great honour. Ralph would claim the Corpus Christi plays for the Church: Robert would see Coventry stand high in civic pride because the Guilds had carried off a great work. The realm would echo to the glory of the Coventry Pageants. Ralph would be hailed as a great bishop: Robert as a great mayor. The long fight against the plague's hopeless misery would be over. The city would stand triumphant.

Sometimes, though, black thoughts and bitter memories came to Robert Meriden. Once there had been another struggle, hard, cruel, for mastery of the city. Alderman fought alderman, brother fought brother, Guilds were riven, families split. There was only one winner. Robert Meriden and his party stood supreme: Ragnal Stow, greedy and envious, was banished.

Robert was mayor – and now, eight years on, he was mayor again, in time for this Corpus Christi Day.

But no one had heard of Ragnal Stow since. Was he dead? Robert hoped so. The fear, that one day the unmistakable figure might be seen again in Coventry and many might rally to him, could keep him awake at night.

There was something else. He had seen a familiar face with the actors when they came to Coventry two days before: that axe-like jaw and dark hair. He could not put a name to the face, but he knew the memory was not good. Why should he see that face *now*, of all times?

He ate well, perhaps too well, at dinner. Later, in the soft bed in the fine mayor's house in Baylie Lane, two minutes' walk from St Mary's Hall and a minute more to St Michael's, he could not sleep the sleep he deserved now the triumph was so near. Nagging doubts and strange, formless premonitions dogged his mind. There was a taste in his mouth as if he had eaten brass, not capon, fine sauces and an excellent syllabub. When he slept he had bad dreams. When he woke with aching head and groaning stomach, they vanished, leaving him with suffocating despair.

Father Anselm was at Compline. The friars' voices rose in plainsong chant and they prayed for Micah and Fulk and the young man whose body lay before the altar. Then they prayed that their labours for the next day would have their reward – but for the folk and Church, not for themselves. When Compline was over, Anselm went to his cell and prayed all night for Bartholomew's soul.

At last dawn streaked the sky and the long vigil was over. Anselm looked back over the days before. He had ended yesterday full of hope for today. A night's prayer should make that even stronger. But it hadn't. He went to the morning's first mass with a heavy heart.

When Joslin did not return, at first everyone was worried. Then Hob said they knew where he'd gone and Sym said that perhaps Thomas Dollimore was a bit more friendly now. The actors went to bed early. "Tomorrow will be a long day and important to us," said Miles. But Crispin sat silent downstairs as folk drank, talked and swore all round him. Nobody spoke to him: something in his eyes told them they should not. He waited – for Joslin, for the morning to come, for *something*. . .

On the way back, Joslin thought hard. There was no way he'd give Crispin up to these people. He just wondered why they wanted him so much. The man with the huge head must have a score to settle with Crispin so great, so extreme, that it warranted a death as terrible as the most squalid public execution. And, Joslin recalled, if he didn't do what they said, he'd suffer it as well. So what was it about?

He tried to relate what he'd heard to everything else. It seemed to boil down to a single mad notion – that Bartholomew was killed because he was funny, so being funny was the one thing which riled them to murder because it must ruin whatever their plot was. But there were others – being Crispin Thurn, for example. Or being poor Lambert. If only Crispin had said more than *He that has ears to hear. . .*

Nobody stopped him as he entered the Bull. It was crowded: curfew was half an hour away. Crispin sat alone in a corner, motionless, watchful, almost in a trance. Joslin sat by him on the bench.

"Well?" said Crispin.

Joslin told him. Crispin's eyes widened, but he said nothing until Joslin had finished. Then he said, "So you'll give me up to them?"

"Of course not. How could you ask?"

"Because though I ask for your trust, I've told too little to earn it."

"That doesn't matter."

"Yes, it does. I gave you a riddle to solve and I think you may be working it out. But I'll tell you more because now it's right that I should. What I tell you now is between us only. Is that understood?"

"Of course," Joslin replied.

"You wondered how I know the forest so well. I know it because I spent years there. Not as a robber or a renegade soldier. We weren't all felons and rascals hiding there. Why I was there I won't tell you. Not yet, anyway. But then I left and spent years away. I was a minstrel: I needed the open road again."

"Is that all?"

Crispin looked at him. "Joslin, you had a father murdered. You were in danger yourself before you left France. Even if you get out of Coventry alive, there are some arms which stretch a very long way."

Joslin was silent. He remembered that last night in the Castle at Treauville: hustled with his dying father into the night, escaping on *The Merchant of Orwell*, arrows shot at them by the Count's soldiers.

"Minstrels live strange lives," said Crispin. "They have entry to the highest and are at home with the lowest. Castle, tavern, it doesn't matter as long as there's an audience. But that's why we're useful. We know, we see a lot – sometimes we see what's to happen before anyone else."

"What are you saying? That minstrels are spies?" asked Joslin.

"I'm saying that when you saw me singing in the tavern in Warwick I intended to do what I told you – go to the cities of the Welsh Marches. But when you saw me that night with my late caller, that changed. I was to go back to the forest. I was needed."

If Joslin got a clear reply to his next question, he felt he would understand more what Crispin had said earlier. "Was that a request or an order?" he asked.

Crispin smiled. "You're assuming the message came from some great man," he answered. "It was neither. It was a cry for help."

"Who from?"

"I had friends in the forest: Lew, Mab, many others. Something was happening there, something disturbing. That's what I did as you got better. I watched, listened, tried to understand. You did see me with Lew's attackers. I had to be all things to all men."

"And what was happening in the forest?"

"I'm ashamed to say that after three weeks I was little the wiser."

"Are there connections between Randall Stone and Coventry?" asked Joslin. "Remember: 'Randall Stone shall come into his own'."

"People say there is no Randall Stone," said Crispin, half smiling.

"Could *Ragnal Stow* come into his own, then?" Joslin asked.

"Stow was thrown out of Coventry, half Coventry happy to see him go. Meriden was left supreme and free to run the city the way he wanted. And Ragnal Stow disappeared off the face of the earth."

"Not into the forest, then?"

"I heard no talk of it. I had left by then."

"And when did the legend of Randall Stone start?"

"Long before," Crispin replied.

"When you were first in the forest?"

Crispin did not reply.

Joslin tried another question. "Could Ragnal Stow be the man with the big head?"

"Not unless he's suffered some awful curse. Anyway, why should a poor band of actors be persecuted, a Hell-mouth built where nobody will see it and a man murdered for being funny?"

"So why should such a death be marked out for you?" said Joslin.

"There's a reason in that huge head. Who knows?"

"That wasn't a proper answer. You must know more," said Joslin.

"It's all the answer you'll get. If I knew, I'd tell you."

"So should we tell the authorities: Meriden or even the bishop?"

"If Anselm won't tell them, how would we be believed? We'd be in the stocks for troublemakers."

There was no more to say. "I must sleep," said Joslin.

"I shall stay here," Crispin replied. "Sleep's far away for me yet."

As the Bull emptied, Joslin left him – waiting, waiting. . .

Before Joslin gratefully slept on his pallet, surrounded by snoring guests and actors, he had some last thoughts. He was past considering what manner of mystery would unfold. But one thing he was sure of – *that monstrous-headed man must have much cause to hate Crispin*. Surely Crispin found *something* out when he was searching the forest? But then, he didn't say he was *no* wiser at the end. He was "*little* the wiser". So there were still things about tomorrow that he wasn't saying.

As Joslin slept deeply, Margery slept happily, Crispin waited, Father Anselm prayed and Robert Meriden had bad dreams, the pageants stood deserted in their appointed places. And deep in the vault under Dead Lane there was movement. Men walked across the open land to the steps hidden by the bushes. They filed down into the vault. Candles were lit: the coffins showed dimly in their glow. The hammers waited for whatever use they would be put to. One man with a huge head and another with long hair and a cast in one eye helped a third down the steps and made him comfortable with cushions and blankets. He was treated with deference, even slight fear, by all there, though he was frail and old and his right arm was missing from the shoulder. Then there was silence, while everybody slept while they had the chance.

Outside, four huge horses, their black coats making them almost invisible in the darkness, grazed contentedly, ready like everyone else to play their part next day.

Corpus Christi Day dawned. The streets filled up with crowds jostling for the best places. From the upper windows of houses, taverns and shops, more people watched although there was still nothing to see. But that would soon change. First would come the procession, from St Michael's, round the streets of Coventry and back to St Michael's Green, ready for the end of the day and the bishop's homily. The bishop, priests, mayor, aldermen and masters of the Guilds would walk dignified and the Communion Host would be paraded before them. When the procession was over and the folk had shown their devotion, the day's real business would start. Ralph Breville might not like it but the plays were what people came for.

At each station a pageant stood. Horses were ready to pull it to its next appointed place. The Creation Pageant, at the northern edge of the city by St John's Hospital, would play first. Next at the same place would come Cain and Abel, then Abraham and Isaac. Meanwhile, the Creation Pageant would trundle round back streets to its next appointed place at Jordan Well. The other pageants would follow until by dusk every play would have been performed nine times, once at each station.

As he lay in bed at home in Greyfriars Street, Thomas Dollimore groaned at what he had let himself in for. How many times would he be a learned doctor that day? Once each at St John's Hospital, Jordan Well, Gosford Street, Newgate, Greyfriars, Smithford Street, Bablake, Cross Cheaping, St Michael's – he lost count. He'd sleep for a week after that. *Then* who'd do all the weaving? There was little time to lie in bed and moan about it either. Hardly had the sixth hour after midnight come than he was ready in Bartholomew's gown on the pageant, waiting to be pulled by two horses which would also be worn out by day's end.

Father Anselm rose at last from his knees and stepped out into sunshine. Yes, it was a bright day and with God's help would remain so. Though a man of God, his day's business was on the pageants seeing all was done aright, not in the procession. Other friars joined him, each bound for his pageant.

Miles's band was up even earlier. Each was also bound for a different pageant. But first, there were matters to discuss.

"How can we do our Judgement play, when we're all scattered over the town, then?" asked Hob.

"Peg and I will make sure you're ready," said Molly. "The Judgement play would be last anyway. We'll pull our cart and wait at every station for you."

Miles smiled benevolently. "What would we do without you?" he said. Jankin laughed and Peg gave him an angry look.

"After today's colour and noise, the folk will laugh

at our miserable apparel," said Sym.

"It's not the dress which matters," said Miles. "It's the actor himself and the words he says. How many times have I told you, Sym?"

Joslin noticed a gleam in Miles's eyes. Miles was looking forward to this.

In St Michael's the great procession formed up. As mayor, Robert Meriden had a place of honour. He stood waiting in his fur-lined robe, shivering slightly, though not entirely from cold. The chair for the bishop waited for his portly form to sit in it. The four bearers fated to carry his weighty body round the streets stood patiently. At the front of the procession, a priest held the Communion Host high. Behind him, lay clerks sang, not stopping until they had completed the circle and come back to the church for the bishop's final sermon.

At last Ralph Breville appeared. He lowered himself into his chair. The bearers lifted it. The procession snaked through the west door of St Michael's. The feast of Corpus Christi had commenced.

The day passed in a blur. Thomas Dollimore found it hard to credit how fleeting it was. His first time as a learned doctor, with Father Anselm seeing all to rights and Miles even at the last whispering instructions left him slightly dissatisfied. He could see his wife and Margery watching, saw Margery's face rapt as if in a trance and said to himself, "What a pity you had to see the first one. I'll do better yet."

The second was better – though still not right. But Margery was there again, willing him, urging him on. The third was better again. Still Margery, wide-eyed, was there. Then the fourth, then fifth. The sun rose and waned. The horses dragged the Weaver's pageant round the city – Bablake, Smithford Street, Cross Cheaping. He wasn't tired but glorying in it. By now, the play seemed real. He wasn't in his own town: he was in that temple thirteen hundred years ago. Nothing of his world existed except Margery's proud little face.

As evening came, the pageant reached St Michael's Green. There they waited for the Shearmen's play to finish. They watched Herod ranting and roaring and heard the mothers sing their lullaby. At last, the Weavers' turn. When this their last performance was over, Thomas felt a sad emptiness. Weaving might keep a roof over their heads but now the yearly Corpus Christi plays were all he would live for.

On the Shearmen's pageant, Joslin finished his day's main business. Under his guidance, the mothers of the innocents had at least sung tunefully. If he was here longer, he might give them a really good song. A haunting tune and words to go with it moved through his mind. "Lully, lullay, thou little tiny child." That would make a good start. But if today ended well he'd soon be miles away so it was too late.

Or he hoped he would. Had they waited at Hell-mouth for him to bring Crispin at the tenth hour? When they realized he would not, had they been surprised? What revenge would they take?

Miles's actors felt they had done well what was expected of them. There wasn't a performance on any pageant which wasn't better because of them. Even Hob and Jankin were content when the last plays were over. "Jankin," said Hob. "This will be a good billet every year from now on."

"You're right," Jankin replied. "At least we'll share the glory. Those plays would be nothing without us."

Molly and Peg, unnoticed, had dragged the actors' cart behind the pageants. Now they had reached St Michael's Green. In front of them the crowds pressed thick. They saw only hundreds of backs. Over the people's heads they could see the tops of pageants ranged round the Green and the roof of the decorated canopy over the bishop's throne.

"We'll never get through," moaned Peg.

"We will," Molly said grimly. "Haven't you noticed? It's the woman's lot in this world to do miracles against the odds."

Peg leant to the cart and heaved. But Molly didn't. "I'm not doing this on my own," Peg complained.

Molly was facing away from St Michael's and looking south towards Dead Lane and the city walls.

"Listen," she said.

Ralph Breville, richly robed and coped, with mitre and crozier, walked towards his throne. He was flanked by priests and preceded by singing clerks. The crowd became quiet. He was helped up to his throne. There he sat, surveying his flock with imperious eye.

The hush was complete. Except – some tiny, irritating noise far off, like the Old Testament's cloud no bigger than a man's hand.

It was nothing. The greatest act of Corpus Christi was here: the final brick in the wall of God's purposes for mankind – and it was in the hands of His bishop, not unworthy common folk.

Ralph Breville cleared his throat to speak.

"What can you hear?" asked Peg.

"Something. I don't know. What do you think?"

Peg strained her ears and heard – what? Mighty blows far away, then a crumbling, crashing roar, as if Jericho's walls were falling. Then, in the silence left by an engrossed crowd, she heard heavy horses walking and big wheels turning over rough ground.

"Do you know what that is?" cried Molly. "Someone is knocking the wall down in Dead Lane. The Hell pageant is free. We must get this cart through the crowd. The devils are coming. Our Judgement play will have to be done while there's still time."

The view was better from the pageants drawn up on the Green than for the jostling folk pushing towards the bishop's throne. Ralph Breville surveyed his flock with an expression which might be expressing God's love to everyone, might be distaste at the human smell rising from so many in one place. Then his voice rang out, strained and shrill out of doors. "My children, sheep of my flock. . ."

"No more plays for us today," said Alban.

Pushing the cart through was like knocking a castle down with bare hands. "Let us through," Peg pleaded. People swore at her. "The bishop needs us," Molly cried. To Peg's surprise, the crowd believed her. Slowly they forced their way through.

When they could see bare grass and the bishop's throne and heard the bishop's voice, Peg said. "Listen. I hear something else."

* * *

"My children, today you have seen the world created, Adam fall and Noah deliver us from the flood. You have seen a birth, a crucifixion and a rising from the dead. Now you shall hear what this will lead to."

Ralph Breville looked up. And there, rising before his eyes behind the ocean of faces was a sight he had never thought to see, not even when he was finally called to Judgement, because he believed he would go to Heaven without the need to know Satan.

Like everyone else, the actors had their backs to whatever Ralph Breville saw. So when Hob too said, "Listen!" and Sym answered, "I am listening," and Hob replied, "No, not to him," they did not know what to make of the new noise. But Father Anselm did. He heard the long note on the horn echoing round the Green and saw the eyes of his bishop widen and stare. He followed their gaze – and then he saw the sight he had seen in his nightmares, unmistakable, worse than the worst imaginings of any painter making a Doom. He groaned, beat his fists against his head and cried, "What are we to do?"

At last they were through. The cart stood on the Green, in front of the bishop's throne. Panting with exertion, Molly and Peg looked towards the Weavers' pageant. "Miles," Molly shouted.

Miles heard. He saw them, then turned to the others. Then the actors, with Joslin and Crispin, jumped off the pageant and ran to the cart. All the while, the high steady note of the horn – blown it seemed by air not from human lungs – sounded on and on, seared into their ears and stifled thought.

Joslin was first to the cart. "Quick," said Molly.

"Here's Bartholomew's gear." He shoved on patched devil's clothes, put a ragged cloak over the top and took his staff. He looked half-devil, half-human. Miles and Hob needed no costumes. Alban and Sym, angel and Jesus, threw on simple white gowns. Peg pinned crude wings to the back of Alban's. Jankin's devil's costume might fit Crispin, but on him it was too tight and looked its age.

They were ready. Behind them, Ralph Breville, his priests and the city worthies stood silent and powerless. The crowd was in fearful quiet. The blast on the horn was not finished. By now the folk were remembering. They had heard it before and they knew in their hearts it came from Dead Lane where they would never go. It was true – Hell really did lie underneath it.

Yes, Hell-mouth, red, cavernous, evil, its jagged teeth ready to devour every victim in sight, the smoke of its eternal fires billowing through with bitter, choking stench, struck final despair into every heart. At the foot of Hell-mouth were the beasts that had brought it there: four massive creatures, jet black, bridled and caparisoned with harness which blacksmiths must have made on the Devil's own anvils.

For a second, the actors were struck as dumb as the crowd. But Miles rallied them. "Come on," he cried. "Make every word count. It's little enough to pit against such an assault, but we've got to stop people's eyes resting on that horror and their ears taking in the blasphemies that are shouted from it. We've never done a play which matters as much as this."

Joslin, though, felt his own despair. It was not so much the Judgement play which their enemies had feared as Bartholomew's part in it. *Whatever secret Bartholomew had,* he thought, *is closed to me.*

27

hell-mouth loomed up and the folk knew their doom – the glowering beasts which brought it there, the devouring jaws and vicious teeth. Soon the sharp incisors would close on them and they would fall to depths unimaginable, airless regions where God's light never came, shot with blinding flames which destroyed but never consumed, peopled by demons who tortured eternally with never-wavering delight. When the folk tore their eyes from the sight and looked wildly round, they saw only each others' fearful faces. Then they knew. There was no Heaven, no God to rescue them. They were judged already and the whole city was found wanting.

Ralph Breville's fine words died. He had no strength now. God had deserted him. Was he judged too? He had lived a life of power. Things came easily to him: rewards and temptations alike. "Lord, I am not as other men, poor and needful," he often said. But now he saw he was. He was to be devoured with the rest.

Robert Meriden felt emotions he did not expect. He knew what he had feared. But this visitation was not it. He should be abased with terror like the rest. Yet he was not. He'd expected a rebellion with swords. Even if Hell and damnation beckoned, he would go as mayor, with his power intact. He was content – no usurpers from the past had come to steal them. He gasped at the stupidity of his thoughts. What did a chain of office count against everlasting torments? But he couldn't help it.

Father Anselm groaned aloud. If he was found not worthy, then so be it. But why everybody else? Was *nobody* to be saved in this city?

Then he remembered. He knew this Hell-mouth for what it was: he'd clambered over its wooden floor and past its teeth. He turned to the groaning, trembling men of the Weavers' pageant, still in their costumes. "Courage. It's not what it seems. It's not Hell itself. It's nothing but a pageant like the one we're standing on now." But no one heard.

The devil blowing the horn ceased at last. But the sound was taken up again as he handed the horn to a second devil. The first devil went to the back of Hell-mouth, out of sight and hearing of the crowd. Here he surveyed the two files of men lined up, quiet and tense as if ready to advance into battle. Bows were slung over their backs, quivers of arrows at their waists. They each carried a short sword.

The first devil, with a head so huge it seemed as if it must overbalance from his body, spoke to them. His voice was such that the armed men, if they didn't know otherwise, might, like Jankin, think it was Satan's himself. "Today we settle an old wrong. Today the one whose birthright was taken away comes into his own again."

He beckoned. The frail, one-armed man walked slowly between the two watching files of armed men. He joined the devil with the huge head. At first he said nothing, as if collecting his thoughts. Then he spoke. "I have so much to thank you for. We have stayed secret, though many have tried to find us. We have found a way to deliver this city intact, so the people are cowed and willing to do whatever we say. We know those few who must die for their sins, for what they did to me once. First is Meriden. You know him well. He knows me. He played me the worst trick of all. Second is Thurn, the minstrel. You know what he did." There was an angry growl. The man felt with his left hand at where his right arm should be. "Thurn will be a sorry man by the end of this day," he said.

"And it will be today because it's fitting," said the huge-headed devil. "We could have taken him at any time in the forest these last weeks when he thought nobody knew him, but we saw fit not to. We waited for him this morning, but his friend foolishly broke his word and it will the worse for him as well. Today is Thurn's death day and here is his death place, so that he and everyone will know why he dies. And it's the death day too of his miserable little friend who reneged on his promise."

The one-armed man laughed. The devil continued. "It's time for our own Judgement play, better than a bishop's ravings, or what ragged vagabond fools can give, a real judgement which will bind the folk for ever to our service. Bring me our first damned souls."

Three armed men pushed forward two stumbling figures in bloodstained habits. The devil laughed, mirthlessly. "To see these go to Hell will convince the folk that the world's turned inside out and Satan's triumph is assured. Hold them here until we show them to the folk. Now, let us start our play."

The huge-headed devil went to the front of the Hell pageant and the folk saw him. He joined the other devil blowing the horn. The long piercing note at last ceased. Every face seemed fixed, tranced, by that long unearthly noise. The huge-headed devil drew breath for the first words of his own Judgement play.

"Dark and desperate dreadful deeds for all of time
*   have been our care.*
Now Judgement Day is come at last and not a
*   single soul we'll spare.*
There's no hope here: no one leaves, no soul can
*   ever hide.*
They'd love to run, they'd love to fly. No! Here they
*   must abide*
And wait in fear and awe for us and see our Justice
*   strike.*
No lawyer's any good to them: everyone's alike,
For mayor or bishop, serf or churl: this is the worst
*   of times.*
It's each man for himself today: they'll answer for
*   their crimes."*

From the nearest watchers came a deep collective groan as they saw their dooms laid out before them.

On the little cart the other side of the crowd, the rival Judgement play started. Hob shrieked and shouted, telling the world how evil he'd been – and nobody heard. They all had their backs to him. Miles made his grave speech of contrition. If Miles could not make an audience listen, then things were out of control. Sym blew his horn but it sounded a tiny squeak compared with the sound which had just rolled round the Green. Still nobody turned. Alban as Jesus had no effect either. When Hob was marked for Hell he'd suddenly had enough of the play. "Oh, where's the sense in it," he screamed. "Who believes I'm going to Hell? Not this lot when they think they're *really* going."

Joslin had worked himself up to go on. But Hob's cry stopped him. *What's the point of doing this*, he thought. *We're finished.*

Anselm strained his eyes and ears to take in everything happening on this appalling Hell-mouth. He heard the devil's first words and thought: *they are ugly. I don't like them.* But what happened next was even uglier. Two figures were pushed on to the pageant. He knew them. The devil's voice rang out again.

"*Now twice cursed be the fathers who let this pair be born,*
Doomed to live short lives which are ending here forlorn.
And twice cursed be the mothers and twice cursed be the morn
That these were born of them. Alas, for shame and scorn.

"*No!*" Anselm roared. He plunged down off the Weavers' pageant, pushed into the crowd and fought his way through with the strength of five men. "Micah! Fulk! Hold on. I'm coming," he yelled.

Joslin saw that Hob was about to jump off the cart and join the hosts of the lost. He felt some of the same terror. But he fought it down. He seized Hob's collar, and shouted in his ear: "Stay where you are. You're one of Miles's men. You keep going." Shame fleeted over Hob's face. Joslin started his own words.

"You'll be frightened: you'll be full of questions.
I'm descended from Satan: I'm one of his sons.
I'm the sort of bad conscience everyone shuns."

Hob forced himself into carrying on.

"Why did I listen? All destiny comes when it's time."

But this time his despair was part of the play. Joslin whispered, "Well done, Hob. Keep going." Then he went on:

"I can prick you with a pin
To tempt you into sin
And then I'll reel you in
With my rod and line.
I've brought down to Hell, I'm so proud to say,
More than ten thousand each hour of the day.
Some I found in the tavern: some were in bed,
Some cursing, some fighting, striking men dead,
Ah, so very many
Whose way I eased here
To our tender, loving care.
And who did I spare?
It's true – there weren't any."

He was no more listened to than last night when he recited *Lay le Freine* to an empty Dead Lane. Except that . . . what was happening now?

* * *

On Hell-mouth, the second devil pushed the two wretched friars forward. The huge-headed devil shouted, "Hear them speak."

One started a confused mumble. The huge-headed devil prodded him with the horn. "Louder."

The young voice rose.

"Alas for all the deeds that, foolish, I have done,
To think that God would save me, as if I were one
That He could love. Now I can see things plain.
He lets you down, He plays you false, His
*   promises are vain."*

Another groan from the crowd. But with his new-found strength Anselm was bundling his way through. *"Don't listen, don't listen. Don't say it, Micah. You don't mean it,"* he gasped. He reached the black horses standing patient and unruffled. For a moment he was lost between their hooves and it seemed they would trample him contemptuously. But then he was through, clambering up on to the stage, between the teeth, grasping at the young friars, hoarsely shouting, *"They've made you say it,"* lunging at the devils – until the huge-headed devil chopped him down with one blow.

Joslin watched Anselm's progress. Some he pushed aside were angry, others startled as if they realized what was happening. Was he distracting the folk from Hell-mouth's terror? Perhaps this was a chance to make them listen, to make them laugh like Bartholomew did. Joslin saw a very fat man indeed. Oh, yes, he was gross. So he concentrated on him and said:

"Some are so greedy they're fatter than hogs,
With buttocks that wobble and faces like frogs."

A reward. The fat man looked straight at him. He was angry. "Do you mean me?" Joslin heard him yell. And three others turned as well. "He got you there all right, Jack," one giggled and they all laughed. Joslin searched again. Yes, there was a woman. Was she dressed and painted up too much, perhaps, with her hat that looked like it had seen better days on a great lady and that fur-lined cloak for such a hot day?

"Has she got cow's horns? No, that's just her hat.
The fur on her collar must have come from her cat.
And her face! What a sight!
Does she mean to look quaint?
It's smothered in paint.
She's been no saint,
I can see that all right."

The folk saw who he looked at. Now the woman was upset. More raucous laughter. "What have you been up to then, Joan?" someone roared. She beat vainly at him with her fists. "Shut up. Don't listen," she cried. The more she did that, the more they howled.

Joslin held his breath. Could he make laughter spread through the crowd like a rash? Because he realized – this was what Bartholomew did. He made them laugh at each other. This was what it was all about.

He cast a quick look at that other pageant: the devils, the wretched friars, Anselm chopped down. Yes, it was a terrible sight and would cow Coventry for ever. But if they were laughing they surely couldn't be cowed. He seemed to hear a voice inside his head which could almost have been Bartholomew's.

"Keep going. A good laugh never killed anyone."

28

Anselm sprawled over Hell-mouth floor and half hung over the side between two of its teeth. Miles saw this and was grieved. *What's happening to the man who gave us our wonderful new chance? He doesn't deserve this.*

He put me in the play. He's opened up a whole new life for me, thought Thomas Dollimore.

And then the same thought came to them both. *We must help our great friend.*

For Joslin, it was search, search, search. He saw a man dressed much more finely than those round him. Was he vain and conceited with probably not a penny to his name? Have a go at him, then. The play had words for it – the sin of Vanity. He concentrated hard on the foppish fellow – and he turned as if he knew he was being looked at.

"Finery's stupid. That's why I mock it.
When vanity leaves you with nowt in your pocket
But such shoes on your feet

214

> As are made of best leather,
> And you just don't care whether
> Your poor children never
> Have anything to eat."

It worked. A knot of people round him heard as well. As the vain man looked angry, they howled with mirth. "That'll show you," shouted one.

Nobody else looked too fat, nobody else looked overdressed. But, over there, he could see a mean, shifty face. He concentrated on it.

> "Here's some good news I've not told you before.
> Liars and cheats I've brought down by the score.
> They swear by God's word: no one could swear
>   more.
> Yet they swindle the very last pence from the
>   poor."

A look of horror crossed that shifty face and those round him laughed derisively. "He knows you through and through, Wilfred," came a cry. Wilfred the cheat and liar put his hands over his head as if he expected revenge there and then. But he only got pointing fingers and more derision. *Don't waste time looking for the people. Just say the words. They'll listen anyway now,* Joslin thought.

> "Chatterers in church? Confidence men?
> I could point them out to you again and again."

That was the first. Bubbles of conscience all over the crowd. What about more words?

"*Anger and envy, there's plenty of those.*
Adultery, cheating, there's them, I suppose.
Meanness and cruelty, carrion crows
At a corpse – I tell you, that's how the world goes."

He paused. More than half seemed to have forgotten Hell-mouth by now. They were too busy laughing at each other and taking the play's words to heart when they fitted them. But how long could he go on for? Had he done enough? He was running out of words. He might improvise a few but. . .

Then he saw that Miles and Thomas Dollimore were on Hell-mouth along with the devils.

The two of them bent over Anselm. "He's only just breathing," said Miles. "What shall we do?" said Thomas Dollimore.

"*Do? Why you'll do nothing, for nothing can be*
done.
Your dooms are here, your hope is gone and
Satan's cause is won."

The devil's voice roared above them, in words which made it seem as if this were part of the play. Fulk and Micah had not moved. They looked helplessly down at Anselm: Thomas slowly straightened up as if the friars' defeat had spread to him.

But Miles looked higher, straight at the devil's horned head, and spoke fearlessly. "I know who you are," he said. "At the tavern, you stopped me and my actors doing what we're supposed to, act our plays. So I'll stop you now if it's the last thing I do."

The devil emitted one explosive burst of laughter.

The other devil turned away and beckoned towards the back of Hell-mouth. The two lines of armed men stepped out and ringed Hell-mouth, their swords at the ready. But they did not have the cowed, scared audience in their power that they expected. The little pockets of laughter Joslin had made had spread to most folk out there. They were prepared to mock anything now. And if they could do that, then they could see straight.

"That's just a painted pageant like the rest," someone shouted.

"And that's no more Satan than I am," yelled another. "What is he but a man like me?"

A great weight left Joslin. He lifted his concentration. At once he felt weariness smother him. *We've won,* he thought. *I don't quite know how I've done it, but I've pulled the folk round to their senses again. All will be well now.*

But he was wrong. He looked at Hell-mouth and realized with a sinking heart that he had hardly started. These people had more tricks than one to play.

The first devil never flinched. "You'll see if I'm Satan come to haunt you or not." The voice rang out over St Michael's Green and quelled every other sound. "Satan has his hordes. And here they are." More men bearing swords and with bows on their backs appeared and ringed Hell-mouth. Thomas Dollimore gasped. "You know that voice, do you, Miles? Well, so do I. And I never thought to hear it in Coventry again."

"Who is it, Thomas?" said Miles.

But before Thomas could answer, the first devil shouted again. "Show me the power in Coventry which could face down the power I bring. If Satan can't beat you on his own then he has plenty of reinforcements. Show me the soldiers to match mine."

By now though, half the crowd was so unruly and disbelieving that they could shout answers. "Of course we can." "By God, we've been watching them all day." And as Joslin stared at the strange turn events were taking, there was movement on the pageants. A great army was stepping down from them, joining up and marching solemnly towards Hell-mouth. It was led by King Herod, his turbaned head as big as the first devil's. His own soldiers followed him. Then came Cain, tall and fierce, holding a wicked weapon, an animal's jawbone. After him came Christ's crucifiers, torturers, scourgers, huge and strong, and after them the soldiers who stood at the foot of the Cross. They marched though the crowd and then formed up in a half-circle as if protecting it. They looked a mighty, threatening force. But the devil merely laughed again.

"Why should we fear actors in plays who carry swords which wouldn't slice an apple and spears which couldn't pierce a leaf? What could such as you do against my men who've fought the French and the Scots and who'd eat all of you alive?"

Herod stepped forward. "These men here have fought for their king as well as any of yours," he said. "But they came back to being honest Guild men when their wars were over. They'd fight again, though. Their forefathers beat the Danes, kept the Normans at bay and stood up for their rights against unjust lords. They'll not be cowed by you."

"You think so, do you, Will Woolman?" said the devil. "Well, after this you'll think different. There are two people here that we want first. When you know why, you may see things changing again."

Before Herod could answer, the devil's voice echoed over the Green. "Bring Meriden out here. And the man who calls himself Crispin Thurn with him. The little French minstrel had better come as well. Joslin de Lay knows what's going to happen to the three of them because I've told him already."

Joslin remembered last night's warning and shuddered. Should he go? He'd have to. It looked as if their play was over anyway. Crispin had jumped down from the cart. "Joslin, we'll have to go together," he said.

"Why do they want you, Crispin?" Joslin said again.

"I'm beginning to understand," Crispin answered. "Perhaps I always have. Let us go." And he led the way, looking strange in Jankin's tight devil's garb.

"Meriden. Where's Meriden?" the devil shouted.

Ralph Breville looked down from his throne. "Go, Robert," he urged. "For God's sake go and get this thing over."

Robert Meriden turned a stricken face to him. Ralph Breville cared nothing for its ashen paleness. "Go," he repeated. "It's God's command. Do as he wants. It is expedient."

Slowly and unwillingly, Robert Meriden stepped forward. From behind him came the bishop's voice again. "Faster, Robert. It's God's will." From in front came the devil's. "Don't stop, Robert. Keep coming. You know there's no escape." Yes, Robert did know there was no escape – God was behind and Satan was in front and he feared to disobey the word of either.

The three reached Hell-mouth almost together.

"Help poor Meriden up, Crispin," said the devil. "He looks near dead with fear. Isn't that good?"

Crispin and Joslin together pushed Robert Meriden up between the teeth and on to Hell-mouth, where he stood shivering. They looked at each other, then hoisted themselves up after him. Anselm sat up, rubbed his neck and looked wonderingly round.

There was silence, from the two devils, the soldiers, all the folk below. It was Joslin who broke it. Because now he was quite sure. "I know who you are," he said to the devil. "You're Ragnal Stow come back to take the city again."

The devil pulled at his head. The horns moved, then the whole thing seemed to come off at the neck. But it left a human head underneath – huge, so that it seemed it should topple from its shoulders, except that a thick and powerful neck held it on. The whole crowd gasped with recognition.

"Wrong, Joslin," the huge-headed man replied. "I am Randall Stone."

In the silence, Crispin laughed suddenly and explosively. Then he said, "No, you're not. I am."

Joslin was thunderstruck. At first Randall Stone was a will-o'-the-wisp, a jack-o'-lantern, a wicked sprite to frighten children with. Though Crispin had a different tale: the hunted stag, the ambushed soldier, the waylaid, robbed and murdered traveller. And now here were two men claiming they were him. And as for Crispin – well, if he meant what he said, suddenly a lot of things fell into place and the song of Gamelyn as the key to his life became clear. Almost. *He who has ears to hear.*

"Well," said Thomas Dollimore. "I don't know about the minstrel here, but the other's not called Randall Stone. He's Seth Broad, who left when Meriden drove out Ragnal Stow ten years ago."

"Who says my name?" a voice called. "Do you *really* want to see me again?" A figure was approaching from the back of Hell-mouth. The ranks of armed men parted to let him through. And there he stood, enveloped in a white cloak, with hair just as white: frail, old but strangely powerful. The folk saw him for the first time that day. Yet many there realized it was

221

not the for first time in their lives. Old, bad memories crowded into their minds. Robert Meriden groaned aloud. The whole crowd in St Michaels' Green was dead silent, so quiet that a bird's wing-beat could be heard and what was said on Hell-mouth echoed round so it seemed like an extra play which would only ever be performed this once.

"You may well despair, Robert," Ragnal Stow said. "Because my time has come round again."

Joslin was watching Crispin, who had turned away as if the new sight was a grievous shock to him. But Ragnal would not let him. "I'm not surprised you look away, minstrel." With his left hand he pulled his cloak aside, to show the stump where his right arm should be. "Who did this to me, *Crispin?*"

Crispin did not answer.

"Of course you won't speak. You don't recognize the name I gave you. Well, I'll ask you again with the name you called yourself when you did it. *Who did this to me, Gamelyn?*"

For the second time. Joslin was dumb with surprise. How many names did Crispin have? How could he have done that to Ragnal? And when?

Anyway, Crispin was answering. "It's true, I did it, Ragnal. And you know very well why. I didn't want to be caught up in your squabbles with Meriden. I was only passing through Coventry. I knew little about the arguments between you and from all I heard I cared less for either of you. If it hadn't been my only way of getting out of the place alive, I'd never have taken my sword from its scabbard."

"You can't save yourself that way. You worked for Meriden. Admit it."

Robert Meriden found his tongue. "That's nonsense,

Ragnal. He supported you. He'd come from afar to help you. I'd have killed him myself if I had to."

"So you say now," answered Ragnal. But for the first time there was doubt in his voice.

" 'He who's not for me is against me.' That's how it went then, wasn't it?" said Crispin. "I came to Coventry ten years ago. I only wanted to sing and make a bit of money. But I never got a chance to. I walked straight into your squabble and bad luck to you both, I thought. But I had to fight for my life to get out of it. I vowed I'd never enter this place again. Until I came back to the forest and soon realized that I'd have to."

So when Ragnal said sarcastically, "You'd have done better to stay away this time, *Gamelyn*," and Crispin replied, "I wish to God I had," Joslin in the midst of thousands felt more alone than he had for all his time in England. But Ragnal now turned to Meriden: it was his turn to wish that things might have been otherwise.

"Robert," he said. "I reckon that after the years that you and your aldermen have made Coventry a dim and sad sort of town, the folk will line the streets and cheer to see me take my place again."

Robert Meriden hung his head and said nothing. Thomas Dollimore answered for him. "Not if they have good memories."

Ragnal cast his eyes over him as if he did not exist. "Wrong, fellow," he said. "There are those here who prayed for my return and did much to help it."

Godric Chase for one, thought Joslin. And the Bull was full of others, did Meriden but know it. Aloud, he asked a question. "Was John Crowe among them? If he was, why did you kill him?"

"I did not kill the draper," said Ragnal.

"Perhaps not, but Seth Broad with the huge head did. And if he didn't, it was Arnulf Long. And they're both your creatures."

Now the crowd, outraged, broke its silence. "They killed our good friend John Crowe," someone shouted. "Get them," yelled another. The roar built up. Two men broke through the ranks of play-soldiers and torturers and ran for the horses. At a word from Ragnal, the real soldiers on Hell-mouth stepped forward, jumped off, marched in order past the horses and faced them. The crowd quietened suddenly. When Ragnal spoke again, his voice was clear across the Green.

"You see?" he said. "I mean it when I say I'm coming back. And if you still have doubts who's master here, I'll still them for ever."

He shouted a command to Seth and the other devil. This devil also pulled at his horned head until it came off. The face exposed was Arnulf's. Seth and Arnulf seized Robert Meriden. Arnulf took his feet, Seth his shoulders. Robert screamed and tried to hit out but the strength of these two was like any four other men. Now came a scene worse than any vision of Hell the folk ever saw in nightmares. They pulled Robert over to the teeth, pushed him down, down on the longest and sharpest. . .

Some watching closed their eyes. But nobody could close their ears to the scream which soared high and terrible over St Michael's Green along with Robert Meriden's soul as it left Hell-mouth and the world itself.

Ralph Breville from his throne watched and heard. At

first he had nothing to say. Then, when he saw his friend Robert Meriden's appalling end, he said, "No bishop will ever be taken by men in devil's clothing." He remembered Ragnal Stow. No matter who was mayor, Stow or Meriden, the Church had to live with the civil power. He called to his priests and lay clerks, "We'll return to St Michael's. Prayer alone can stop these deeds."

And, gathering his robes round him and tucking his crozier under his arm, he made off for the cathedral as fast as his legs would take him.

Robert was dead. The great tooth projected through his body and Joslin realized anew how Bartholomew had died on that very spot, with no one to see or hear him. Then, as he watched powerless, Seth and Arnulf seized Crispin. Crispin was not as easy as Robert. Though his ill-fitting devil's costume looked ridiculous compared with the others, yet he had kept his sword by his side and now he used it. Except that Seth dashed it out of his hands and kicked it away. They pulled him to the next tooth. Though he arched his back, yet he could not stop the point piercing his devil's skin, his tunic, reaching his skin. . .

Free of soldiers ringing them round and with both devils doing other deeds, the two young friars were on their knees and Anselm had struggled up to join them. The fury of their prayers seemed to ascend from Hell-mouth like an extra smoke. But now Anselm rose to his feet. Praying time was over. He must see if the prayers were answered. Fulk and Micah rose with him. Ragnal Stowe stood watching the devils and Crispin, a faint smile of approval on his

225

face. Anselm said, "Nobody guards him now. You can seize him." The young friars looked at Anselm aghast. "He may be wicked, but his body's weak," said Anselm. "Do it." They jumped into movement and held him fast, one at each side.

Now Anselm stepped to the front of Hell-mouth. "Miles?" he said. "Thomas? Will you join me?"

They came out of their shocked trances and did as he asked. "Now," he said. "The three of us have made these plays today into Coventry's greatest glory. Friar, actor, Guild man. The folk know us and trust us, which is more than they do anyone else here. So together we'll stop this evil from going further, because nobody else can."

And now he lifted up his voice and shouted, as the tooth began to pierce Crispin's back and the first blood flowed: "People of Coventry, what you see is wrong and God calls on you to stop it now. You've shaken off the power of the devil once today by laughing at it and the time has come for you to do it again through your anger."

Miles shouted as well. "There are thousands of you. There's but a score and ten of these."

And Thomas shouted, "Guild men are free men."

The people heard. There was a sudden great roar like a tidal wave sweeping through the city. The crowd surged forward. The soldiers saw the weight of numbers, sensed their great anger and knew that not even swords could help them. The plan had failed: the folk were not cowed and pliant but angry and dangerous. The soldiers stood aside as men, women and even children swept through. A shout rang out. "Seth, let the minstrels live to sing another day or be killed on your own devices." The two devils realized at once what power had been released against them and pulled Crispin off. He fell to the ground, blood soaking his back. Joslin knelt beside him to see what help he could give.

As the first of the folk came to the edge of the stage and clambered up past the teeth, Seth and Arnulf looked at each other. Then they turned and ran, away down the ramp, down the steps, out of St Michael's Green and towards Dead Lane. When they reached it, the people following paused, unwilling to go further. But Seth and Arnulf were already through the vault and out into the open land, making for the forest. The folk turned back. "Disappeared," said one. "Perhaps they've really become devils."

They called over to the next men climbing up. "Stop there. They've gone. We've won."

There was a new cry, almost of disappointment. It had all been so quick. The soldiers were dispersed among them and suddenly there seemed no point in hounding them down. All that was left was the white-haired old man looking so insignificant, held with strength yet gentleness by the two young friars. "What will you do with me?"

Joslin remembered what Crispin said – that he'd be hung from the nearest tree. *No, not that,* he thought. *There's been enough bloodshed.* And he bent again to Crispin.

After two men had come up to remove Robert Meriden's body, the great mass of people were at a loss what to do next. Anselm saw this. He shouted: "You have no mayor now."

"Who wants one?" someone growled.

"We'll have nobody who was to do with Stow – or

Meriden, for all he's had a dreadful death," said another.

And then came a shout so unexpected that it amazed even Anselm. "Thomas Dollimore's a good man and he came to the front and stood up for us. I say Thomas Dollimore should be mayor." The shout was repeated and spread and spread, until St Michael's Green echoed with it. "Thomas Dollimore shall be mayor."

And while Thomas listened thunderstruck, then wondered if it would be allowed, then wondered if he could cope, then thought they were right, there was nobody better, somewhere in the crowd Margery swelled with pride, while her mother said, "Now I'll be left to do all the weaving myself."

"It contents us all," said Anselm.

"And Anselm shall be bishop," came another cry. Before it spread, Anselm quelled it. "That will never be," he said. "But word must be got to Ralph Breville about today's outcome. The King's Justices must be called to deal with Ragnal and with the other two when we find them and he should do it."

While this went on, Joslin was bending over Crispin, staunching the blood as best he could. And at last he was rewarded. Crispin opened one eye and grinned. "Don't worry on my account," he said. "It's just a scratch and a good poultice will cure it. I'll go to the apothecary again tomorrow."

30

'Robert Meriden's body was decently covered, placed on the actors' cart and taken to St Michael's Church with two Guild masters between the shafts. Ralph Breville, his dignity restored, received it solemnly. Ragnal Stowe was taken to the cells under St Mary's Hall where he would be well treated because he had once held high office there, but close watched until the King's Justice arrived.

On the Green there was confusion. In it all, Ragnal Stow's soldiers did what seemed prudent. They quietly lost their weapons and merged with the crowd. Some stole out of the town and made for the forest again. They aimed to follow Seth and Arnulf and resume their outlaw lives. Randall Stone's name might still frighten children to sleep. Others thought they'd stay and try their luck at town life again.

The black horses were led away by the Master of the Smith's Guild. "If they were stolen from an honest man and he can prove title, I'll willingly return them. If they were Stow's, he can whistle for them, because they're Coventry's now," he said.

When the horses were safely gone, folk swarmed over Hell-mouth, uprooting teeth, tearing down the roof, ripping up the boards of the stage. Until someone shouted, "Hey, what are we doing? This could save months of work." So they stopped, the pageant was roped off and later pulled away to be stored with the other pageants until next Corpus Christi Day, when it might be a proper Judgement play.

So this tumultuous Corpus Christi Day ended, Coventry sighed with relief. Some, though they would never say so, were sorry Ragnal Stow hadn't come back. Life might have been bad for many when he was mayor, but it was good for some. For most, though, it was relief and a feeling that they were delivered from a great scourge. Most weren't sorry to see Meriden go. Coventry had been a sad place under him and his like. But they asked if he deserved such a terrible end and when they came to the answer they felt a guilt that they could not understand, for what could they have done to stop it? Still, as with kings and barons, so with mayors. The rich and powerful thought nothing of killing each other, so let them get on with it. The folk resolved to shake a bad memory off and looked forward to life under a new mayor.

Next morning, Jankin led the way to the apothecary who had dressed and poulticed his ankle. He willingly opened his shop and prepared a poultice and dressing for Crispin's wound. "You were very lucky," he said as he cleaned it out and Crispin lay face down with gritted teeth. "You are a strong man. Only the skin is pierced. It will soon heal." When he had finished, he stood up. "My daughter Eleanor will apply the poultice and the dressing. She needs the practice if she's to take this shop over one day." Now Joslin could see this girl who had made Crispin so thoughtful two days day before. Eleanor was tall, with dark hair: a serious, grave girl who, Joslin estimated, was in her mid-twenties. She worked dexterously and Crispin's teeth seemed to be ungritted as he relaxed. When all was finished, they went back to the Bull. Crispin seemed deep in thought again and Joslin knew why.

The tavern was full. When the actors and minstrels entered, the talking stopped and every face turned towards them. Then, one man stood up and said, "Welcome. And thank you." After him, another stood, and another. Sym looked bemused, Jankin angry as if suspecting a trick, Miles happy and satisfied. For a moment the Bull was full of embarrassed silence. Then everyone burst out cheering and, as actors and minstrels came forward, hearty hands slapped them on the back. "Careful," shouted Crispin and dodged out of the way. "Ale for them all, Godric, from the good barrels you never tap for us," one man shouted.

Godric looked away, shame and guilt on his face. So there should be, thought Joslin. But he wouldn't make an issue of it. This town must forget the resentments of the last years.

So the evening wore on. Hob and Sym ended it nearly unconscious with free ale: Jankin ended it happy, forgetting his sore leg and hugging Peg as if life depended on it. "When we come back to Coventry next year, we'll get wed, you and I," he shouted. "I won't let you forget you said that," Peg answered. Only Alban, Molly and Miles seemed to have any cares left and as curfew came, Miles showed why. "To bed," he ordered. "We must rise early and sober tomorrow to bury our Bartholomew as he deserves."

The sun had risen an hour when they met in Greyfriars chapel. Anselm, Fulk and Micah were waiting for them and it was Anselm who performed the rites necessary for Bartholomew's soul. Then Miles, Alban, Sym and Hob bore his body to a plot in the corner of the friars' garden. All the friars followed as Anselm consigned him to the earth. Joslin watched and grieved at the manner of man the actors had lost.

When they had said their farewells to Anselm and Miles had promised they would be back a month before Corpus Christi next year, they left Greyfriars. "A day to rest," said Miles. "Then we move on. We go north."

"I go westward," said Joslin and looked to Crispin. But Crispin was quiet: there was a look on that enigmatic face Joslin had not seen before. "I'm going to the apothecary for my wound to be seen to," he said. "Will Eleanor do it?" asked Jankin innocently, but Crispin didn't answer.

Joslin felt slightly nettled. He had assumed they would travel together as Crispin went for his business in the Welsh Marches. But he wasn't able to ask more, as Crispin strode off to the apothecary's at an alarming speed and was gone all morning.

Joslin spent the time packing his panniers and seeing that Herry was well-shod and rested. Miles went to St Mary's Hall. There he found that Anselm had done well for them: payment for their work was waiting. When he returned he found Godric. "We leave tomorrow early," he said. "I'll settle up now."

Godric looked shifty. "No payment," he said. "It's

free. Have your stay on me. The same goes for the minstrels."

It was, Joslin thought, the least he could do.

Crispin returned from the apothecary in great good humour. Eleanor was with him, hanging on his arm and looking happier than she had yesterday. But she would not come inside the Bull: Joslin saw her walk away up the street with Crispin watching after her.

"Crispin, are we moving on together as we said?" he asked.

"You go," was the answer. "As to whether I'll be with you, I'll tell you after I've had my wound dressed tomorrow."

That afternoon, they were at two more burials. Robert Meriden was laid to rest in the sunniest part of St Michael's graveyard, where one day a fine tomb would be raised. A mass was sung for his soul. John Crowe was buried simply in a remote corner under the wall. Later, they saw the coroner and told him everything they knew of what happened to John Crowe. "I still grieve that he died because of my question to him," said Miles.

Whether or not Crispin left Coventry tomorrow, tonight was the last time they would have with the actors. For hours in the Bull that evening they talked over the last four tumultuous days.

"Where have Arnulf and that bighead Seth Broad gone then?" Hob wondered.

"Back to the forest, I should think," Crispin replied. "And there I reckon they'll lie low for a long time. The justices will send soldiers to scour the whole of Arden, but my bet is they'll never be found. They know Arden too well now: besides, they know things would go hard with them if they were caught. The only thing I'd be certain of is that Arnulf won't be master of the tavern any more."

"So Slad will take over after all," said Hob.

"Poor, put-upon man. He deserves it," said Molly.

"Why was Arnulf there in the first place?" asked Alban.

"I'll have to go back a long way to explain that," said Crispin. "Some of it I've only just realized."

"Why did you say you were Randall Stone?" said Joslin.

"Because I *was* Randall Stone," Crispin replied.

The rest looked mystified.

"When I was a young man, I suffered a grievous wrong. I was cheated of all I had: family, friends, possessions, land."

"Like Gamelyn was," said Joslin.

Crispin paused. "Yes," he said after a moment.

"And it was on the Welsh Marches, where you're bound for now," Joslin said again.

"You've worked a lot out for yourself, haven't you?" said Crispin.

"I think I have," said Joslin. "'*He that has ears to hear.*' Remember? Well, I heard Gamelyn's story and now I've made it yours and I reckon I know what you're going to say."

"Then let's see if you're right," said Crispin. "Anyway, I fled, eastwards, into the forest of Arden. And there, as I hid shivering, the outlaws found me. I gave myself up for dead, but, they looked after me, took me in as one of their own. Randall Stone himself, the first, the real Randall Stone, told me how they were strong, fearless, on the side of the oppressed, because they'd all been oppressed themselves. Their own stories were much like mine. Soon I found out

234

how loved Randall Stone was by the forest folk, by serfs and bondmen round about, how hated by barons and lords. I knew this was how I wanted to be. I fought alongside the outlaws. I found I was strong and brave myself as well as being a good minstrel to them. It was then that I learnt the song of Gamelyn. But I never knew how true it would become. When Randall died, he passed his mantle on to me. I was acclaimed the outlaw king. And what better to do but say that now my own name would be Randall Stone?" He stopped. "Have you made Gamelyn's story fit yet, Joslin?" he asked.

"We haven't reached the end of his story yet. So we can't have reached yours either. But it all fits so far except the wrestling match."

"Be patient," said Crispin. "For four good years I led them. But it always stayed in my mind: this was not my real life. I'd lost my inheritance. I wanted it back. Nobody would give it to me, so I must do it all myself. But it would never happen if I stayed in the forest."

"So what did you do?" asked Jankin.

"I left my friends to try my luck in the outside world again," said Crispin.

"Why didn't you go straight back to your home?" Molly asked.

"I knew there'd be no point straight away. There wasn't much I could do. Much better to roam the land singing and listening. I said to Joslin only the other night that the minstrel is ideal to pick up each piece of gossip that goes: that's why we make good spies. I listened for years, in taverns, on street corners, in lords' halls if I had to."

"And what did you hear?" said Miles.

"Nothing – at least nothing which was of interest to

me. Except that other travellers were saying that Randall Stone had changed: he was now a threat and scourge to folk passing though the forest. That troubled me. Whatever sort of wretch had my friends acclaimed to succeed me? But I vowed I'd never go back to find out – those days, I thought, were gone."

"Yet you did," said Joslin.

"Two months ago in Leicester, in a fine tavern after I had sung well and been paid what I deserved, I fell to talking with a traveller on his way to Norwich from Hereford. He told me something – what it was doesn't matter now – which shrieked out to me: 'Go back. Your time is near.' So I set off westwards again until I reached Warwick."

"And there you met me," said Joslin. "And that night I saw your encounter with the stranger in the night."

"That's right," said Crispin. "He was one of my oldest friends from the forest. He'd dared to venture out by night because somehow they'd heard that I was near. They had to warn me before I reached the forest. New people had come into the forest years before: hundreds of them. They were different: cruel, merciless, evil: they didn't care what they did. They'd taken the name of Randall Stone for themselves and turned it into a curse. And now there was worse. My friends were certain that something new was being planned: some great campaign, attack, onslaught, call it what you like. But they had no idea who it would be aimed against. There was one clue. They did not know who these renegades were who'd hunted and killed them – but they knew where they'd come from."

"Where?" asked Miles.

"Coventry," Crispin answered. "And when I knew that, I remembered something which happened just after I'd left the forest all those years ago. Could these things, I wondered, be connected?"

"Well, what happened? Come on, tell us," demanded Jankin.

Crispin did not answer at once, as if this was painful to him. Then he said, "It's a strange story. It was ten years ago. I'd been on the road as a minstrel for a year or more. When I came to Coventry I thought I'd find good pickings. I remember I entered the town through Newgate. Nobody asked what my business was: the place seemed deserted. But I heard a great, confused noise coming from the middle of the town: shouting, screaming, the clash of swords. This was no place for me, I decided, and turned to go. Then two men burst round a corner and nearly knocked me over. One seized the other by the shoulders and was about to drive a knife into his back. Well, I couldn't have this. I jumped in between them and separated them. I stopped the man with the knife in his tracks. I couldn't help it: it's my nature."

Joslin could see the scene plainly. That tall figure would make anyone quail.

"Well, the man with the knife turned on me. 'You're Meriden's man,' he yelled. 'I don't know what you mean,' I said, but I made him drop the knife and he ran off. The other dusted himself down and said, 'Thank you. What's your name?' One thing certain was that I wasn't telling that to anyone in this place. So I said the first name that came into my head. 'Gamelyn,' I answered."

"What other name was there?" said Joslin. "You'd hardly say 'Randall Stone'."

Crispin nodded and went on. "'Come and meet Robert Meriden, Gamelyn,' said the man I'd saved.

'Let him thank you for what you did.' I thought I might as well: what would this be but a town brawl soon over? I stowed my baggage in a doorway for safe keeping and went with the man I'd saved. I saw Meriden. 'Join us,' he said. 'We need you.' 'I know nothing about you,' I replied. 'I have other business.' I left before he could object. But before I'd gone ten paces, I was set on by a crew led by the man whose knife I'd seized. Before I knew it, another set of ruffians jumped on them and I was in the middle of a fight such as I'd never known for its ferocity. I didn't know which side was which. I laid about everybody because they all seemed as bad as each other. I saw the leaders there, Meriden and Stow, and they saw me and both must have concluded that I was on the other side and doing them as much damage as four other men. My sword was drawn and nobody was keen on coming near it. But I was chased round the town nevertheless, and got an idea of its streets in my desperation that I knew I wouldn't forget. Then I worked my way back to near where I came in, where I'd hidden my minstrel's gear. But who was barring the way? Ragnal Stow himself and a henchman with straggling brown hair and a cast in one eye. Yes, it was Arnulf. No wonder he had bad memories of me and didn't know me either as Crispin Thurn or as minstrel.

"Well, I had to take them both on, and in the fight I wounded Ragnal so badly that it seems his arm had to be cut off later to save his life. I never knew that. Arnulf turned to him at once, calling for help which didn't come. I picked up my gear and ran for it and didn't stop until I was a good mile out of Coventry, lost in trees and fields as far from the road as I could be. I vowed then never to go back there willingly."

"Was that your nearest thing to Gamelyn's wrestling match?" said Joslin.

"Looking back now, I suppose it was. The strange thing was that I saw and heard nothing of any man called Seth Broad with a big head when I was in Coventry. If I had, we'd have sorted all this out in half the time. But I reckon he saw me."

"It seems your visit was so fleeting that I'm not surprised you didn't know who was who," said Miles.

"Anyway," Crispin continued. "In Warwick that night, my friend from the forest begged me to interrupt my journey and try to find out what was happening. I didn't want to, but for old times' sake I agreed. It was there I found Joslin and helped him. But as for what was afoot in the forest, I had little inkling. Until the night in the tavern. I met Arnulf again and then I saw the way you actors were treated, for no reason as far as I could see. Something told me then that I had to go back to Coventry, for that's where the answers would lie."

"What do you mean, *something*?" said Jankin. "You must know what it was."

"All right. I didn't like the way you were pushed off the stage. I wondered why you were warned off Coventry and Corpus Christi. Why shouldn't you see for your-selves? I was worried about Bartholomew, especially if the tavern was the last place he was seen alive before he came here. I thought the minstrels' contest was nothing more than a play, which Arnulf and Seth Broad set up. They wanted that result and they made sure they got it. Lambert stayed in the tavern so Seth could kill him; we were outside, so that I could travel on. Arnulf knew well that once I saw him I'd want to go on to Coventry: I believe he knew why I was in the forest."

"But why was Arnulf in charge of the tavern anyway?" asked Sym.

"He was their look-out – an advance guard. The tavern was perfect for seeing who came into the forest from Coventry and to control who left it to go there. Yes, he was very useful to Seth and Stow. They wanted me to go to Coventry. Then they could kill me in style in front of all the folk: a far better revenge that a secret death like Lambert's."

"But *why* kill poor Lambert?" Sym was agitated once again at the London minstrel's memory. "Nobody knew him and he'd done no harm."

"That's what I said. They killed him *because* nobody knew him," said Joslin.

"I think it's clear," said Crispin. "They thought that killing him would frighten you actors so you wouldn't go to Coventry. In a sort of way he was one of your number so it was a blow against you. But if it had been any other of you, you'd have been angry and become a nuisance to them. They calculated that this way you'd get discouraged and go away. But knew it would make me start thinking, especially when his body disappeared, so that I probably would go to Coventry. They didn't bargain for us all going together."

"And all because they didn't want our Judgement play in the town," said Miles. "Even though they'd killed Bartholomew, they couldn't risk it in case another of us could take his part."

"Our puny little Judgement play," said Alban.

"Ah, but it worked, didn't it," said Jankin.

"I still don't see how," said Hob. "Or why."

"I think I do," said Joslin. "I remember Miles in the Bull wondering what would happen if the plays turned out wrong, if Abraham murdered Isaac and

Herod killed Jesus with the other innocents. Alban said the folk would die. You kept thinking about that, didn't you, Alban? You said it again while we were watching Herod together. Then Anselm told us of his terrible dream when we saw Hell-mouth with him. Well, all of you were right, weren't you? The folk depend on these plays, more than any scripture or priest's homily. The plays show these things happening in front of their eyes. They're what the folk depend on most. If these things aren't so, what hope is there? Isn't that what they think? Isn't it what *we* think?

"These devils, then, they used the plays for their own ends. What do we make of a Judgement which isn't made by God but by the devil because there's no God there? There wasn't any God there, was there? There wasn't a place for Heaven on this awful pageant. It was a Judgement where everyone was guilty and everyone was damned. The folk would see it happen in front of them. They'd be filled with such misery that they'd be straw in the devil's hands. Evil men could walk into Coventry and take it for themselves knowing nobody would try to stop them because they thought it was all they deserved."

Miles looked hard at Joslin. "You're right," he said. "But what you say chills my heart so much that I feel I don't want the responsibility of acting ever again."

There was silence. Then Jankin said, "You will, Miles. A good night's sleep and you will."

"But it didn't happen like you said, Joslin," Alban objected.

"I know," said Joslin. "We turned the devil's weapon against him. That's why they had to kill Bartholomew. They couldn't have a Judgement where people might laugh. They didn't want any chance of you doing it, either."

"But they could have killed us here in the Bull before Corpus Christi started. Godric would have let them in," said Jankin. "When I was trying to get away from them, I thought I'd find you all dead."

"But we'd been given a job by Anselm," said Molly. "We were important. If we'd been killed, there would have been a huge hue and cry. The plays might even have been stopped, and then what might have happened? Perhaps building a pageant where nobody would go might not be secret enough after all and their plot would be foiled."

"Well, it was foiled anyway," said Jankin. "Joslin's right. The best way to deal with evil is laugh at it. Once he started horsing around out there, a man in a devil's garb would look a right fool."

"But it's more than that," said Miles. "It's *how* you laugh at it. Bartholomew made our play stronger, not a mere jester's piece. It didn't just say, 'You've been bad so you're damned whatever happens.' It said, 'You'll be found wanting and I can tell you why, so think on.' That's what the play's for. At least, it should be."

There was silence. Then Molly said, "Let's put this behind us now. We came into Coventry and found a bad place. But next year we'll be back and it will be a good place again. We should be content with that."

There was another silence. Then Alban asked, "Crispin and Joslin, will you sing to us?" "Yes, Come on, Crispin and Joslin." The shout spread from the actors out across the whole tavern. Crispin fetched his drum and flute and Joslin fetched his harp. Crispin sang a song new to Joslin, from the north country: a tale of King Arthur's knights such as he'd never heard before. "Sir Gawain and the Carl of Carlisle" it was called. Joslin vowed that before he and Crispin's ways parted he'd learn it in full, because it made the listeners laugh and shudder by turns.

Then it was his turn. "Sir Orfeo" he sang, as he had in Randolf Waygood's hall the night before he was to ask Alys to marry him, then "The Tournament of Tottenham", as he sang in the tavern at Henley, when Dafydd told him to go north to Oxford: then ballads from France, of Melusine the snake woman, Huon of Bordeaux, Roland and Renaud, then sad songs of travel and exile – "I am of Ireland and the holy land of Ireland" – and he remembered his voyage to England on *The Merchant of Orwell*. Long into the night, for hours after curfew, he sang and Crispin sang and everyone in the tavern seemed in a trance. At last they could sing no longer. Joslin put his harp down and said, "Crispin, I've never heard such wonderful songs so wonderfully sung as yours." Crispin replied, "You're a fine minstrel, Joslin. Finer than me by a mile."

So they went to their beds. Joslin slept to wake refreshed and strong enough to face anything.

Thus passed his last night in Coventry.

The actors left early. "They tell me there's a horse fair not ten miles distant," said Miles. "Now we have the money, we'll be there first thing to buy a horse. We need it with carrying Jankin on the cart."

So they said their farewells. "May both your quests end happily," said Miles. "And perhaps, Crispin, the end of your story will be as fortunate and richly deserved as Gamelyn's was."

As he watched them leave, Joslin knew he would not easily forget the actors. Sym and Hob pulled at the shafts of the cart and it rattled over the stones out of the Bull. The last sight Joslin had was of them turning left into Cross Cheaping to take the road northwards. He and Crispin were left standing alone.

"Well?" said Joslin.

"I'm going to the apothecary," said Crispin. "Wait until I return. Then I'll tell you what I'm doing."

Joslin knew Crispin and his new love Eleanor would be seriously talking while his wound was dressed – and her father as well. And it wouldn't be the state of his wound which would keep him in Coventry.

I'll watch his face as he returns, Joslin thought. *If he's smiling, he's staying: if he's glum, we're going together.*

When Crispin had gone, he went down to Greyfriars Street and Thomas Dollimore's cottage to say goodbye to Margery. First he saw Thomas, still reeling from the prospect of being mayor and the thought of moving into the fine house in Baylie Lane. Then he saw Margery.

Margery was sorry to think the nice man was going. But when Joslin wished her well in her life she knew she would never see him again. She also knew that if he hadn't come to Coventry, none of these exciting things would have happened to the Dollimore family.

Back at the Bull, Joslin waited. After two hours, he saw Crispin appear at the end of Smithford Street. The nearer he came, the clearer was the broad smile on his face. Joslin prepared to mount Herry and start off on his own.

"Right, let's be on our way," said Crispin as he reached the tavern.

244

"Has she refused you?" said Joslin, puzzled. "I'm sorry. Why are you smiling?"

Crispin led his horse out of the stable. "I'm a mere travelling minstrel and Eleanor's the daughter of a prosperous apothecary. It's little enough I can give her now. But when my business in the west is finished, I can return with something worth offering. Eleanor would have me today, but when I return, her father will consent with a good heart and I'll be content in life at last."

They rode down Smithford Street together, passed through Spon Gate and set out on the road ahead. Coventry receded behind them.

As they rode out, a horseman watched, hidden from their sight by a large tree. He watched them pass and waited until they were a good two hundred paces ahead.

"Well done, Joslin," he said. "That was a fine piece of entertainment. Oh, I do love watching a good play. But I'm glad you're safe out of that city and on the move again. It makes our final meeting, for good or ill, all the nearer. And nothing matters to you so much as its outcome. Or to me, if it comes to that."

Then he rode after them, making sure his cloak half-hid his sallow, pock-marked face and twisted mouth.

Here ends the fourth story concerning Joslin de Lay's journey to Wales.

AUTHOR'S NOTE

There's a lot about Coventry and the Corpus Christi Mystery Plays in this story which is true. There's a lot which might have been true – because so few records have survived nobody can ever say for sure. There's also much which most certainly isn't and I've invented it for the sake of the story.

First, what might seem surprising. In 1369, Coventry wasn't actually a city yet so St Michael's Church was not a cathedral. But all over the world nowadays, Coventry is known for its cathedral. The old St Michael's had only been a cathedral since 1918. Along with most of the rest of the wonderfully pre-served medieval Coventry, it was destroyed in a few hours in 1941, the terrible night of the great air raid. After the war a wonderful new cathedral, world-wide symbol of peace and reconciliation, was built. So why, if Coventry didn't have a cathedral in 1369, did it have a bishop? That was just one of the strange anomalies of the time. The bishop was Bishop of Coventry and Lichfield. Lichfield had the cathedral. But Coventry was one of the leading four English

246

towns in the fourteenth century and for the bishop to preside over its Plays would be only fitting. Though whether he actually did, nobody knows.

Now for what's definitely not true. Ralph Breville, the bishop, is a fictional creation. The name of the real vicar of St Michael's at the time was John de Tuftis. To avoid too much confusion between fact and fiction I have left him out. For this information about the bishop and vicar, I am indebted to the Archivist of Coventry Cathedral.

Robert Meriden and Ragnal Stow are my own inventions and so was the feud between them. To find that Coventry really did once have rivals for the mayoralty with those names would be like winning the lottery jackpot twice a week for a whole year. Though it is true that there was a lot of anger and unrest in the town thoughout this time. The remark Joslin overhears in the Bull about people not having their rights until they had struck a few heads from off the churls that ruled them was an actual remark written down by a very angry citizen some years after this story is set.

There was never a Robin Hood-like outlaw in the Forest of Arden called Randall Stone. But forests in the Middle Ages were strange places and hiding places for many who had good reason not to be seen. If Robin Hood could range round Sherwood, who knows who might have haunted Arden?

About the plays. These certainly existed – and still do. We know that plays like them were performed all over Europe. In England, many have been lost for ever, but the play cycles at Chester, York and Wakefield survive intact. There's another complete cycle existing which could have been performed anywhere – the "N-Town Cycle". Once it was thought it was from Coventry. Now we are sure it wasn't. The two real Coventry plays which do survive both appear in this story – the Play of the Shearmen and Taylors, about Christ's birth and the slaughter of the innocents (including the famous Coventry Carol, "Lully, Lullay, thou little tiny child" which Joslin regrets he didn't have time to compose!) and the Play of the Weavers, about Christ in the temple. Shakespeare saw these plays. That's why Hamlet talks of actors "Out-Heroding Herod" when they act anger, because the famous stage direction says: "*Here Erode ragis in the pagond and in the strete also.*"

There were at least eight more plays, all lost. I have adapted all the other plays which appear in this story from the Wakefield cycle – the "Towneley Plays". The origin of the part Bartholomew created for the Judgement play which Joslin finds himself acting was a mocking devil called Tuttivillus in the Wakefield Play of Judgement. He was a creation of the shadowy "Wakefield Master" who wrote a few plays which in their irreverent humour and savage satire are different from any other miracle plays. His Pickharness, Cain's servant in the Cain and Abel play, and Tuttivillus look forward to Shakespeare's clowns who keep appearing at the moments of highest seriousness – and Tuttivillus works in the same way as Shakespeare's porter at Hell-gate in *Macbeth*, or the clown in *Antony and Cleopatra* who brings the snake for Cleopatra to kill herself with. So poor Bartholomew was at the start of something important in English drama.

At first, Corpus Christi plays may well have been done by professional troupes of actors. But gradually the Guilds took them over. The first written record of Guilds doing the plays at Coventry comes in 1392, when the Drapers' Guild pageant for their new Judgement play is mentioned. By then, they were well established. So it seems quite possible that the changeover time could have come at about 1369, when this story is set. Many believe that the friars helped with – and wrote – a lot of the Corpus Christi plays. In Chester, one is known by name – Ranulf Higden. In a way, Father Anselm is my Ranulf Higden.

But we also know that there were many bands of wandering actors who went from place to place performing plays – and miracle plays were among them. Big towns on Corpus Christi Day would pay easy and good money. But what about when the Guilds started to take over?

These plays are still performed – the full York, Chester and Wakefield Cycles very often. Brought to life again, they are marvellous. One thing shines out. They are not easy to do. Playing the same part ten times or more in one day must be killing, as Thomas Dollimore found out. Ordinary people play in the York Cycle when it is done nowadays, just as they did in the Middle Ages. But they get a lot of help from professional actors – and they need it. It seems to me very likely that the wandering bands of actors, like the one led by Miles, would be there to give this help six hundred years ago. What I've depicted here is like what sometimes happens now.

The plays were performed in different ways in different places. But we know well that in Coventry they were performed on pageant wagons: there are detailed records to tell us. We also know where most of the different stations were, and those I have used. Though I'm not sure which play used each station: I had to guess.

There was, it seems, a station at the end of Little Park Street, near where it joins Dead Lane. I don't know how Dead Lane got its name. However, to put a vault for plague dead underneath, such has been found in excavations in London, seemed a reasonable thing to do.

Would the people of Coventry – or anywhere else – really have been so frightened of an unexpected Hell-mouth pageant? I've no way of telling: but I've long been haunted by the idea that they would. In an age when we can talk about *EastEnders* and *Coronation Street* characters as if they were real people, I don't think we should regard those far-off folk as stupid because they saw their mystery plays as somehow magically real. Remember, the story the plays told was for these people the whole of human knowledge and God's truth. Most couldn't read and anyway their Bible wasn't in English, so wall paintings in churches, sermons by priests and friars and these plays were the only ways they had of having this knowledge. If the plays turned out wrongly and had a terrible outcome, far different from the one expected, what were they to feel? I don't know, but I believe they'd feel panic, distress and despair. God, angels, devils were close to them. There's an often-told story of a play performed in Exeter two hundred years later where more devils than could be accounted for appeared on the stage – and the audience ran away screaming!

DENNIS HAMLEY